PRAISE FOR CAROLYN BROWN

The Magnolia Inn

"The author does a first-rate job of depicting the devastating stages of grief, provides a simple but appealing plot with a sympathetic hero and heroine and a cast of lovable supporting characters, and wraps it all up with a happily ever after to cheer for."

—*Publishers Weekly*

"*The Magnolia Inn* by Carolyn Brown is a feel-good story about friendship, fighting your demons, and finding love, and maybe, just a little bit of magic."

—*Harlequin Junkie*

"Chock-full of Carolyn Brown's signature country charm, *The Magnolia Inn* is a sweet and heartwarming story of two people trying to make the most of their lives, even when they have no idea what exactly is at stake."

—*Fresh Fiction*

Small Town Rumors

"Carolyn Brown is a master at writing warm, complex characters who find their way into your heart."

—*Harlequin Junkie*

"Carolyn Brown's *Small Town Rumors* takes that hotbed and with it, spins a delightful tale of starting over, coming into your own and living your life, out loud and unafraid."

—*Words We Love By*

"*Small Town Rumors* by Carolyn Brown is a contemporary romance perfect for a summer read in the shade of a big old tree with a glass of lemonade or sweet tea. It is a sweet romance with wonderful characters and a small town setting."

—*Avonna Loves Genres*

The Sometimes Sisters

"Carolyn Brown continues her streak of winning, heartfelt novels with *The Sometimes Sisters*, a story of estranged sisters and frustrated romance."

—*All About Romance*

"This is an amazing feel-good story that will make you wish you were a part of this amazing family."

—*Harlequin Junkie* (top pick)

"*The Sometimes Sisters* is [a] delightful and touching story that explores the bonds of family. I loved the characters, the story lines, and the focus on the importance of familial bonds, whether they be blood relations or those you choose with your heart."

—*Rainy Day Ramblings*

The Strawberry Hearts Diner

"[A] sweet and satisfying romance from the queen of Texas romance."

—*Fresh Fiction*

The Lullaby Sky

"I really loved and enjoyed this story. Definitely a good comfort read when you're in a reading funk or just don't know what to read. The secondary characters bring much love and laughter into this book—your cheeks will definitely hurt from smiling so hard while reading. Carolyn is one of my most favorite authors. I know without a doubt that no matter what book of hers I read, I can just get lost in it and know it will be a good story. Better than the last. Can't wait to read more from her."

—*The Bookworm's Obsession*

The Lilac Bouquet

"Brown pulls readers along for an enjoyable ride. It's impossible not to be touched by Brown's protagonists, particularly Seth, and a cast of strong supporting characters underpins the charming tale."

—*Publishers Weekly*

"If a reader is looking for a book more geared toward family and long-held secrets, this would be a good fit."

—*RT Book Reviews*

"Carolyn Brown absolutely blew me away with this epically beautiful story. I cried, I giggled, I sobbed, and I guffawed; this book had it all. I've come to expect great things from this author and she more than lived up to anything I could have hoped for. Emmy Jo Massey and her great-granny Tandy are absolute masterpieces not because they are perfect but because they are perfectly painted. They are so alive, so full of flaws and spunk and determination. I cannot recommend this book highly enough."

—*Night Owl Reviews* (5 stars and top pick)

The Wedding Pearls

"*The Wedding Pearls* by Carolyn Brown is an amazing story about family, life, love, and finding out who you are and where you came from. This book is a lot like *The Golden Girls* meet *Thelma and Louise*."

—*Harlequin Junkie*

"*The Wedding Pearls* is an absolute must-read. I cannot recommend this one enough. Grab a copy for yourself and one for a best friend or even your mother or both. This is a book that you need to read. It will make you laugh and cry. It is so sweet and wonderful and packed full of humor. I hope that when I grow up, I can be just like Ivy and Frankie."

—*Rainy Day Ramblings*

The Yellow Rose Beauty Shop

"*The Yellow Rose Beauty Shop* was hilarious and so much fun to read. But sweet romances, strong female friendships, and family bonds make this more than just a humorous read."

—*The Readers Den*

"If you like books about small towns and how the people's lives intertwine, you will love this book. I think it's probably my favorite book this year. The relationships of the three main characters, girls who have grown up together, will make you feel like you just pulled up a chair in their beauty shop with a bunch of old friends. As you meet the other people in the town, you'll wish you could move there. There are some genuine laugh-out-loud moments and then more that will just make you smile. These are real people, not the oh-so-thin-and-so-very-rich that are often the main characters in novels. This book will warm your heart, and you'll remember it after you finish the last page. That's the highest praise I can give a book."

—Reader quote

Long, Hot Texas Summer

"This is one of those lighthearted, feel-good, make-me-happy kind of stories. But, at the same time, the essence of this story is family and love with a big ole dose of laughter and country living thrown in the mix. This is the first installment in what promises to be another fascinating series from Brown. Find a comfortable chair, sit back, and relax because once you start reading *Long, Hot Texas Summer*, you won't be able to put it down. This is a super fun and sassy romance."

—*Thoughts in Progress*

Daisies in the Canyon

"I just loved the symbolism in *Daisies in the Canyon*. As I mentioned before, Carolyn Brown has a way with character development with few, if any, contemporaries. I am sure there are more stories to tell in this series. Brown just touched the surface first with *Long, Hot Texas Summer* and now continuing on with *Daisies in the Canyon*."

—*Fresh Fiction*

the Family Journal

ALSO BY CAROLYN BROWN

CONTEMPORARY ROMANCES

The Empty Nesters
The Perfect Dress
The Magnolia Inn
Small Town Rumors
The Sometimes Sisters
The Strawberry Hearts Diner
The Lilac Bouquet
The Barefoot Summer
The Lullaby Sky
The Wedding Pearls
The Yellow Rose Beauty Shop
The Ladies' Room
Hidden Secrets
Long, Hot Texas Summer
Daisies in the Canyon
Trouble in Paradise

CONTEMPORARY SERIES

THE BROKEN ROAD SERIES

To Trust
To Commit
To Believe
To Dream
To Hope

THREE MAGIC WORDS TRILOGY

A Forever Thing
In Shining Whatever
Life After Wife

HISTORICAL ROMANCE

THE BLACK SWAN TRILOGY

Pushin' Up Daisies
From Thin Air
Come High Water

THE DRIFTERS & DREAMERS TRILOGY

Morning Glory
Sweet Tilly
Evening Star

THE LOVE'S VALLEY SERIES

Choices
Absolution
Chances
Redemption
Promises

the Family Journal

CAROLYN BROWN

Montlake
Romance

Text copyright © 2019 by Carolyn Brown

Published by Montlake Romance, Seattle

www.apub.com

Amazon, the Amazon logo, and Montlake Romance are trademarks of Amazon.com, Inc., or its affiliates.

ISBN-13: 9781542015370
ISBN-10: 1542015375

Cover design and photography by Laura Klynstra

Printed in the United States of America

*To my aunt Mildred Chapman Edwards
and my cousin Doris Chapman Mead.
You are both more like sisters to me than an aunt and
a cousin.
I appreciate all the love and support you lavish upon me.*

Chapter One

*W*hen you come to the end of the rope, it's time to tie a knot and hang on. Lily Anderson had reached the place where there wasn't even enough rope left to tie a knot. She'd thought about her problem for a whole day, made a few phone calls, and now her mind was made up. She was moving her kids out of the city of Austin and to her hometown of Comfort, Texas—population a little more than three thousand.

She hated to always be the bad person, but since the divorce five years ago, she'd had no choice. A kid could find a dozen friends on every street corner, but they only had one mother. And in her kids' case, only one parent—thanks to no help whatsoever from her two children's father. Knowing all that didn't make anything easier for Lily on Friday morning. Her hands were clammy and her pulse raced. She felt like gravity was pulling her heart right out of her chest. At least she owned a house in Comfort, and the move wouldn't be difficult.

She had almost changed her mind and decided to stay, but then her daughter, Holly, gave her one of those go-to-hell looks that was meant to fry her on the spot.

"You've got less than twenty-four hours to pack your clothing and whatever else you want to take to Comfort." Lily's voice landed somewhere between a whisper and an icicle. "The movers will be here at seven in the morning. Until then, I'll be taking your cell phone, laptop, tablet, and all the games you play on the television."

"You can't do that!" Fourteen-year-old Holly jumped up from the sofa and screamed at her mother. "I won't leave my friends! You can't make me! We've got parties planned this weekend, and I'm not going to miss them. I'll go live with Daddy!"

"You should have thought of that before you took a marijuana joint into the library bathroom on Wednesday afternoon." Lily's finger shot out like a pistol at her daughter. "Sit down and lower your voice."

Holly fell back onto the sofa and glared at her mother. "You had no right to come in the bathroom and spy on me."

"So this is my fault? Do you realize what would have happened if the police had come into the bathroom instead? You'd be in jail, not moving to Comfort."

"Why do I get punished, too?" Her twelve-year-old son, Braden, pouted. "I wasn't the one who got caught smokin' pot in the public library."

"No, you"—Holly did a head wiggle—"you and your little buddies have been sneaking out at night to smoke cigarettes and drink beer. I don't see what the big difference is between smoking pot and cigarettes." She turned back to her mother. "If I'd gotten caught with cigarettes, you would have taken my phone for a week. But your precious little angel of a son is doing that, and you didn't even know it. I'm calling Daddy."

Lily focused on Braden with his dark hair and big brown eyes that, at that very moment, were trying in vain to look innocent. Surely this was a nightmare. The walls seemed to be closing in on her, and she had to lean against the back of a recliner to keep from dropping. How did things get so out of control? She was a therapist, for heaven's sake, and she didn't even see the signs concerning her own children's behavior. Talk about having her head stuck in the sand.

"Is that the truth?" she asked.

He shrugged. "I only smoked a few and drank two beers. I didn't do nothing like she did."

"Yeah, right," Holly almost snorted. "You and your little friends think it's sooo cool. You strut around with them like you're too cool for the other kids."

"Do not," he protested.

"Sweet Jesus," Lily muttered. "You just lost all your techie devices, also. Both of you will have to earn them back, and that won't happen before summer."

Holly ripped her phone from the hip pocket of her jeans in a dramatic gesture. "I refuse to live like a prisoner. I mean it! If you force me to give up my phone, I will go live with Daddy."

"Tell him I want to live with him, too," Braden said.

Lily folded her arms over her chest and waited. The children thought their world was tumbling down around the toes of their cute little boots—it was about to take another major nosedive when Holly called her father, Wyatt Anderson.

"You can use your phone for one more call, but you have to put it on speaker," Lily said.

Holly rolled her eyes toward the ceiling, hit speed dial, and laid the phone on the coffee table. Her father, Wyatt, answered her call with, "Hello, princess, did you have a good Christmas?"

"Wonderful, Daddy, but it would have been better if I could have spent some time with you." She smirked at her mother.

"Darlin', I would have liked that, too, but Victoria had plans for us to spend the holiday in the beach condo. It's just not big enough to fit us all," Wyatt said.

Lily fought the urge to roll her eyes. Wyatt could weave a lie so sweetly the angels in heaven would believe him. Why didn't he just tell the kids the truth? He liked his new, rich lifestyle with his second wife, and she didn't want to share him with children.

"Mama's bein' a bitch, so me and Braden are going to come and live with you," Holly said.

"Add riding the bus to school for the whole semester for calling me a bitch to your punishment," Lily said.

"No!" Braden yelled. "Daddy, she really is being a bitch."

"That puts you on the bus with your sister," Lily said.

"Only geeks ride the bus!" Holly whined. "You can come get us tomorrow morning at seven, Daddy."

The silence that filled the room was so heavy that it seemed to suck out every bit of the oxygen. Even though Lily was still angry with her children, she felt sorry for them. If she'd been paying more attention to them, maybe none of this would've happened.

"Are you still there, Daddy?"

Lily knew what Wyatt was about to say to them and that it would almost literally break their hearts. Poor Holly's tone was so desperate that Lily wanted to hug her, but right then tough love was the only way to get through to her children. If it kept those two out of trouble and out of jail, it would all be worthwhile.

"Honey, I'm real sorry," Wyatt said. "But you can't live with me. Victoria and I made an agreement about children when we married. I'll come see you real soon, and we'll have a day all to ourselves. Maybe in July we can even have a whole weekend while Victoria is in California on one of her business trips. If free time comes up between now and then, I'll call you for sure."

"Daaa-deee." Holly dragged the word out into several syllables. "Mama is moving us to Comfort. I don't want to live in that Podunk town," she whined. "You just have to come and get us. I'll die in that place. You just have to go to court and get custody of us."

"Me, too," Braden yelled from across the room.

"You have to understand. I simply cannot have you kids living with me and Victoria. It wouldn't work, and you'd be more miserable here than in Comfort." Wyatt was beginning to sound frustrated. "Put your mother on the phone, and take it off speaker."

Holly hit the right button and tossed the phone toward her mother. Lily caught it in midair and said, "Hello, Wyatt. So no deal on helping raise your children?"

"I told you when we divorced that I'd pay child support and see them when I could, but I didn't want custody then, and I don't want custody now. Victoria and I have a lifestyle that doesn't . . ." He paused. "Why are you going back to Comfort, anyway, and at this time of year? Can't you do what's best for the kids and at least stay in Austin until summer?"

"I *am* doing what's best for them. I caught your daughter smoking pot in the public library bathroom two days ago, and I just now found out that your son has been sneaking out at night to smoke and drink with his little preteen buddies. So I'm taking them out of the city, and they aren't getting their phones or tablets for a long time." Lily carried the phone into the next room. "If you think you can do better with them, maybe they could spend some quality time with you that involves more than taking them to dinner every six months, or to a hotel for a couple of days while Victoria is off somewhere on one of her business trips."

"Good God!" he gasped. "I wouldn't know what to do with them, and believe me, Miami is worse than Austin."

"Then Comfort it is," Lily said.

"Good luck," Wyatt muttered, and the call ended.

Lily returned and dropped the phone into the tote bag she had sitting on the end table. Then she turned to face Holly and Braden, who were still pouting on the sofa. "I expect all your electronic devices to be in that bag in ten minutes."

Holly groaned and Braden moaned at the same time.

"Until you earn the right to have your phones back, you can talk to your father when he calls on the house phone in Comfort. Oh, and FYI, it's a corded phone that hangs on the kitchen wall. Since you won't have anything else to do this afternoon, you can start packing. Set your alarms for six thirty in the morning."

Braden pulled his phone out of his hip pocket and dropped it in the bag. He looked longingly at it, as if he were looking at his best friend lying in a casket. Finally, he let out a heavy sigh and started down the hall toward his bedroom. "What am I supposed to pack in?"

"The moving company is bringing boxes in . . ." Lily paused when she heard a truck outside. "Looks like they're here now. You'll have your own bedroom in Comfort, but we'll all have to share one bathroom. So remember that. And one more thing—if either of you ever call me a bitch again, I'll add another punishment to the list. Believe me, it will be something I can guarantee you will hate worse than giving up all your devices. Now, you can bring your tablets, your video games, and your laptops to me."

"Our laptops, too? That's not fair," Holly whined.

"Fair flew out the window like the smoke you were blowing in the library, Holly," Lily said, "and was drained like the beer you were drinking, Braden."

"I can't survive without my own bathroom." Holly's whining took on a whole new level. "I refuse to share one with Braden." She jumped up from the sofa and glared at her brother.

"Sorry, princess." Lily used the same nickname that Wyatt had given their daughter before she was big enough to walk. "It's either share one with me and Braden or else you can use the one that's out behind the storage shed. No one will fight you if you want that one. It was still standing the last time I was home. Just remember to take toilet paper with you."

"I hate that house! I hate Comfort! I hate—" Holly's mouth snapped shut.

"And right now you hate me, but that's all right. I love you both, but I don't like either of you very much today," Lily finished for her. "And for your information, I hate leaving this apartment, too. I hate leaving my clients, my few friends, and our church. I hate that you and your brother's misbehavior has made this move necessary. So, darlin' girl, I don't have much sympathy for you right now." She pointed down the hall. "Go pack. If you ever even think about smoking another joint, I'll homeschool you, and you'll have no social life at all."

"Not that there'll be much of a possibility for a social life up there in the middle of nowhere, anyway," Holly grumbled, and started down the hallway at a snail's pace.

Lily remembered feeling the same way about Comfort when she was growing up in the small town. Her family lived three miles south of town, and they'd only had one vehicle, which her dad took to work every day. That hadn't left much opportunity for the kind of socializing her kids were accustomed to having.

I think your words were that you couldn't wait to go to college and get away from Comfort and all its prying eyes. Her mother's voice in her head scolded her, but just imagining Vera Miller's sweet voice took the sting out of the words.

"And now, after twenty years, I'm going right back to it," she whispered.

Welcome home, baby girl. You should never have left. Vera's voice was so real that Lily's mother could have been in the room with her.

"You got that right." Lily went to the front door and opened it before the doorbell even had time to ring.

An older guy with a rim of gray hair around his otherwise-bald head brought in an armload of flat boxes, dropped them in the corner of the living room, and left her six rolls of packing tape. "You do know that we'll be glad to pack everything for you?" he asked.

"We're not moving out permanently—at least not yet. These should be enough for now. See you early tomorrow morning."

"Not me, but Skipper will be here to load up for you. Y'all have a safe trip." He nodded toward her, and she closed the door behind him.

She glanced around the large living room in her apartment and sighed. She had rented the place because of that feature—lots of space so she could be with the kids more. At first, it had been great—they did their homework in the living room while she made supper. They ate around the table every evening, and they played games together. A little bit at a time, that all got away from her somehow, and a few months ago, she'd realized she was eating alone and the kids were spending all their time in their rooms or with their friends.

With another long sigh, she took stock of what had to be moved. Her lease wasn't up until June, and her mother's old house was still fully furnished, so the furniture would stay. If she had a pickup truck, she could probably move what they packed in it, but her compact car wouldn't hold it all.

She picked up two of the flat boxes, folded them into shape, sealed them with tape, and carried them down the hall. She knocked on Holly's door but didn't wait for an invitation to enter. "Here's your first box. When you get it filled, call me, and I'll tape it shut and get you another one."

Holly turned away from the window. "I'm sorry. I'll do the dishes by hand for a year. I'll never smoke weed again. I'll even miss the parties this weekend."

"Thank you for the offer," Lily said, "but the weed was the last straw, not the first one. You've been getting more and more belligerent and disrespectful. I'd expect some of that out of a senior in high school, but not a freshman. We're moving to Comfort. It's up to you and your brother whether we come back to Austin for the next school year, or if we stay there until both of you graduate."

"You are the meanest mother in the world. All the other kids . . ."

Her daughter's unfinished sentence reminded Lily of what her own mother used to ask: If all the other kids jumped off a cliff, would you follow them? The memory almost put a smile on her face. She crossed the room and hugged Holly, who looked a lot like pictures of Lily's mother when she was a young girl—same size, same height, same face shape. Holly had inherited her blonde hair from Lily, but those beautiful blue eyes had come from Wyatt's gene pool. The rest of her genetic makeup was straight Vera Miller.

Holly squirmed away and shot a dirty look toward her mother. Lily felt the sting of Holly's glare as if it had been a sharp knife stuck all the way through her heart.

"All the other kids don't have mothers who hate their kids like you do." Holly glared at Lily.

Lily tossed the box on the bed and left before she lost her resolve.

She found Braden sitting on his bed, looking bewildered. That wasn't hard to understand. They'd moved into the apartment when he was only seven years old. Lily had done the packing as well as the unpacking that year, but if he was old enough to smoke and drink, then he could figure out what he wanted to take to Comfort all on his own.

"I brought your first box," she said. "When it's finished, you can take it to the living room, and I'll get another one ready for you."

"Mama, what do I do first?" His voice broke.

For a minute she thought he was about to cry, but the expression on his face denied there were tears on the way. His voice had begun to crack last month. That meant he was starting to go through puberty. Next thing she knew, he would be shaving and chasing girls.

"I'd suggest that you pack your clothing first. Leave out something to wear tomorrow, though. Good luck." She eased the door shut and went straight to the kitchen, where she took a bottle of Jack Daniel's from the cabinet, poured herself a shot, and threw it back like a cowboy in an old western movie.

With the burn still in her throat and stomach, she taped up half a dozen more boxes. Then she pulled her cell from her hip pocket and called the home phone at the house in Comfort.

Mack Cooper kicked off his work boots and left them sitting just inside the utility room. The sun hadn't peeked out from behind a layer of gray clouds in almost a week. Even the goats were huddled up together in the shelters closest to the house. That morning, he'd seen the first sunrays doing their best to split the clouds. They'd reminded him of the light from a single bulb trying to sneak down through a layer of smoke in an old honky-tonk.

The Christmas break from his regular job as the vocational agriculture teacher at Comfort High School would be over in a few days. Teaching was his passion, and he was eager to get back to school.

He stopped in the kitchen for a cup of coffee and had just reached for his favorite mug when the old black wall phone rang right beside his ear. In the five years he'd rented the house from Lily Anderson, he could count on the fingers of one hand the times he'd heard the phone ring. Two of those had been wrong numbers.

He set the pot aside, put the phone to his ear cautiously, and said, "Hello?"

"Mack, this is Lily," the husky voice on the other end of the line said.

"Why are you using this phone and not my cell?" he asked.

"I'm so rattled that I didn't even think of that," she replied. "The kids and I will be in Comfort in the morning."

"Before noon? I'll have dinner ready for y'all," he offered. "Are you coming to town to go through your mother's things?"

"Dinner would be great. Thank you. But I've decided to move the kids to Comfort, so we're coming to stay for a while. We'll be there until summer, at the very least," she said.

He felt like all the air had just been knocked out of his lungs. "You're what? I've got forty goats, and—"

"I'm not asking you to move out. The house is big enough for us all. The kids and I will take the upstairs bedrooms and bathroom. You can go on about your life as usual in the downstairs. You and the kids will be in school after this next week, so it'll only be in the evenings that we'll be sharing the living room and kitchen," she told him.

"Are you sure you want to . . . ," he stammered before trailing off.

"We are adults, you and me, and we'll be roommates, nothing more," she said.

"Comfort is a small town. You do remember that, don't you?"

"Oh, I remember that all too well," Lily said. "But a couple of days ago, I took Holly to the library and . . ." She told him what had happened that day. "I've got to get them away from this big-city life. They aren't happy about it, but neither am I."

"Kids will be kids. They're easily influenced by whatever their peers are doing," he said.

"I know that," Lily said. "I wasn't hatched out as a full-grown adult, but I also know that the way to fix it is to change the environment and their group of friends. And for me to spend more time with them."

"I'll have a pot of soup ready when you get here." As long as he didn't have to move, he could survive with having people stomping around upstairs. If living with a couple of city kids who hated country life got to be too much, he would find another place to rent.

"Sounds great. I'll stop along the way and pick up a dessert," she said. "See you then."

His thoughts swirled as he put the phone back on the base. He leaned back against the cabinet and tried to settle his mind. Then his twin brother, Adam, yelled from the front door, "Hey, where are you?"

"In the kitchen." Of all the people occupying the planet, Adam was the last person Mack wanted to see or talk to that day. He bit back a groan and got down two mugs, filled them both with coffee, and added two spoons of sugar to his.

It was a surprise to see his brother in Comfort on a Friday morning.

Adam had followed in their father's footsteps and gone into business after college. Orville, their father, had been the president of a small bank right there in Comfort, and raised goats as a hobby. Adam was the head honcho of a huge bank in San Antonio, but Mack could never see him doing anything that would get his fancy shoes dirty.

No one would ever guess that he and Adam were twins by looking at them. Adam had a standing appointment with his hairstylist every Saturday morning to have his blond roots touched up and styled, and he went to the gym at least three days a week. Mack had jet-black hair that he seldom even thought about until it was time to go to the barbershop—maybe once a month. Adam had a movie-star face and body—the former from birth, the latter with help from his protein supplements and weight lifting. Mack hadn't been quite as blessed in the good looks department, but he wasn't ugly by any means, and his muscular chest and arms bore the proof of his hard work.

"What are you doing so far from the big city?" Mack asked. "I poured coffee for us. Have a seat."

Adam removed his suit coat and hung it on the back of the chair before he sat down. "We're foreclosing on the old Bailey property. I had to drive over and take a look at it. You should buy it. There's forty acres and a house that's not a hundred years old out there. Not a new brick, but a nice little two-bedroom frame house that's pretty sturdy. You're wasting your money renting this place."

"I like the location and the house." Mack carried both mugs to the table. "And the rent is less than I'd pay in property taxes and insurance on a place of my own."

It was evident that Adam wasn't happy with his response. Mack had always been able to read his brother, though they'd never been close. They'd grown even farther apart as the years passed. In high school Mack was interested in vo-ag classes; Adam played football. Then Mack went to Texas A&M and Adam left for Baylor, and the separation got even wider a couple of years after that when Adam stole Mack's girlfriend.

They had nothing in common anymore, except for their parents and the blood in their veins.

Adam sipped at his coffee, careful not to get it on his white shirt or his $100 tie. "There's another reason I came by. Charlene and I are getting a divorce."

"I'm not surprised. Who'd you screw around with this time?" Mack drummed his fingers on the table. "Have you told Mama and Daddy?"

There was the familiar old Adam shrug. Translated, it meant that Mack would most likely be the one breaking the news to their folks.

"Oh, no! Not this time." Mack shook his head. "You can go by and tell them while you're in town. I told them when you and Brenda divorced and when you and Natalie split up. I'm not doing it a third time. Man up and do your own talking. What happened anyway?"

Another shrug. "She caught me in a motel with my secretary, Darcy."

"Good God, Adam!" Mack raked his fingers through his dark hair, which was peppered with gray. "Aren't you ever going to settle down? You must like paying alimony."

"Only on the first one." Adam grinned. "After that, I insisted on prenups. And I really don't like upsetting Mother. She takes things so much better from you than from me. So come on, be a decent brother and break the news to her for me."

How two boys could be raised in the same household and turn out so differently was a total mystery to Mack. He loved kids and animals. That's why he had become a teacher. Mack had raised show goats when he was in high school. Adam had been the quarterback. Mack had always been shy and withdrawn. After he'd had the mumps, Adam wasn't able to have kids, and he always had a girl hanging on his arm—a girl he seemed to change more often than his socks.

"Well, brother, you're on your own this time," Mack said. "*You* can tell them or you can wait for the gossip to get to Comfort. Mama really loved Charlene, so good luck."

"You're really not going to help me out?" Adam asked. "Could you just maybe even hint that Charlene has been acting strange, and that maybe she's been having some problems, like with drinking or depression? That way it wouldn't be my fault."

"Nope." Mack refilled his coffee mug and sat down at the table. "I told you last time that I'm not paving the way so you can keep your glory-child crown anymore. We're forty-one years old. You need to own up to the fact that you can't keep your pants zipped when a pretty girl is anywhere close to you."

"You're just jealous because Mother loves me most, but then why shouldn't she? I'm making three times what you do. I've always been better-looking, and damn, Mack, you could put on a thousand-dollar suit and still look like you just walked across a cow pasture." Adam's tone had turned nasty.

That was as predictable as his famous shrug. When Adam didn't get his way, he turned off the charm and flipped the switch on downright meanness.

"Maybe so, but this time, you tell the folks that this divorce is your fault," Mack said. "And I'm comfortable in my skin. I don't need Mama's approval. I've lived with the fact that you're the fair-haired child for a long time. It doesn't bother me anymore."

Mack's cell phone rang, and he slipped it out of his hip pocket, laid it on the table, and put it on speaker. "Hello, Mama. What's going on in San Antonio?"

Adam waved his hands and mouthed, "Don't tell her I'm here."

"Charlene is here," his mother said.

With just those three words, Mack could tell that his mother was upset about something.

"She's cried until her poor eyes are swollen. Have you seen your brother? If you do, tell him he'd do well to steer clear of me for a while. Cheating on her like that with a secretary that's twenty years younger than he is. What can he be thinking? Now I'm wondering about those stories he told about his first two wives. I might take a switch to him even if he is a grown man," Nora Cooper fumed.

"If I see him, I'll give him your message," Mack said. "You and Dad should make a trip up here soon. I've got five new baby goats, and you know how he loves to watch them play."

"We'll do our best to come visit when the weather clears up. His memory gets worse every day, but you're right, he does love your goats and has a good time when we're there. I've got to get back to the living room and console Charlene. Bless her darlin' heart. If I'd caught your dad with another woman, I would have shot the both of them. Bye, now."

"Bye," Mack said.

"Well, crap!" Adam moaned.

"Maybe it's time to talk to your wife about that counseling," Mack suggested.

Adam pushed back the chair and put on his coat. "Don't gloat."

"The goat boy never gloats." Mack followed him to the door and held it open for him to leave.

Chapter Two

olly sighed in the passenger seat of the car, but Lily ignored it for the fiftieth time. Poor little darlin's probably felt like they were in solitary confinement with no cell phones or tablets or even their handheld video games to use on the two-hour trip. They both should have thought about the possible consequences before they made the choice to smoke pot or sneak out of the house to drink beer and smoke cigarettes.

"You've made your point, Mama. Can we turn around and go home?" Holly asked when they'd left the city and started driving through nothing but ranching country on either side of the road.

"We're headed in the right direction. *Home* from now on will be in Comfort," Lily answered.

"Please, Mama. I won't ever sneak out of the house again. I promise," Braden said from the back seat.

"And I'll never even look at another joint," Holly promised.

"I know you won't, because we'll be in Comfort, and I'll be keeping a much closer eye on both of you. I'm going to have weekly visits with your school principal." Lily caught the next exit onto Highway 290.

The GPS would have routed her through San Antonio, but the smaller highway kept her out of the big-city traffic.

"I can't believe we have to go to school in that little-bitty town," Holly groaned.

"It's your choice. You can be homeschooled or . . ." Lily paused.

"I'll go to school," Holly blurted out.

"Good." Lily nodded. "If the schedule is still like it was when I was in school, the bus will pick y'all up at seven fifteen every morning."

"You've got to be kidding, right?" Holly spit out. "We can't ride the bus! That's for nerds and geeks. You'll have to take us."

"Sorry, darlin'. You'll just have to get out your nerd shirts and your geek jeans." Lily turned on the radio and found her favorite country station.

"Are we going to have to listen to that the whole way?" Braden whined from the back seat.

"Can't we just have our Nintendos until we get there?" Holly begged.

Lily shrugged. "They're packed in a box, and it's in the moving van."

"This is too much punishment for just smoking one joint," Holly fumed.

"You think so?" Lily asked. "Just imagine what would have happened if the police had caught you, especially since you had a little bag of the stuff stashed in the lining of your purse."

"You went through my purse?" Holly raised her voice.

Lily turned up the volume on the radio. "Yes, darlin', I did, and we'll have random checks of your purse and your room until you earn back the trust I've given you all these years."

"God! All over one joint! What if you'd found . . ." Holly stopped and glared at her mother.

"Did I miss something in your purse, sweetheart? Do I need to unpack all your boxes and make sure there's nothing tucked away with your cute little bikini underbritches?" Lily asked.

"No, Mama," Holly sighed. "It's just that pot is such a minor thing. My friends do all kinds of worse things."

"Then it's time to get away from those friends. I'm not your friends' mother. I don't watch my children ruin their lives. Sit back. Enjoy the ride. And listen to some good old country music," Lily said.

"No, *you* ruin our lives *for* us," Braden said from the back seat.

Lily ignored both of them. When she had left Comfort to go to college, she'd vowed that she would never live there again. Small-town life wasn't for her, especially in a historic little town that catered to tourists looking for a trip back in time. She had wanted to go *forward* with her life, not live forever in the past, with historical markers everywhere. That was twenty years ago. Now the idea of historical markers didn't seem so bad.

The kids remained silent until she turned south in Fredericksburg. That's when Holly moaned dramatically. "We're dropping off the edge of the world."

"And falling into—"

Lily shot a look into the rearview mirror that stopped Braden's sentence short, and he blushed. That was a good sign, in her book. At least he wasn't so hardened that he couldn't turn red when he was about to say a dirty word.

"We'll be in the place we're 'falling into' in about thirty minutes, tops. You'll have the same bedrooms that you always had when your grandparents were still with us. I don't expect the place to look much different than it did when we came for your grandmother's funeral five years ago," she said.

"That means the historical marker is still in the front yard. The porch swing still squeaks, and the most exciting part of the whole day is when you hear a second car go by out on the road." Holly sighed again, this time with lots of self-pity.

"Because the house is so far back on the lane, you damn . . . darn sure can't *see* the cars going by." Braden blushed again.

"Ain't life grand?" Lily looked up in the rearview mirror at the reflection of her son in the back seat. "Only now, we'll be sharing the house with Mack Cooper, the vo-ag teacher at the high school, and the pasture is full of goats."

Holly threw her hands over her eyes. "This gets worse and worse."

"Goats? You mean real animal goats we saw at the petting zoo when we were little kids? I kind of liked them," Braden said.

Holly whipped around to glare at him. "Traitor."

"Well, I did." He shrugged.

Lily wasn't looking forward to being back in the house that held so many memories, or living with Mack, either, but that was the price she was willing to pay to keep her kids out of jail. The last time she'd been home was for her mother's funeral. She'd planned on driving back over to Comfort every weekend until she got the place cleaned out and put up for sale, but she'd been so busy with the divorce and the move to the apartment soon after that she just let that business slide. Thinking of the divorce still made her angry, even after all these years. Right after she'd buried her mother, Wyatt revealed that he'd fallen in love with one of his clients, oil baroness Victoria Banfield—he had told her in a tone that sounded like he was discussing the weather. He was willing to give Lily the house they lived in at the time, but there was no way that her salary as a work-at-home mom could ever make the mortgage payments. So they'd sold it. She'd put her part of the equity into a college fund for the kids and paid the first year's rent on an apartment that was really too expensive for her budget, but it gave the kids their own bathroom and privacy. They deserved that much when their sorry father didn't even want normal custodial rights.

Wyatt was married within days of the divorce, in another state or another country. She had moved herself and the kids into the apartment, and life went on. The house in Comfort had been on the back burner. She had seldom thought about it. With everything going on in her life at that time with the pain of a divorce, she just couldn't put herself through the heartbreak of sorting out her mother's things. Two months went by, and Mack Cooper called to ask if she'd be interested in renting it—as is—with everything inside the place included in the rent. As the new teacher in Comfort, he needed a place outside town with a few acres to run his goats. They'd agreed that he would move the furniture from her parents' bedroom to the empty room upstairs.

Lily remembered Mack from her high school days. He had a twin brother who was downright sexy and always had a harem around him, but Mack was withdrawn and shy. Adam had been the football hero. Mack had been into the ag program. They sure didn't act or look like twins. Even so, she'd checked out all his references and settled on an amount for the rent. He'd never been late on a single payment, and Lord only knew how much the money helped her get by.

She'd been a high school counselor before Holly was born, but Wyatt had wanted her to stay home with the baby, so she'd given up her job and run a counseling service out of the house. They'd had a sweet little guesthouse that worked great for that business, and then when she moved to the apartment, she managed to keep up the work out of the tiny office she'd fixed up in the guesthouse. As she neared Comfort, she slapped the steering wheel in anger. She'd been blind to the way her own children were getting out of hand. Looking back, the signs had been there, but she'd had her head buried in the sand so deep that she'd ignored them. Things were sure enough going to be different from here on out.

"Almost there." She made a sharp right-hand turn onto her old homestead, where she'd grown up back before she'd married and when she was Lily Miller. "We're actually on your grandparents' property right now. It looked a little different the last time y'all were here. If you look to y'all's left, you'll see the goats. To the right, well, darlin's, that's more goats."

"Kind of cute," Braden said.

Holly narrowed her eyes, turned around, and gave him another drop-dead look.

"Well, they are." He crossed his arms over his chest.

Lily came to the end of the drive and parked her car in front of the house. When she had come home for a visit, her mother, Vera, had always been on the porch swing, waiting for her. But not today. The old blue swing looked lonely, like it was waiting to tell stories, and it could sure enough tell a lot. That was where Lily had gotten her first kiss when she was Holly's age. That was where she would've lost her virginity after the junior prom if her mother hadn't switched on the porch light five minutes before curfew.

She took a deep breath and got out of the car. "Y'all can come on in or freeze out here. It's up to you, but it looks like rain. That means all those boxes on the porch could get wet. It would make for a lot of laundry. Which reminds me—Saturday mornings will be for cleaning and getting the laundry done. I figure that a few chores might help keep you out of trouble. Be sure not to wash your white things with red or you'll have pink underwear."

"God!" Holly moaned. "Is there anything else? Like maybe making us live on bread and water for a year?"

"Don't give her any ideas." Braden flung the rear door open, got out of the car, and started toward the house.

Holly did the same, only she stomped every step of the way. When she reached the door, Lily called out, "You might as well pick up one of your boxes and carry it upstairs to your room. They aren't going to grow wings and float up there for you."

Holly looked over her shoulder and rolled her big blue eyes toward the gray skies. "Why didn't the movers put them in the rooms where they belonged?"

"Because I told them to leave them on the porch," Lily answered. "And I told Mack not to bring them inside. So get on with it, my darlin's. It'll be a big mess if it rains on them."

She almost felt sorry enough for Braden to help him, but then she remembered her own shock, dismay, and disappointment over the preceding events.

Mack threw open the door. It had been years since she'd seen him, and her first impression right then was nothing short of shock. He was a little heavier than he'd been five years ago when he'd attended her mother's funeral, but it was in all the right places. His broad shoulders and huge biceps strained the seams of his oatmeal-colored knit shirt. Faded jeans hugged his big thighs, and his cowboy boots were scuffed and worn, marking him for a real rancher, not a Saturday-night wannabe. She'd forgotten what a good-looking man he was, and now she was going to be living in the same house with him.

"Hey, y'all made it. I thought I heard a car drive up. Come right in. Here, Braden, let me help you with that. It's about to drag you down, boy."

Braden glanced at his mother. Lily sighed. "If Mack wants to help, that's fine by me. But you have to do the unpacking. I'll check your rooms later to see that everything is put away."

"Thank you, sir," Braden said respectfully.

Lily picked up one of her own boxes and followed them into the foyer and up the narrow staircase to the second floor. Holly fell in behind her and huffed all the way to the top as if she were toting a pregnant elephant up the steps, when in all actuality, the box had *nightshirts and underwear* written on the side of it.

"I've got a pot of loaded potato soup simmering, and corn bread is ready to go in the oven. Where do I put this, Braden?" Mack asked.

"Mama says we'll have the same rooms we did when we were little kids and came to visit Grandma and Grandpa, so this one." He pointed to one of the four bedrooms. "Potato soup's the best—I'm starving."

"You unpack that one while I bring the rest of your stuff up, and then I'll help Holly," Mack said.

"I can get my own," Holly smarted off.

Lily's stern look must have had an effect, because Holly added, "But thank you for the offer."

"Sure thing," Mack said. "If you change your mind, I'll be glad to help out."

Braden had ripped the tape off the top of his first box and was busy taking things out when Lily and Mack started back down the stairs. Memories seemed to reach out from the corners and grab her. Nothing had changed, not even the pictures of herself and her sister lining the staircase wall. The one of them together on the swing set out in the backyard sent a single tear down Lily's face. That was the last picture taken before Rosemary was diagnosed with a brain tumor and died six months later.

"I remember when you and your sister looked like that," Mack said.

She wiped the tear away. "I should've come back and taken care of this place years ago, but I had too much on my plate."

"Facing old memories isn't easy," Mack said. "You haven't changed much since high school. I would have known you anywhere."

"You either," Lily said. "Except I don't remember you wearing glasses back then. Do you and Adam look any more alike now than you did then?"

"If anything, we look even more different." When they reached the door, Mack held it open for her. "He's a banker in San Antonio and—"

"Still chasing anything that wears a skirt?" Lily asked.

"You got that right. He just told me this morning he was about to get his third divorce." Mack looked up at the sky. "Hey, I just got the first drop of rain on my face. Let's just push all these inside to the foyer so they don't get wet."

"Thank you for helping, and for not minding if we move in here." She picked up a couple of lightweight boxes and shoved them to the back of the foyer, past the hall tree and the two ladder-back chairs. Work boots were shoved up under one of the chairs. They belonged to Mack and weren't the same style her father had worn, but they still reminded her of seeing Frank Miller's boots in the same place. He had passed away a year before her mother. The things she'd missed the most when she came home when her father was alive were seeing his boots under the chair and his favorite coffee mug right beside the old percolator.

"Mom-maaa . . ." Holly's pitiful scream floated from above.

Lily stopped what she was doing and flew up the stairs with Mack right behind her. She was out of breath when she hit the top step, but she caught her second wind and rushed into Holly's room.

"What is it?" Lily panted.

Holly spun around, pointing at every wall. "There's no closet in this room. The dresser only has three drawers, and look at that tiny mirror. The lighting is horrible. How am I supposed to put on my makeup, and where am I supposed to hang my clothes?"

"You sounded like you were dying!" Lily grabbed the doorjamb and fanned herself.

"You've taken away everything, including my closet, where I—" Holly stopped herself short and threw herself backward on the bed.

"Where you what? Hide your marijuana?" Lily asked. "See that?" She pointed toward a sturdy clothes rack in the corner. "That's what I used for a closet when I lived here, and I'm still alive. I don't expect it will kill you to use it until you go away to college."

Holly sat up and let one trained tear roll down her cheek. "Please take us home. I will never smoke pot again in my life, or drink or sneak out at night or—" She clamped a hand over her mouth.

Lily sat down on the bed beside her and gently wiped away the tear with her fingertip. "After that confession, honey, we aren't even going back to Austin for a visit until summer gets here. You'll graduate in a little more than three years. Then you can go to college and have a real closet. Or hide a whole rope ladder under your bed."

Holly's expression changed from one of pure repentance to absolute rebellion. "When I get out of this prison, I'll never come back, not even to your funeral."

"I won't know it. I'll be dead." Lily stood up and headed for the door. "It's raining. The boxes are all inside the house. At least their contents will be dry. And FYI, one of the boxes with your name on it is filled with hangers. I remembered to pack them while you had breakfast this morning. Holly, darlin', I do love you."

Holly sprang off the bed and tipped her chin up in the air. She whipped around dramatically and ripped the tape off a box. Lily turned and headed back down the stairs as if nothing had happened.

"Whew! That was intense," Mack whispered as he followed her.

"That was just a little bit of temper and a well-trained tear. Intense was when I walked in that library bathroom and caught her smoking a joint," Lily said. "Are you sure you can handle us living here?"

"I'm a teacher." He stacked one box on top of another and started back up the stairs. "I've seen a little bit of everything."

"I was a school counselor until Holly was born, but living with a kid twenty-four, seven is different than having them in a classroom for an hour a day," she said.

"You want a job as a substitute teacher? I can probably get you one at the school. We're always short on qualified subs."

"I hope I can build a little counseling practice here in Comfort. If I do, I wouldn't have time to sub, but thank you." She followed him up the staircase. "It'll take a while to get clientele built up, but maybe in a few months, it'll show some kind of profit. As long as I have a computer and Wi-Fi, I'm good."

He turned around at the top of the staircase. "Guess you'd better call someone to install Wi-Fi, then, because we don't have any technical stuff here. I've got a cell phone, but I don't even use all the data I'm given every month."

"We really are living in the boonies." She managed a smile, but it didn't reach her eyes.

"Yep, and I love every single minute of it." He disappeared into Braden's room with the boxes.

She couldn't quite agree with him, but she hoped that someday she'd be able to say, "Amen." Right at that moment, Lily felt a whole lot like her daughter. She had been jerked out of her church, taken away from her friends, and didn't even have a closet, either. But deep down in her soul, she knew this was the right move. She'd brushed so many incidents under the rug, and told herself each one of them was just another phase they were passing through. Now it was time to jerk her head out of the sand.

She reminded herself again that a kid could kick any bush between the Red River and the Gulf of Mexico and a dozen friends would come rolling out, but they only got one mother—mean or otherwise. With a fresh start here in Comfort, she hoped she'd do a better job of being the mom they needed.

Fresh start? I'd say you're coming back to your roots. Her mother's gravelly voice, so much like her own, was so clear that Lily whipped around to see if she was coming out of the kitchen.

"Well, there's that, too," Lily muttered.

Chapter Three

*L*ily turned around slowly, taking in the whole room that had been hers before she left for college. The lace curtains were the only things that were the same. When Mack had moved into the house, he'd cleaned out everything from the downstairs bedroom into the room that had been emptied when Lily moved into her first apartment.

Why oh why hadn't she come back to take care of things? She threw herself backward onto the bed and stared at the full rack of her mother's clothing on the far wall. Vera had known that her time was short, so she'd taken care of all the legal business with her lawyer, and even arranged her own funeral. She'd made it so easy for Lily to simply lock the doors, put the key in the hands of Teena, her friend from high school and a real estate agent, and just walk away.

"Lily, where are you?" A voice floated up the stairs.

"Speak of the devil." Lily raised her voice. "In my old bedroom."

Teena didn't even knock on the closed door, but came right on in and bent to give Lily a hug. A tall brunette without an extra ounce of extra weight on her slim body, she'd changed very little since high school. Not even having a set of twins had widened her narrow hips or put another inch on her waist.

"I figured I'd given you enough time to get here," Teena said. "Mack was just getting in his truck to leave, and he said for me to come on in. Sally is on the way. We've got a couple of hours to help you get unpacked." She glanced over at the clothes rack. "Those are your mama's things. I remember that blue dress. She wore it to your folks' anniversary party at the church the year before your dad died. All us girls went shopping with her to pick it out. Good God, Lily! Why haven't you taken care of some of this before now?"

Lily drew in a lungful of air and let it out slowly. "I planned to, but if I didn't, then I could pretend she was still here. If I didn't come back to Comfort, well, y'all understand."

"Yes, we do, but it's time to let your mama go." Teena straightened. "And that starts by taking care of some of her things. I'll put all that on the bed so you can hang up your clothes. We'll use the boxes you brought your stuff in to pack all Vera's stuff. Sally and I will take everything to the church clothes closet when we leave today. Someone can get some good out of it."

"Good out of what?" Sally leaned on the doorframe, huffing. "I'd forgotten how steep those stairs were."

"Lily hasn't even gone through her mother's stuff," Teena said. "Come to think of it, she hasn't been home in five years."

"I don't blame her. When my mama dies, I'm going to give that job to my sister." Sally met Lily halfway at the foot of the bed, grabbed Lily's hands, and jumped up and down like a little girl. "We're all together again. I'm so happy I could dance a jig in a pig trough on Main Street."

Sally's blonde hair was pulled up in a ponytail. Shorter than Lily, she'd always carried a few extra pounds, but she'd been the life of the party when they were kids. Now she was divorced, had no children, and owned a cute little vintage boutique in Comfort.

She pulled a box cutter from the hip pocket of her jeans and asked, "What do you want opened first?"

"You got a concealed carry permit for that weapon?" Teena started piling clothing on the bed.

"Yep." Sally nodded as she sliced through the tape on the nearest box. "It's called a business license to sell antiques."

Lily got to her feet. "Thank you both for being here."

"Hey, that's what friends are for," Teena said. "I'll take the clothes off the hangers and fold them. Sally, you can hang up Lily's stuff and repack the boxes. Lily, you start going through the dresser drawers."

"Yes, ma'am, Miss Bossy Britches," Lily teased.

"I'm the organizer, remember?" Teena wrapped her arms around the last load of clothing from the rack and put it on the bed. "Do you want to keep anything from all this?"

Lily shook her head. "I've got lots of memories. I don't need a shirt or a dress to remind me of her. Anything in there you can sell at Yesterday's Treasures?"

"It's not old enough to be vintage," Sally said, "but if she's still got that pair of cat-eye glasses she wore stuffed in a drawer, I'll pay you top dollar for them." Sally was already busy putting Lily's clothes on hangers and taking them across the room to the rack. "I get two or three requests for those every week."

"If they show up, you can sure have them." Lily opened the top dresser drawer and fought back the tears welling up in her brown eyes. The faint aroma of the little floral sachet in with her mother's nightgowns brought back memories of all the times her mama had tucked her in at night, right up until she was in junior high school. The rose scent that her mother loved had lingered behind in Lily's bedroom a long time after Vera had left the room every evening.

Teena sniffed the air. "I smell roses."

"Mama's sachet." Lily held it up. "You'd think it would have lost all of its scent after five years."

"Probably no one has even opened the drawer in all this time." Sally pushed an empty box over to her. "We could give the nightgowns and underwear to Granny Hayes if you don't mind. She'd be glad to get them."

"That's fine," Lily agreed.

It was common knowledge in Comfort that Granny Hayes only came to town on Sunday morning. She lived five miles west, way out in the sticks, and rode Dusty, her trusty old mule, to church. She sat in the back pew and was usually the first one to shake the preacher's hand and leave. Sometimes she stopped at the grocery store to pick up a few items, but usually she just rode back to her shack out west of town. She hitched the mule to a wagon about twice a year to come into Comfort for supplies, but other than that, she remained a hermit.

"I'd forgotten about her. She's about the same size Mama was. Are you sure that she'd want such personal things?" Lily carefully took them out of the drawer and packed them into a box. "Does she still have that 'No Trespassing' sign up on her fence? She might shoot first and ask questions later if you enter her property without permission."

"She likes me," Sally said. "I'll take them out to her this evening."

"Well, she sure don't like me." Teena started stacking shoes under the clothes rack.

"She's just a lonely old woman," Lily said. "I wonder what her story is. We always thought her place was haunted and she kept ghosts in that old log cabin."

"That's why she doesn't like me," Teena said. "I asked her about the ghosts when I was a little girl. She glared at me and told me to leave her alone."

"Y'all ever known anyone to go inside her place?" Lily asked.

"She lets me come up on her porch, but not inside the cabin," Sally said. "That's probably because I buy some of her craft items for the store."

"I can't imagine living like that." Teena opened the last box, saw that it was underwear, and slid it across the floor toward Lily. "You're on your own with this stuff, and now I've got to get going. I've got a two o'clock appointment to show a house."

"And my long lunch hour is over, so I'm going, too." Sally stepped out into the hallway. "Hey, you two beautiful kids. Come out of your rooms and give me a hug."

Holly's door cracked a little and then flew open. "I thought I heard voices," she said as she wrapped her arms around Sally.

"When did y'all get here?" Braden asked as he came out of his room with a smile on his face.

Lily felt a pang of jealousy that they were so warm and sweet with her friend. She and Teena joined the three of them in the hallway, crowding up the small space.

"We've been here about an hour, helping your mama unpack. And now, we need some help getting those three boxes down the stairs," Sally said.

Without so much as a sigh or a grumble, Braden and Holly each picked one up. Teena got the last one, and they all five paraded down the stairs together. The kids even took the boxes out to Sally's bright-red vintage Mustang and helped her get them in the trunk—in the drizzling rain.

"Have they forgiven you?" Sally asked.

"Nope, but it's good to see they still have some manners," Lily answered in a soft voice.

"It'll take time. I remember when my boys were fourteen. The world would have come to an end if I'd jerked them out of their school and took them away from their friends," Teena said.

"I didn't have much choice. I thought about every possibility for two days before I made up my mind," Lily told her. "How are the twins?"

"They're moving back into the dorms on Sunday. I've loved having them home for a month, but truth is, I'm glad they're going back to college. Ryder spends every waking minute he can with his girlfriend, and Creed stays up all night playing video games with his friends and sleeps all day," Teena answered. "They didn't make all As, but they did pass all their courses, and they didn't get kicked out of school, so I guess I shouldn't bitch about them."

"You don't mind having an empty nest?" Lily asked.

"I did at first, but then they came home every couple of weekends, so it wasn't a big deal," Teena replied. "Okay, girl. I'm leaving now."

"Call if you need anything. We'll see you in church tomorrow morning, right?" Sally got into her car and waved out the window.

"We'll be there, and thanks again." Lily waved at both vehicles until they were out of sight.

The kids stopped on the porch to wave for a few seconds, and then they went back inside. When Lily got to the living room, Braden was sacked out on the sofa with a disgusted expression on his face. Holly was sitting in the recliner, frowning and picking at her nails.

"Mama, we don't even have cable," Braden moaned.

"I told him that we were going to live back in the caveman days, but he didn't believe me," Holly smarted off.

"This is back before that, even," Braden said. "I keep expecting a dinosaur to peek in the windows."

"There's a whole assortment of movies in that cabinet. Take your choice," Lily told him. "I'm going to make a pitcher of sweet tea. Y'all want some?"

"Nope." Holly flipped back and forth between the three channels on the television, finally settling on a rerun of *Friends*.

"I'll take a glass," Braden said.

It got him a hateful look from his sister, but he just shot one right back at her. "You ain't the boss of me. If I want tea, I'll drink it," he said. "Why couldn't we bring our televisions from home? Holly always hogs the remote."

"We're going to be a family from now on, not three people who live in the same house," she answered. "We're going to share everything."

"Hello, house." Mack's big deep voice echoed as he came in through the back door. "I brought two friends with me."

Lily got misty-eyed again when she saw Polly Dillard coming in ahead of Mack. Polly had been Vera's lifelong friend. She had more gray streaks in her dark hair and a few more wrinkles than the last time Lily had seen her. Polly set a chocolate sheet cake on the cabinet and opened up her arms. Lily walked right into them. Hugging her was so much like hugging her mother that Lily had to fight back tears.

Mack carried in a covered dish and a bag of chips and placed them beside the cake.

"Thanks so much, Mack, for helping me get this stuff into the house." Polly stepped away from Lily and said, "Girl, I could just take a switch to you for not coming home more often. I've missed you. I made seven-layer dip and your favorite cake." She pointed at the cabinet. "You look more like Vera every day, except for that blonde hair, but then your grandmother had lovely blonde hair. Still don't seem right that Vera is gone. Or that she left me behind. We made a pact when we were twenty-one and got drunk off our asses that we would do everything together. We even got married the same summer, and we were supposed to die on the same day. I guess she went on so she could get the place ready for me. Lord knows I'll need all the help I can get."

Polly always did use a hundred words where five would do the trick, but Lily was so glad to see her that she didn't mind the way she went on, especially about Lily's mother. It was comforting to hear the same things that she'd been told more than once.

Lily couldn't imagine her straitlaced mother drunk. She had only drunk an occasional glass of wine, and that was at a wedding or a New Year's party.

"She didn't have kids at the same time I did, though," Polly said. "Bless her heart, it was several years after she and Frank married before

Rosemary came along, and then she had you. If it hadn't been for you, she'd never have survived Rosemary's dying so young."

"It's sweet of you to say that." Lily's voice cracked a little.

"A mother should never have to bury a child," Polly said. "We're born with the knowledge that we will have to lose our parents, and that's a natural grief. But to mourn a child is unnatural grief. I was glad that Vera had her kids later in life. That way we never had that empty-nest thing because we still had you around." She took off her coat and hung it on the back of a kitchen chair. She towered above Lily and was thin as a rail, yet her blue eyes still sparkled with lots of life. "Let's all gather 'round and break into that dip. Then we'll have some cake for dessert and call it all an afternoon snack. Where are the kids? And why did you decide to move back here in the middle of the school year? Sally told me yesterday that you were coming, but she was busy with a customer so I didn't ask for details."

"Kids are in the living room. I had to get them out of the city. Have to explain later," Lily whispered, and then yelled, "Hey, we've got chips and dip and chocolate cake if y'all want to . . ."

Braden was in the room with Holly right behind him before she even finished the last words. Mack took a gallon jug of sweet tea from the refrigerator, got down five glasses, and asked, "Braden, you want to help put ice in these glasses?"

"I'll help him," Holly offered.

"Sweet Jesus!" Polly laid a hand on her heart. "They've grown up so much. They were just little things when Vera passed on."

"I was expecting them to look like they did at Vera's funeral, too," Mack said as he took down a stack of small plates. "Guess we get a picture in our minds of the last time we saw a person, and we don't think about the passing of time."

He handed the stack to Lily. She took it and dealt the plates around the table. She couldn't remember the last time she'd sat at the kitchen table with her kids. They usually heaped a plate and either took it to the living room or to their bedrooms. She scooped out two big spoonfuls of the dip and passed it on to Mack, who was sitting beside her at the round table. There was a slight tingle when his hand brushed against hers, but she chalked it up to nerves.

"Thank you," he said. "It's kind of nice to have folks to share food with. Gets lonely in this big house all alone."

"Big house?" Holly fussed. "I don't even get my own bathroom, or a walk-in closet."

"But you get to live in a house that's more than a hundred years old." Polly piled dip onto her plate. "Just think of all the stories this place could tell."

Braden poked her on the shoulder. "I bet ghosts live in your bedroom. When you hear spooky music, that will let you know they're coming out of the walls."

Holly shivered. "Be quiet!"

Braden hummed spooky music.

Holly narrowed her eyes at him and said, "If anything scares me, I'm going to open the door and shoo them over to your room. You better keep a light on. I hear they slip into your head and turn you into an alien."

"Spoken like a true smart-ass." Polly giggled. "I swear, her *voice* is even like Vera's."

Braden grinned impishly and poked his sister on the arm. "Maybe Granny's ghost has already crawled inside your head. Any day now, you're going to start wrinkling up all over your face."

"You're mean!" Holly ran her fingers over her flawless face. "Mama, tell him to shut his mouth."

"You started it, Holly Jo," Lily told her.

"I did not," Holly protested. "Braden did, and if I start getting wrinkles, I'm going to run away."

"The goats turn into zombies at night," Braden said. "You better stay in the house after dark."

"They only eat little boys. They hate girls," Holly told him. "So you better not go outside to smoke. Did you throw away that pack you had hiding in your underwear drawer?"

"Yes, I did, tattletale," Braden replied. "Did you throw away that joint you had in your purse?"

"I flushed it down the toilet." She blushed.

"That's enough out of both of you," Lily said.

Mack chuckled under his breath. "This is going to be an adventure."

"More like a nightmare," Lily whispered.

Chapter Four

The first major fight between Braden and Holly came about on Saturday evening. They both wanted to have first dibs on the single bathroom on the second floor. Lily came out of her bedroom and got between them before they started throwing punches. "Braden, you go take a bath and get to bed. You can read until eleven since this is Christmas break. Lights go out at ten on school nights."

"Ten! That's for babies," Braden argued.

"You always take his side." Holly crossed her arms over her chest and fumed.

"You will take a morning bath." Lily turned and waggled a finger at her daughter. "The bathroom is off-limits for putting on makeup or primping, and that goes for both of you. You each have a mirror in your room. And ten o'clock is bedtime, and there will be a bed check."

"I don't primp," Braden declared. "And I want a shower, not a bath."

"You're out of luck, kid. Our bathroom only has a tub, and the weatherman says there's no chance of rain for a couple of days," Lily told him.

"What's rain got to do with it?" Braden asked.

"Duh!" Holly snorted. "You have to go outside and dance around naked if you want a shower." She clamped a hand over her mouth and groaned. "How am I supposed to wash my hair with no shower?"

"See that plastic pitcher sitting on the ladder-back chair?" Lily pointed.

"Are you serious?" Holly asked.

"Yep, I am, but on the positive side, that big old claw-foot tub is deep enough that you can sink down in it all the way to your chin," Lily said. "You might even learn to like it after you take a few baths."

"Yeah, when them goats out there sprout wings and fly." Holly stormed off to her room and slammed the door.

Lily remembered the last time they had been there, Braden had called the deep tub his swimming pool. In those days, Holly had been content to read her Harry Potter books in the evenings, and there was no problem with sharing a bathroom. Wyatt was still with her then and had comforted her all through the days leading up to the funeral and even on the way back to Austin when she'd been so sad. Two days later, he'd told her that he wanted a divorce.

She went back to her bedroom and closed the door, sat down on the bed, and stared at the old oak secretary without really seeing it. "The bastard," she whispered. "He was holding me and thinking of Victoria the whole time. Thank God I didn't get pregnant that last night we were in this house."

She blinked, bringing the secretary into focus. Lily had played at her mother's feet when Vera would lower the little flap to make a desk so she could answer letters every Sunday afternoon. Her mother had warned her constantly to be careful with the curved glass door, behind which Vera's most prized knickknacks were kept.

Lily stood up and lowered the flap. Each of the little cubbyholes was filled—one with stationery, another with matching envelopes, and still another with a roll of forty-nine-cent stamps. In the space under the cubicles sat a leather-bound book about two inches thick. Thinking it might be a first edition of one of the classics that her mother loved, she slid it out slowly and laid it on the desk. A thin piece of leather wrapped around a big brown button on the top kept it closed. She ran her fingers over the tooled title: *Family Journal*. Why hadn't her mother ever showed it to her or even mentioned buying it?

She unwound the leather latch and opened the book. "Holy smoke! It's not a book. It really is a journal. I wonder where Mama got it." She opened it and started to flip through it when Holly peeked in the room.

"Mama, I hate it here. You've proven your point. Please take us home," she begged. A tear slowly made its way down her cheek, showing that she was truly miserable.

Lily almost caved, but then a voice in her head reminded her to *deliver what you promise.* She remembered her mother saying those very words.

"But you haven't proven your point," Lily said. "When you've proven that you can be trusted, then we'll have this discussion again. Until then, we're staying right here."

Holly wiped the tear away with the back of her hand and glared at her mother. "I'll never forgive you for making me do this." She turned around, crossed over to her room, and slammed the door.

Feeling as if she was reading something sacred, she stared at the first entry—small, neat handwriting from someone named Ophelia Smith.

June 1862, Vicksburg, Mississippi: My heart is broken. My life is in shambles and I have no idea what to do. I can run a household, but William took care of the plantation, and now he's dead and gone. I've kept things going, but it hasn't been easy. A woman doesn't have the authority that a man does. William left six months ago to fight for the Confederacy. They brought his body home yesterday, and we buried him today. Now I have two children, a daughter, Matilda, and a son, Henry, to raise on my own. Times are hard right now, and children need a father, especially Henry, who isn't old enough to help me run this place, and is already showing rebellious signs. I fear he'll run off and join the fight as soon as he's old enough. Our foreman left today, and several slaves have already run away, too. I can see nothing but disaster in the future. Our way of life is gone, but it's all I know, so what do I do now?

Feeling as if she were peering into the window of a woman's soul, Lily couldn't force her eyes away from that first entry. She read it several times and thought of Braden. Evidently, there had been single mothers trying to raise children on their own for a century and a half. She carefully closed the journal, put it back in the secretary, and lifted the flap back into place. She wanted to read more, but just reading that much made her feel guilty about peeking at someone's intimate thoughts. Besides, tomorrow was Sunday, and that meant going to church, so she couldn't stay up reading about Ophelia's life half the night. She got dressed for bed, turned off the light, and slipped beneath the covers.

She closed her eyes, but the words from the journal still ran through her mind. Had Ophelia and William slept in a four-poster bed like this one? Had she soaked her pillow with tears for him every night that he was gone to the war, or did she have so much to do, trying to keep her children fed and clothed, that she had no time for tears?

~

Lily seldom ever dreamed, and when she did, she usually woke up with every detail still fresh in her mind. The next morning, she sat up in bed, and for a split second, she was Ophelia, and Braden and Holly were Matilda and Henry. She rubbed her eyes and looked around at the room. Then she remembered who and where she was. She turned the alarm off two minutes before it was set to ring and threw back the covers.

"That was one crazy dream." She longed to read more of the journal that morning. She felt like a moth drawn to a flame, as if she should read it from the first to the last. Maybe by the time she'd read the rest of Ophelia's story, she'd figure out who the woman was and why Lily's mother had the journal. Maybe Ophelia just needed someone to sympathize with her even though more than 150 years had passed. But Lily had breakfast to cook, and then it would be time to get ready for church. The kids had been used to sleeping in on Sunday, so there was no doubt that there would be groaning and moaning.

She dressed in jeans and a baggy T-shirt, pulled on a pair of socks, and padded down the staircase. When she made it to the foyer, she could smell coffee, and she saw that the light was on in the kitchen.

"Good mornin'," she said as she entered the room and headed for the coffeepot. "Are you an early riser, too?"

"I've been up for a couple of hours," Mack told her. "Five o'clock is when I start my day. I've already fed the goats and chipped the layer of ice off their water tank. Do y'all go to church?" He beat her to the coffeepot, filled two mugs, and handed one to her.

"We do today." She leaned against the counter and sipped her coffee. "We haven't been in more than a year. The kids didn't want to go, and I let them make the decision. Do you go?"

"I'm the Sunday-school teacher for the twelve-to-fifteen-year-old group. Are y'all just going to church or to—" he started to ask.

She butted in. "We'll be going to both. Sunday school still starts at ten, right?"

He nodded. "Then church right after at eleven."

"Just like when I was a kid," she said.

"Things don't change too much in Comfort." He grinned back at her.

"Thank God for that," she sighed. "Have you eaten yet? I checked last night and found everything I need to make sausage and pancakes. I'll replenish the grocery supplies tomorrow morning."

"I haven't had breakfast, and you're welcome to use whatever is here whenever you want," he told her.

"We need to talk about your rent, too." She set her coffee on the counter and got the sausage out of the refrigerator. "I figure since we're staying here, it's not fair to charge you rent."

Mack got the flour and other ingredients for pancakes from the pantry. "That's pretty generous of you. How about I still pay all the utilities, and we split the cost of the groceries?"

"That's more than fair." She found her mother's cast-iron skillets right where Vera always kept them and got out two—one for sausage and the other for pancakes.

"I like to cook, so I don't mind sharing the workload," he said. "I've got a roast thawed to put in the oven this morning. It should be ready when we get home from church."

"Mama always made roast for Sunday dinner." The memory put another smile on her face.

"My mother still does, and until they moved to be near Dad's doctors, I ate with them on Sunday. It'll be nice to have family around me again." He reached into the cabinet for a bowl to stir up the batter for pancakes, and his arm brushed against Lily's shoulder. Sparks flew, but Lily attributed them to the fact that she hadn't been in a relationship in years. She'd be crazy not to be attracted to a good-looking man like Mack.

Lily had worried about how things would work with Mack in the house, but it looked like she'd fretted for nothing. He was agreeable to a really good financial arrangement, and he liked to cook. She couldn't ask for anything more out of a roommate—unless he also liked to wake up grumpy and belligerent kids.

While the sausage cooked and Mack flipped pancakes, Lily set the table for four. She waited until breakfast was cooked before she went to get the kids. Dreading even talking to Holly, she decided to rap on Braden's door first. He threw it open and sniffed the air.

"I smell food." He ran down the stairs in a blur.

She crossed the hall and knocked on Holly's door, but there was no answer. She cracked the door open and saw that her daughter's bed had been slept in, but she was gone. Lily's heart rose up in her throat, and her chest tightened.

"What are you doin'?" Holly asked right behind her. "Already inspecting my stuff to be sure I didn't sneak any pot in with my things?"

Lily turned around. "No, smarty-pants, I came to call you to breakfast. We'll be having three meals a day around the table from now on."

Holly frowned and unwound the towel from her wet hair. "I haven't even got my makeup on yet."

"Breakfast first, then makeup and getting dressed for Sunday school and church." Lily put her hands on Holly's shoulders and turned her toward the stairs. "We're having pancakes."

Holly set her heels and shrugged off her mother's hands. "I'll bring mine up to my room after I get my makeup on, and I'm not going to church or Sunday school."

"Joining the rest of us around the table was not a request. Neither was church." Lily pointed to the stairs. "If you aren't sitting in your place in three minutes, I'll be taking all of your makeup away for a week. Your choice on that matter. But you don't have a choice about church. We will be going as a family every week. I'd hate for you to have to show up your first two times without a drop of lipstick or eye shadow on."

Holly threw the towel at the bathroom door and stomped into her room.

"Towels go in the basket in the utility room, not on the floor," Lily said as she started down the stairs.

"What happens if I don't pick it up?" Holly called out. "Will you lock me in my room and give me nothing but bread and water?"

"Maybe water, but don't push your luck about bread. You've got three minutes, starting right now." Lily didn't remember being so sassy at Holly's age. She thought about Ophelia again and wondered if Henry ever got over that rebellious stage.

Holly pushed it to the last fifteen seconds, but she was sitting in her place within the allotted three minutes. She reached for a sausage patty with her fingers, but Lily shook her head. "Grace first, and then you'll use a fork."

They bowed their heads, and Lily said a short prayer. "We'll take turns saying the prayer before meals. If it's okay with Mack, either he or I will say the breakfast prayer, and you two will alternate on supper."

"I'm not prayin'," Holly declared.

"Then you don't eat." Lily put two sausage patties on her own plate and handed the platter to Mack. Then she took three pancakes from the stack and sent them around the table.

"If I'd known that smokin' a joint would cause this much trouble, I never would have done it. I might as well be a nun." Holly slathered butter on four pancakes and topped them off with lots of maple syrup.

"I never knew a pot-smokin' nun," Braden said. "Are you going to start a brand-new church where all the people smoke pot on Sunday?"

"Sure, I am, and all your little friends will have to put their cigarettes and beer in a big box at the front door before they can come into my church," Holly shot back at him.

Lily ignored the both of them, but she noticed that Mack was chuckling under his breath. It might be funny today, but wait until he had to put up with it for weeks on end. He'd be ready to load up his goats and leave Texas altogether.

~

Mack thought about Lily all the way to church that morning. He'd left half an hour early so he could get his Sunday-school room put in order and think about the week's lesson. When he saw her get out of that car on Friday, something stirred in an area he thought for sure was stone-cold dead. Sure, he'd known her—kind of, sort of—in high school. In a town the size of Comfort, with only three thousand people, everyone knew everyone else. The big joke was that they read the local newspaper just to see who got caught because they already knew what had gone on in town all week.

Lily Miller—as she was back in those days—had been a sophomore when he was a senior, but he'd forgotten how pretty she was with that mane of blonde hair flowing down her back and those big, beautiful brown eyes. When she spoke to him in that husky voice, he'd definitely felt something, but he told himself that it was useless. Adam had stolen the love of his life—twice. It could happen again, if his brother thought he was interested in Lily.

He set up the folding chairs in a circle and tried to put Lily's full lips out of his mind and think about the Sunday-school lesson. Of all things, it dealt with loving your brother as yourself. It might be a lively discussion with Holly and Braden in the mix. They squabbled about anything and everything. He didn't mind. Actually, he kind of enjoyed listening to them.

If he'd had misgivings about living with Lily and the kids, they had disappeared with that first look at her and the way the kids entertained him with their constant bickering. Lily was being very fair about the financial end of things, and if every day started off like that day when they had worked so well in the kitchen together, this arrangement would be great.

"Hey!" The preacher of the church, and one of his oldest and best friends, poked his head in the room. "There's doughnuts in the nursery."

"Thanks, but I had a big breakfast," Mack said.

He and Drew Donovan had graduated from Comfort High School together more than twenty years ago now. They'd formed a friendship way back in elementary school because they were the two shy boys who didn't fit in with the rest of the kids. Drew was tall and lanky, with a thick crop of black curly hair he had inherited from his black father, and green eyes from his white mother. Drew had known when he was in middle school that he would be a preacher someday, just like Mack had known from a young age that he wanted to be a vo-ag teacher.

"Walk with me to my office. We've got a little while before it's time for Sunday school," Drew said and led the way to his office.

"What's on your mind?" Mack opened the door for him.

"I hear that Lily Miller has come back to Comfort and is living in her folks' place with you. How do you feel about that?" Drew took a seat behind his desk.

"They just arrived yesterday, but so far, it's fine," Mack answered. "Only she's Lily Anderson now, and she's got a couple of kids. Braden is twelve, and Holly is fourteen."

"Are they going to be in church?" Drew asked.

Mack nodded. "And Sunday school, pretty much against their wishes, but . . ." He went on to tell Drew the reason why Lily had taken them out of the city.

"Smart mother." Drew finished off the last of his doughnut, stood up, and went to the small refrigerator in the corner. He took out a diet root beer and held it out to Mack.

Mack shook his head. "I should be getting on down to my classroom."

Drew twisted the lid off the bottle and set it on his desk. "You'll be a good influence on those two kids, Mack. I have faith in you."

"Thanks." Mack stood up.

"You get part of the credit for my boys being good men." Drew placed a bookmark in his Bible to save his spot.

"I just kept them focused. You were the guiding light." Mack waved at the door.

Drew had met a wonderful woman at seminary, married her when they graduated, and come straight back to Comfort to the church. They'd had three cute little boys in about four years. The oldest had been in Mack's agriculture classes and in his Future Farmers of America program. The two youngest still were. Their oldest son had joined the air force right out of high school. The middle one was a senior this year, and he already had an academic scholarship to Baylor University. The baby was a sophomore, and it looked like he would be following in his father's footsteps.

Mack found Clay Donovan, Drew's youngest, already in the classroom. Unless a miracle fell out of heaven, Clay would never be a tall man. He was about five foot seven, had straight light-brown hair like his mother and brown eyes like Drew's dad, and had a slim build. But he'd been blessed with a deep voice, and when he spoke, most folks paid attention.

"I came in with Dad this morning, so I went ahead and got things ready," Clay said.

"Thank you." Mack sat down in one of the chairs. "Are you ready to go back to school next week?"

"Might as well be." Clay chose a chair on the other side of the circle. "I kind of hate to see the year come to an end, though. I'll miss Barry when he goes to college. It wasn't the same around the house last year when Randall left, but it'll be even worse when I'm the only one at home."

"Spend all the time you can with your folks. I sure wish I had," Mack told him.

The door opened and five teenage boys came in. They plopped into chairs and slid down until they were practically sitting on their backbones. Mack checked the time on the clock at the back of the room. Five more minutes and he'd begin the lesson.

Another minute ticked away, and Braden peeked into the room. "Is this the right place?"

"Come right on in." Mack motioned with his hand.

All six boys sat up straighter when they saw Holly enter behind Braden.

"Take a seat anywhere," Mack said. "We've still got a couple of minutes before we begin, and . . ." He turned to look toward the door when he heard laughter in the hallway. "There are the twins right now."

Two girls with long black hair and brown eyes carried their Bibles into the classroom and took seats. Rose and Ivy Sanchez were fourteen. They'd just moved to Comfort a year ago, so they were still considered newbies, both in school and in church. They got seated, and then Isaac and Faith Torres arrived. Mack stood up and the room got quiet.

"We've got two new members today, so we should introduce ourselves. I'm Mack Cooper, and I'm your teacher. Clay, you can go next. Tell us your name and how old you are, maybe what grade you are in school." Mack half expected either Holly or Braden to pop off a smart remark, but they both sat still. The only things that moved were their eyes, shifting from one kid to the next.

After everyone else had given their names, Braden and Holly introduced themselves, and Mack dug deeper by having everyone share whether they had siblings. Then he segued into the lesson about loving your brother. He could tell by the look on Holly's face that she wasn't buying a single bit of it—no way was she going to love Braden like she did herself.

While he was listening to the kids' arguments about why they didn't love their siblings, he thought about when he and Adam had been in that same classroom, right along with Drew. Mack loved his brother then, but he sure didn't like him. Truth was, nothing about that situation had changed.

$\sim$

Lily wasn't quite sure where she should go. The last time she and Wyatt had come to church in Comfort, they had gone to the young married couples' class, but now that she wasn't married anymore, she just stood in the middle of the sanctuary and wondered what to do. Sally came up behind her, looped an arm in hers, and steered her to the left.

"We go to the singles' class," she said. "Divorced or never married go in this one. We can't go to the young married class anymore for two reasons. We're damn sure not young." She raised a hand toward the ceiling. "Forgive me, Lord. That Saturday-night language just slipped out."

Lily giggled. "And the second reason?"

"We're those wild divorcées who might steal one of those poor women's husbands if we go into that class. We're so bad that Preacher Drew teaches this one himself," Sally whispered.

"You are not old," Drew said right behind them. "And that's not the reason we have this class. It's for the fellowship."

"Busted!" Sally laughed and gave Drew a hug.

Drew nodded over her shoulder toward Lily. "Welcome back to Comfort—we're all glad to have you in church with us."

"Thank you." Lily entered the room first to find four other people already seated around a table.

"We've got a newcomer," Drew said as he took his place and opened his Bible. "Y'all might remember her as Lily Miller. Now she's Lily Anderson, and she's moved back into the old Miller house south of town where she was raised." He introduced the other four people by name. They must've moved to Comfort in the last few years, because she didn't recognize any of them.

She made a concerted effort to put names with faces, though, as Drew began to talk about the responsibilities of being a good Christian. According to him, it went beyond showing up in church on Sunday morning and in knowing the Bible upside down and backward. It had to do with what was in the heart.

Lily's mind drifted off as she wondered what was hiding down deep in her soul. She was still thinking about that when the time was up and they all filed out of the room to go to the sanctuary for church. Moving back, sleeping in the old house, cooking with her mother's skillets—memories flooded her mind that morning as Drew preached on kindness. If she hadn't had two teenage children sitting between her and Mack, she would have thought she'd taken a couple of giant leaps back in time. Nothing had changed. Not the house where she grew up. Not the church with its two rows of pews and a center aisle—the same one that she'd walked down on her daddy's arm when she married Wyatt. Thinking of that, she remembered the journal. What would she write in one? Would someone read it in a hundred and fifty years and see themselves in the sorrows and joys, like she had when she read Ophelia's first paragraph?

~

Holly had spent part of the afternoon on the phone with a couple of girls she'd met in Sunday school that morning. She'd rolled her eyes every time anyone walked through the kitchen, where she sat on the floor with the corded phone on her shoulder as she did her fingernails. From the little Lily had heard when she went to get a glass of tea, those two girls didn't have cell phones, either.

Braden and Mack had gone outside after Sunday-dinner dishes were done to play catch. Braden didn't even seem to mind that his sister gave him another one of her looks that branded him as a traitor. He'd stuck his tongue out at her and then run out the door before she could retaliate.

Lily wandered through the house—memories continuing to wash over her like floodwaters in every room, from her father's office, to the living room, to the dining room and the big country kitchen. There were pictures of her and her sister everywhere. The first one she removed from the piano in the living room was her wedding picture.

"Why is this even still in here?" she muttered as she took it out of the frame and tossed it in the trash. She could almost hear her mother's voice saying that when she had passed away, Lily and Wyatt had still been married. Well, they damn sure weren't anymore, and she didn't need reminders of the pain that she had endured.

She found five more pictures of herself and Wyatt and put them into the trash can before she slowly climbed the staircase and looked at photos of her life from birth to graduation from college on the two walls. When she reached the landing, she peeked in Holly's open door, but her daughter didn't even look up from the book she was reading.

That reminded Lily of the journal, so she went to her room, got it out, and crawled into her bed with it. The pages had crumbled at the edges, so she turned the first one slowly and respectfully. The second entry was dated November 1862:

I'm numb with shock, disappointment, and even more with worry. Henry ran away from home two weeks ago and joined the Union army. He's only fifteen. I feel like he has betrayed his father by doing this, and it's hard for me to hold my head up in town as well as in church. People look at me like I have leprosy, and sometimes I feel like maybe I do. How did I fail my son so much that he'd betray what we believe? What great sin have I committed that I have to bear this burden? I believe Henry did it because of Malachi, who is a son to one of our slaves. Malachi's mother was Henry's wet nurse, and he bonded with her and with her son who is just days older than my Henry. They've played together like brothers their whole lives. He took Malachi with him, and left a note for me, saying they were both joining the Union troops that had marched through here. He's always said that when the war is over he'll be old enough to take over the plantation, and he will free all our slaves. Such an optimist, he is, and so foolish. Who's going to work the cotton fields? Who will take care of his everyday needs, like cooking and laundry? He's just a child with big dreams. So now it's just me and Matilda in this huge house. There was no cotton crop this year. The Yankees burned what we had. I wonder how much longer we'll be able to hold out. I may have to walk away from everything William and I have built and go live with my brother in Georgia. Matilda will throw a fit if that happens.

Lily thought of the tantrum Holly had thrown about leaving Austin, too. Lily was about to turn another page when Holly rapped on the edge of her open door.

"Mama, can I invite Rose and Ivy over tomorrow? You met them after church, remember? They're the twins. Their mama said they could come after dinner and stay until suppertime if it was all right with you. They're in my grade at school, and I'd like to know someone when I go there on Wednesday." Holly was using her I'll-be-nice-to-get-what-I-want voice.

"Sure." Lily nodded. "Do we need to go get them, or is their mother bringing them to the house? And what are you planning to do all afternoon?"

"Their mama is bringing them, and we're going to do pedicures and see what hairstyles look best on us. I'll go call Rose back and tell her it's okay," Holly said.

"Hey, wait a minute," Lily called out. "Why didn't you ask me sooner? Did you cheat and get your cell phone out of the bag?"

"Nope, and I didn't ask you sooner because you were busy throwing pictures of you and Daddy in the trash. You looked madder than you did in the bathroom at the library," she answered. "I didn't want you to say no, so I waited until you were in a better mood."

"That may be the smartest thing you've done in days," Lily said. "I'm glad you're making friends."

Holly just nodded and raced down the stairs to the kitchen to make the call.

"Maybe next time she'll remember to say thank you," Lily said out loud.

"Thanks, Mama," Holly yelled from the bottom of the stairs.

Lily hugged herself. Just those two words made her day. She went back to the journal and read on:

Times have already changed so much since this damnable war has begun that I dread to see what it will be like when it is over. No matter what side wins, both the north and the south will come out with dead bodies to bury. I shudder to think about how this fighting will tear apart families. I cry myself to sleep at night, but all the tears don't bring peace. I still worry, and I'm still an outsider in a world where I used to be respected.

A tear left a shiny trail down Lily's cheek. Reading what Ophelia had written was like long fingers reaching deep into Lily's soul. How could she feel such overwhelming empathy for a woman she'd never even known existed until she'd opened the journal?

Chapter Five

With three giggling girls in the house, and even more important, with those girls being right across the hall from his room, Braden opted to go outside that Monday afternoon and help Mack round up three goats that had gotten out of the fence. Lily was glad to hear Holly laughing and having such a good time with her two new friends and hoped to God neither Rose nor Ivy were pot smokers.

She was roaming around the house, trying to decide what would go and what would stay if she didn't go back to Austin in the fall. She was about to pour herself a glass of sweet tea when the back door swung open and Sally called out, "Anybody home?"

"In the kitchen," Lily called, raising her voice. "Want a glass of tea?"

"Love one." Sally came into the room, taking off her scarf and coat. She tossed them on a chair, and then opened the cookie jar. "I skipped lunch, so I can have chocolate cookies."

"Want a plate of leftovers?" Lily asked. "There's lasagna on the stove."

"Yes, and thank you." Sally put the lid back on the cookie jar and got down a plate. "Does it ever seem like Vera is just gone to town or off to get her hair done? Everything in this house is still the same as it was five years ago when she was still bustling around in here."

"Oh, yeah." Lily nodded. "I've been trying to decide what to sell, what to give away, and how to make the place mine if I decide to stay past the end of summer. It seems like I'm throwing Mama away when I think of changing things." She started to tell Sally about the journal, but she couldn't. It had touched her so much that she couldn't share it.

Sally heaped her plate and heated the lasagna in the microwave. Lily poured two glasses of tea, set them on the table, and then put a dozen chocolate cookies in a bowl. "There's also ice cream if you want dessert," she said.

"This is probably enough fat calories for the whole week." Sally brought her plate to the table. "Is this Vera's recipe?"

"Yep, that's just the way Mama made it." Lily sat down across the table from Sally. "What brings you out here in the middle of the day?"

"I got this brilliant idea," Sally said. "I've decided that you need a change in your life. It needs to be more than just bringing your kids here to Comfort. Lord have mercy! Your mama died. You got a divorce and had to move from your home right after that. And now this with the kids. Woman, you definitely need something new in your life."

"You think so? I thought I'd put a little ad in the newspaper about a counseling service here in Comfort. I can live on my savings until I get a clientele built up." Lily sighed. Just thinking about marketing gave her a case of hives.

"Oh, yes, I do think so," Sally said between bites. "And I've got just the thing for you." She accentuated each word by poking her fork at Lily. "But before we talk about my offer, I should let you know that two people already provide private counseling here in Comfort. One is a certified psychiatrist who has a practice in Austin and sees clients in the evenings. The other works as a psychologist up at the Kerr State Hospital and sees folks on the side. I think you'd be wasting your money to put an ad in the paper. The town is too small to support three counselors."

"You've got to be kidding me," Lily groaned. "I don't have anywhere near that kind of training. I'm just a counselor. I guess I should listen to the kids and go on back to Austin. Maybe I can get my old clients back. I referred them to a friend when I decided to leave on such short notice."

Sally laid a hand on Lily's arm. "You need a change, so hear me out." She put another bite in her mouth and washed it down with a sip of tea. "What's your annual salary with the job you have? I know I'm prying into your personal business, but I need to know before I go on."

Lily gave her a rough idea of what she'd made the previous year and then added, "But I do get a healthy child-support check from Wyatt. That money goes for whatever the kids need, and I still get to put away a small amount each month for their college funds."

"I'll pay you fifty percent more than what you were making as a therapist to come work for me at the vintage shop," Sally said.

"Have you lost your mind?" Lily gasped. "You can't make enough money at the shop to do that."

"Yep, I do, and I need help," Sally told her. "I have to lock up the place to go to lunch, and I practically have to walk around wearing an adult diaper so I don't miss a customer. I should be out looking for stock at garage sales and especially estate sales, but I can't leave the shop until after five. By then, everything is picked over. I want someone I can trust working with me. Someone who has a little bit of business savvy. You're a perfect fit."

"Can I think about it until the end of the week?" Lily asked.

"Sure, you can." Sally pushed her empty plate back and picked up a cookie. "But I really think it will be good for you to get out of the house. I've been opening at nine, but if you want to come in at eight and leave at three thirty, that's just fine by me. Oh, and I cleared it with my CPA before I even came out here. She says that I can offer you insurance and vacation time."

"You're making it very tempting," Lily said. "But what if things don't work out here and I go back to Austin? I'd be leaving you in a bind, and what am I going to do if I go back without any clients?"

"You can always go back to working for a school. You know how the state is always crying for school counselors." Sally pushed back her chair and stood up. "Even with that, you'd be getting out of the house. I've got to run. Thanks for the lasagna and cookies. Think it over and we'll talk again in a couple of days."

"I will." Lily stood and walked her friend to the back door. "And thank you for the offer."

"Hey, I couldn't think of anyone I could work with every day until you came home. Seems like a win-win to me." Sally gave her a brief hug and put on her coat and scarf. "It's colder'n a mother-in-law's kiss out there. I see Mack and Braden comin' this way. They look half-frozen." She hustled on out to her business van and honked the horn as she left.

Mack threw up a hand in a wave, but Braden kept his hands tucked into his coat pockets. Their shoulders were hunched against a fierce north wind that rattled the tree limbs. The weatherman had said there was a cold front on the way, but she hadn't realized that it had arrived. She checked the thermometer hanging on a porch post and saw that it was below freezing—that meant the temperature had dropped more than twenty degrees since she had looked at it that morning.

"Mama always said that if you don't like the Texas weather, just stick around twenty minutes and watch it change," she muttered to herself as she got down everything she needed to make hot chocolate.

As soon as he and Braden were inside, Mack removed his stocking hat and gloves, shoved them into his mustard-colored work coat, and hung it on one of the hooks by the back door. He kicked off his rubber boots and set them beside Lily's father's old boots. Lily's mother had said that she just couldn't part with the last boots he'd worn or his old stained work coat that hung on a nail above them.

Braden kept his jacket on and slumped down in a kitchen chair. "I think my blood is frozen."

"Think hot chocolate will thaw it out?" Lily asked.

"Is it that stuff out of a package or the real thing?" Braden shivered so hard his teeth rattled.

"It's homemade, like you like it," she answered.

"We've got to get him a warmer coat. A hooded sweatshirt isn't enough on cold days," Mack said. "My blood isn't frozen, but hot chocolate sure sounds good. What can I do to help?"

"You can get down a couple of mugs," Lily answered.

"You aren't going to have any?" Mack asked.

"I just finished a glass of sweet tea, so I'm good," she answered as she used a whisk to mix cocoa, sugar, coffee creamer, and a little vanilla together. The milk in the pot came to a boil, and she stirred in the other ingredients and poured the hot chocolate into the mugs. Before she took them to the table, she topped both mugs with whipped cream. When she handed off the first cup to Mack, her fingertips brushed against his. There was that tingle again.

Braden took a sip and picked up a cookie. "I feel my blood thawin' out."

"Amazing what a little heat, cookies, and really good hot chocolate will do for you, isn't it?" Mack agreed.

"Mama makes the best." Braden used his cookie to skim off the whipped cream and then popped the whole thing in his mouth.

Lily couldn't remember the last time Braden had said anything to her other than smart-ass remarks and a few grunts. She would've hugged him but didn't want to jinx anything. They'd only been in Comfort a few days, and each of the kids had said something kind to or about her. Miracles did happen.

"It's the best hot chocolate I've ever had for sure," Mack said. "Thanks for making it for us, Lily."

"You're very welcome."

"Are those girls still up there with Holly?" Braden asked.

"For about thirty more minutes"—Lily nodded—"then their mother is coming to get them."

Braden sighed. "I guess I can stand it for that long. It would sure be better if I had my tablet or my Nintendo."

"But you don't." Lily was not giving in, no matter how pitiful he sounded. "But I noticed a package of earplugs in the secretary in my bedroom. Daddy used them when he was out in the garage running the table saw. They're bright orange. Why not go see if they'll work?"

Braden frowned. "What's a secretary?"

"It's that big piece of furniture with a glass front," Lily explained.

"I guess that's better than nothing." He finished his hot chocolate and picked up another cookie to take with him. "See y'all at suppertime."

"If you want to help Mack feed the goats this evening, you can wear your grandpa's coat," Lily said. "It's hanging over there on the hook beside Mack's."

"That would be dorky." Braden wrinkled his nose.

Mack chuckled. "I don't reckon the goats would mind."

Braden shrugged and left the room.

"He's a good kid. He just got mixed up in the wrong crowd," Mack said.

"You know the kids here. Will you tell me if he does the same thing in school?" Lily sat down in the chair Braden had just vacated.

"Yes, I will."

Lily hadn't had to make a job decision since Holly was born. She'd been in her counseling office through the last day of school, gone into labor that evening, and had Holly on May 28. She'd already started her home sessions in the evenings and had continued with them all these years until she'd moved to Comfort. Now, it appeared, she'd be banging her head against the wall if she tried to set up another practice.

"Sally offered me a job," she blurted out.

"Are you going to take it?" Mack went to the stove to refill his cup.

"It's tempting," she answered. "She's even said I can open the shop at eight and leave at three thirty. That way I can leave after the bus picks up the kids in the morning and be home by the time they get back here in the afternoon."

"You could take them to school, and I could bring them home if they don't mind waiting until four. I have to be there for thirty minutes after the last bell rings," he suggested.

She shook her head. "Riding the bus is part of their punishment, but thank you."

"You got to deliver what you promise. That's what my mother always preached to me." He sat back down.

"I got the same preachin'." Lily nodded.

"Our parents were of the same generation," he said. "I have to go to school tomorrow for a professional day, and then the kids start on Wednesday. The administration office will be open if you want to enroll the kids tomorrow. You'll need to tell them that Braden and Holly will be riding the bus so their driver will know to come down the lane to get them."

"Thank you," she said. "I'll do that. How many kids are there in the school these days?"

"A little over three hundred total in the high school. We still graduate about the same number each year as we did when we were going to school there—seventy to eighty. Maybe a few more in middle school," he answered.

"The high school Holly attended had more than two thousand in each grade. Braden and Holly will be in for a culture shock." Lily had forgotten just how small Comfort was.

"Probably, but kids are kids wherever you go. We've got potheads, drug users, and alcoholics just like every other place. There's just fewer of them," Mack said.

"How much trouble do you have with gangs?" Lily was almost afraid to hear his answer.

"None," Mack told her. "We nip that in the bud every time it rears its ugly head. Basically we're still a rural school, even if"—his smile brightened the whole room—"the Bobcats do play a mean game of football."

"You still go to all the games?" Lily asked.

"Oh, yeah," he replied. "Haven't missed one in years."

"Why didn't you play in high school? I kind of wondered," Lily asked.

"I'm not the aggressive type." He pushed back his chair and stood up. "Never was, probably never will be. That was Adam's personality, and still is. Guess we split the personality traits before we could even walk."

"That's the way it happens sometimes with twins. I wish Holly and Braden had split some traits. They're both headstrong and mouthy." Lily picked up Braden's empty cup and carried it to the sink, and then the giggling from upstairs turned into thunderous noise.

In reality, there were just three chatty teenage girls stomping down the wooden stairs, but it sounded like a herd of elephants. And then the door opened and slammed, and silence filled the house.

Lily poked her head around the door to see Holly starting back upstairs. "I thought maybe their mother would come inside so I could meet her," she said.

"She doesn't speak much English," Holly told her. "Rose and Ivy are teaching her."

"That's Conchita Sanchez." Mack washed both mugs and set them in the dish drainer. "She and her husband work out on Preston Ranch. Rose and Ivy are the youngest of six or seven kids. All the others have already graduated and left home. You don't have to worry about them. Conchita and John are strict, and they don't put up with any sass. Rose and Ivy are also active in my Future Farmers of America class. They show steers at the local fair, and as far as I know, they're good kids."

"That helps." Lily picked up a dish towel, dried the cups, and put them away. "Now if I could just figure out what to do about this job offer."

"Make peace with it," Mack suggested. "Get out a piece of paper and write down the pros and cons of each job—the one you have now and are comfortable doing, and then the one that Sally offered you. Make a decision and then forge ahead with no regrets."

It sounded like good advice, so she went up to her room, got out a notebook, and began to write. When she finished, she was amazed to see that the side with Sally's offer had the most pros. She'd have to think about it another day or two, but she liked the idea better and better.

She was about to close the drop-down flap of the secretary when she noticed the journal again. Still feeling like she was reading a friend's personal diary, she opened it and turned the first two pages. This entry was dated May 1863:

I have no heart left to break. It's all shattered into a million pieces that will never be put back together. I hate being under my brother's thumb, and hearing him curse my son every day, but we have no choice. My niece treats Matilda like her own chambermaid, and Matilda rebels. There is so much tension in this place that I wish the Union soldiers would have shot me instead of William. I'd do it myself if it wasn't for the fact that Matilda needs me. I've started taking in sewing for extra money, but Walter requires nearly all of it for our room and board. The rest I'm saving to go home when this miserable war ends. Maybe we can reclaim our home there, if there's anything left.

Part of Lily wanted to read more, but the desperation in Ophelia's words broke her heart again. Now that she'd started reading the journal, she intended to read it all, but she'd have to do it in small doses. She flipped over to the last page and was surprised to see her own mother's handwriting.

"Good Lord," she gasped as she realized that this wasn't just a journal Vera had picked up at an estate sale. By her mother's writing, it must mean that this was a history of her own.

Lily closed the book and put it back in the secretary, vowing that she'd read it more slowly now that she realized what she had in her possession. She thought about her ancestor, Ophelia, and the circumstances she was living in during the Civil War.

Lily had a home that had been left to her by her parents. She'd never had to worry about coming back to nothing like Ophelia did. Lily had two kids who'd disappointed her, but like Ophelia, she still loved them both—even if both of them had pulled some crazy stunts. A mother might not *like* her children at times, but she always loved them.

Chapter Six

*L*ily could feel the angst in the car on Tuesday morning when she drove to the school. Of course Holly had dressed in a pair of her best jeans and the boots she'd gotten for Christmas. Her cute little pink hoodie was zipped up to her neck, so Lily had no idea what kind of shirt was under it—she just hoped that it was school appropriate. Her makeup was perfect, and her hair had been curled. Braden wore a pair of jeans—thank God they were pulled up to his waist and not showing his underwear—his oldest faded black hoodie, and a T-shirt with Blake Shelton on the front. Hopefully, the school didn't have a problem with writing or pictures on kids' shirts.

Braden and Holly were both wide-eyed when she pulled into the parking lot in front of the school. There were only somewhere between ten and twenty vehicles there, so she had her choice of spaces. She chose one closest to the front doors.

"Is this the whole thing?" Holly gasped. "Our science department was bigger than this."

"It's the whole enchilada." Lily turned the key, undid her seat belt, and opened the door. "Just be thankful that it's a small school. You won't have trouble finding your classes."

"I'm more thankful that Rose and Ivy ride the same bus as me so I'll know someone," Holly said as she and Braden got out of the car and followed their mother.

The last time Lily had been in this building was the night she'd graduated. A few things had changed, but not much. She had no trouble finding the principal's office. She knocked on the closed door, and a woman's voice called out, "Come on in."

Lily eased the door open and let the kids go in ahead of her. "Ruth-Ann Becker? Is that you?" she asked when she was finally in the room.

The woman looked up and smiled. "Lily Miller. It's good to see you again."

"Only now it's Lily Anderson," Lily said.

Ruth-Ann held up her hand to show off a set of wedding rings. "Ruth-Ann Winkler. I married Justin Winkler. Remember him? He was the geek about two years ahead of us. He's now the head of an IT firm in Fredericksburg."

"Who would've thought it?" Lily shook her head. "I figured you'd end up with Adam Cooper."

"I had a little more sense than that," Ruth-Ann laughed. "I heard you'd moved back. Saw you in church on Sunday, but you were gone before I got to speak to you. Let's get you two enrolled. The email from their old school with all their records came through just this morning. That'll make things a lot easier. Y'all have a seat and we'll get the ball rolling."

"Are you the principal now?" Lily asked.

"Oh, no, honey, I'm just the school secretary. Mr. Stewart is the principal. You remember Kyle Stewart? He graduated a couple of years before we did. He's been here fifteen years," she said, "but I can get your kiddo enrolled."

While she looked over the paperwork, Ruth-Ann brought Lily up to date on all their old classmates—who was married, who had kids, who wound up in jail, and who was divorced. "It looks like everything is in order. We offer the same classes that you had in Austin, Miz Holly. We can slip you right into accelerated English, math, and science in the morning so you can get the heavy load over with before lunch." In less than fifteen minutes, she had arranged Holly's schedule, printed it out, and handed it to her. "Your locker number is right there on the top of the page. If you want a lock, you'll have to provide it yourself." She opened a drawer and brought out a blue-and-gold booklet. "Read this, especially the dress code. The school has gray sweats in all sizes for any kids who come to school dressed inappropriately."

Lily reached out a hand. "Maybe you'd better give me one of those, too."

Ruth-Ann got another one out and handed it to her. "I wish *all* parents would read the booklet."

"I intend to stay on top of things," Lily said. "I will be calling each week to see if things are going well."

"Feel free to do that or stop by anytime," Ruth-Ann said. "If you'd like, I can call down to the elementary school and make sure our principal is still in his office."

"Braden is in the seventh grade. Isn't that middle school?"

"Sorry about that, yes," Ruth-Ann apologized. "Welcome to Comfort, kids, and call me sometime, Lily. We'll have lunch."

"Sure thing," she said, but she had no intention of having lunch with Ruth-Ann. The woman had been the biggest gossip in high school, and she'd already told her everything she knew about everyone in town. Lily didn't need to hear a weekly update on anything or anyone except her own kids. "Let's go get Braden enrolled, and then maybe we'll stop by Sally's store and see her."

"Yes!" Holly pumped her fist in the air.

The middle school had been the old high school and was a little over two miles away and closer to town. It was where Lily had gone to school her freshman and sophomore years. Mack's class had been the last one to graduate from high school in that building. She was thinking of him when she parked the car and got out for the second time that day.

"Can I just stay right here?" Holly asked. "I brought a book, and I'll lock the doors."

"You don't have to lock the doors," Lily answered. "But don't get out and go wandering around if you get bored. We may be a little while getting everything done."

"If I had my cell phone, you wouldn't have to worry," Holly sighed.

"But you don't, and I will." Lily tucked her car keys into her purse, made sure her phone was in the outside pocket, and opened the door. "If you decide to join us, the office is through the doors and about halfway down the hall on the right."

"I won't." Holly already had her nose in the book.

"Just my luck," Braden huffed as they crossed the parking lot. "Holly gets the new school, and I have to take the old one."

"I'd hardly call the high school new anymore," Lily informed him. "It's been there for more than twenty years now."

"Then that makes this one ancient." Braden hung back a few seconds when his mother opened the door. "Does it even have bathrooms?"

"Sure, it does." Lily went on in and headed down the hall.

Braden had to run to catch up with her. "Real bathrooms. Not one at the back of the school in an old wooden building."

"When did you ever really see a bathroom like that?" Lily asked.

"I haven't seen one in real life, but Holly made me watch reruns of *Little House on the Prairie* with her when we were little kids," he answered.

Lily pointed to a door with a "Boys" sign on the front. "Does that ease your mind?"

"Whew!" Braden let out a whoosh of air. "It sure does."

"Hey, I was hoping I might catch you while you were here." Mack waved from a room where several other teachers were leaving from both doors. "I'm free to work in my office until eleven. Y'all want to go down to the Dairy Queen and get a snack when you get done?"

"Yes," Braden answered before his mother could say a word. Then he turned to her. "Please?"

"Love to," Lily agreed.

"I'll meet you there in half an hour." Mack waved and disappeared down the hallway.

The principal was a no-nonsense guy, newer than she was in the town, who handed Braden and Lily over to his assistant—an older lady whom Lily didn't know either—and rushed out to a meeting. The lady was about as warm as an iceberg, but she was efficient. Braden was enrolled and had his own blue-and-gold handbook in less than fifteen minutes.

~

Mack arrived at the Dairy Queen just as Lily and the kids found a booth. Lily and Holly were sliding into one side, Braden the other. He waved from the door and joined them. "So what are we having?"

"French fries and a chocolate malt," Braden said.

"Tater tots and a chocolate chip cookie dough Blizzard," Holly answered.

"Just a cup of coffee." Lily slid out of the booth. "I'll go with you to help."

"Have you made up your mind about the job?" Mack asked as they waited in line to order. He'd forgotten how good it felt to simply take a woman out for ice cream.

"Not yet, but we're stopping by Sally's shop on the way home. I'd like to take a look at the place and get a feel for what I'd be doing," she answered.

Their turn finally came. Before Lily could open her purse, Mack had his wallet out, rattled off the order, and handed the lady a twenty-dollar bill. The young woman made change and gave him a receipt.

"We'll bring it out to you as soon as it's done," she said. "Are you ready for school to get back in session, Mr. Cooper?"

"Might as well be," Mack answered. "When do you go back to college?"

"Tomorrow," she answered. "Just one more semester and I'll have my degree."

"That's great. I'm glad you stayed with it. Still going to teach vo-ag somewhere?" Mack asked.

"Plannin' on it." She grinned and looked over his shoulder at the next customer.

Mack ushered Lily back to their booth with his hand on her lower back. A few customers smiled and others waved. He could almost read their minds—Mack was dating Lily Anderson. They were happy for him. There was chemistry, at least on his part, but he wasn't sure that he'd ever be able to trust another woman, no matter how much he wanted to do so.

Lily slid into the booth beside Holly. "Thank you for treating us today."

He took a place across from her beside Braden. "My pleasure. Ice cream is my ultimate weakness."

"Mine, too," Braden said. "I like it even better than cake, and I love Mama's chocolate cake."

Mack's knee brushed against Lily's under the table, and even through his jeans and her stretchy pants, he could feel electricity between them. What would it be like to hold her in his arms, or even kiss her? Just thinking about it made the dining area so hot that he removed his coat and draped it over the back of the booth.

Their order arrived, and each of them reached for their part of the food. Mack picked up his sea salt caramel Blizzard. Lily took her coffee from the tray. The ketchup bottle was on the table, and the kids grabbed for it at the same time. The argument over who got to use it first was settled with a contest of rock, paper, scissors. Braden won and took his time squeezing it over his fries.

Mack remembered having the same fight with Adam—more than one time. Adam nearly always won at everything, so by the time he was a teenager, Mack usually just gave over to his twin brother. Dozens of memories flashed through Mack's mind—none of them had to do with ketchup, and all of them had to do with women. He wondered how Lily would react to Adam. There was no doubt that his brother would show up before long. Adam wouldn't be able to stand the temptation of an available woman living with Mack. Oh, yes. He would definitely show up with all his charms as soon as he heard that Lily had moved back to Comfort.

Mack looked up from his Blizzard to see Lily staring right at it. He stood up and went to the counter for an extra spoon. He handed it to Lily. "Help me out with this. I shouldn't have ordered a large one, especially when there's a potluck at the school today for the teachers and the folks presenting the programs."

"Are you sure?" She took the spoon from him.

He pushed the cup to the middle of the table. "Yep, I'm glad to share." Truth was, he wanted to see if he got that little spark every time their hands touched. Sure enough, he did.

~

"Mama, what's in Sally's store, anyway? Does she have stuff in my size?" Holly finished off her tater tots and started on her Blizzard.

"I've never been in it, but it's a vintage store, so I doubt you'll be interested in anything," her mother answered.

Lily dug into the ice cream a second time and let her mind go back to when Sally had said she was putting in the store. It was the month after Lily's mother died, and they had all met in Blanco, the halfway point between Austin and Comfort, at the Dairy Queen there. Sally had been divorced for three years at that time, and looking back, Lily didn't know how she would've survived that first year without Sally's support and love.

Lily had thought her friend was out of her mind when she had told her that she was quitting her job and putting in an antique store in Comfort. A single woman needed job security with a benefits package. She damn sure didn't need to use all her savings to open an antique store in a small town. Little did Lily realize just how smart Sally really was. Comfort, like Fredericksburg, was a tourist town that specialized in the past. People flocked to both of them to see hundred-year-old buildings and historical markers on houses and some structures that were even older than that. While in that frame of mind, they bought antiques.

"You're a hundred miles away right now," Mack drawled.

Lily jerked herself back to the present. "I was thinking about how crazy I thought Sally was when she quit her steady job and put in her shop. I've never been a risk taker, so . . ." She shrugged without finishing the sentence.

"Me, either, but sometimes a door opens that isn't really a risk, but an opportunity." Mack checked the time on his watch. "I should be going. Y'all enjoy the rest of the day."

"Thanks again for treating us," Lily said.

"Thank you," both kids chimed in at the same time.

"You're very welcome. See y'all at home," he said.

There had been something between her and Mack when they both dipped into the ice cream at the same time. If anyone ever had a type, Lily did. She liked men who weren't so tall that she had to tiptoe to kiss them. She leaned toward dark hair and was drawn to blue eyes. Mack was over six feet tall and had dark hair, but his eyes were green. He wasn't flirty, and was basically a little shy. So why in the devil were there vibes between them? It simply didn't make a bit of sense.

She was still pondering the situation as she drove back into town and parked the car in front of Yesterday's Treasures. Braden opted to stay in the car this time with his book, but Holly seemed eager to go inside. As usual for her, any store that had a fancy dress in the window had to be a good place.

The bell above the door rang when they walked into the shop. Sally had been dusting a floor-to-ceiling bookcase that held white milk glass pieces of every size and shape. To her left was another case with nothing but cut crystal in it, and to her right was a third one with carnival glass.

She laid the dusting rag on the counter. "Welcome to my shop. I was hoping you'd come by today. I heard that you and Mack took the kids to the Dairy Queen for ice cream."

"I'd forgotten how fast gossip travels in Comfort," Lily sighed.

"Oh, honey, with all these new techie toys, it can make the speed of light look like a snail. If you burp, someone will put what you ate for dinner on Twitter." Sally laughed. "So what do you think of my store? What was your first impression?"

Lily tried to take it all in with one sweeping glance. "It's bigger than I thought it would be—"

"Mama, look at all these gorgeous earrings," Holly interrupted from across the store.

"Granny Hayes makes those," Sally said. "She also crochets the hats and shawls spread out on that old buffet. Oh, and she was delighted with all those gowns and the underwear I took out to her."

"Who is Granny Hayes? Am I kin to her?" Holly asked.

"Why would you ask that?" Sally took a pair of earrings off the rack and held them up to Holly's ears.

"Because Mama said once that there's lots of folks in this town that are kin to other people in some way." Holly looked at her reflection in the tabletop mirror and shook her head. "I like some of the others better."

"No, honey, as far as I know, you aren't related to Granny Hayes. She lives out in the country in an old log cabin. I actually went out and checked on her since she missed church. She had a head cold and didn't feel like saddling up Dusty."

"She's got a horse?" Holly's eyes lit up. "I always wanted a pony."

"Dusty isn't a horse, darlin'," Lily chuckled. "Dusty is an old gray mule, and she's been riding him to church since I was a little girl."

"I want to meet Granny Hayes and learn how to make earrings like these with feathers on them," Holly said. "Can I have a pair today to wear to school tomorrow for my first day, Mama?"

"Pick out your favorite ones," Sally said. "I'll give them to you as a present to celebrate you moving to Comfort."

"You don't have to do that," Lily whispered.

"I want to," Sally said in a low tone. "It's free advertising. If the other girls like them, they'll come in and buy some for themselves."

Holly looked over at her mother. "Please? I love this pair with turquoise stones and feathers. I'll wear my new jacket and boots that I got for Christmas, and I'll pull my hair up in a ponytail and—"

"All right! All right!" Lily laughed.

"Thank you, Mama," Holly said. "And thank you, Sally. I can't wait to wear them." She held them up to her ears in front of the mirror. "I just love them. They look like something Taylor Swift would wear."

"Come see the rest of the shop," Sally said. "The clothing room is through here, and then the furniture is in the back room."

"Good Lord! How big is this place?" Lily asked.

"The front door opens on one block, and the back door is all the way to the alley," Sally answered. "It started off years ago as three stores. I bought each piece of property as it came up for sale and expanded. As you can well see, I need help." She led the way to the next room. "Now," she whispered, "do you think there might be something between you and Mack?"

"Holy hell, Sally!" Lily gasped. "I've only been home a few days. We're barely even roommates."

"I believe in love at first sight," Sally said.

"If that was the case, then I would have fallen in love with Mack when we were about three years old. That's my first memory—of being in church with him and Adam." Lily fingered a lovely lace shawl that had to date back fifty years or more.

"Adam," Sally sighed. "Now that was one sexy boy."

"I always thought he was fake and kind of full of himself," Lily said.

"Yeah, but he's so pretty." Sally fanned herself with her hand.

"I had a pretty man, and look where it got me," Lily said. "I don't know that I could ever trust another of that kind."

"Me, either, darlin'," Sally said, "but I believe that Mack is really trustworthy."

"Then why haven't *you* asked him out?" Lily asked.

"No sparks," Sally said. "If I can't have electricity and chemistry, I'll stay single. I had the ho-hum marriage, and it just didn't work for me."

Looking back, Lily could say that her marriage hadn't been ho-hum, at least not at first, but in all honesty, she had to admit that the romance had died several years before Wyatt said he'd found another woman.

~

Lily could hardly wait that evening to get up to her room and dive into the journal again. The pages were so old that they felt as if they could crumble in her hands, so she turned them carefully. The ink had faded in some places more than others, and she had to get the bedside lampshade adjusted just right to see the words clearly.

Matilda Smith Bedford, June 1870

Lily glanced back over the last pages she'd read and realized that she'd turned two pages at once. She read those before she went on to what Matilda had written.

This entry was dated May 1, 1865:

This is my first time to write in this journal. I feel like I should continue Mama's path, but there's so much to write that I don't quite know where to begin. I found this journal among Mama's possessions, and it broke my heart to read what she'd written, but I was glad to know those things since she didn't talk about the past. My stepfather, Everett, and my mama, Ophelia, died last month. I felt like life had given me a second chance when Mama married Everett, and we finally got to move away from Uncle Walter. That was the most miserable year of my entire life. I felt so sorry for Mama, working her fingers to the bone sewing every day, and then having to give her money to Walter. Everett was a good, kind man who loved my mother, and she had good years with him before they passed from the fever. I got the news by telegram, and Henry and I traveled to Georgia with my two young children to take care of their affairs. I wept for days because Mama had never gotten to lay eyes on her grandchildren, and Jenny, with her pale blue eyes and dark hair, looks so much like her.

Lily's first tear fell on the page and blurred the ink on the last word. She grabbed a tissue from the nightstand and wiped her wet cheeks as she mourned for Ophelia, who had died before she met her grandchildren. Lily regretted not bringing the kids to see their grandparents more often than she did. They only lived a couple of hours away, but somehow every weekend had been filled with events. Those were excuses, not reasons, especially in the summertime, she reminded herself as she went on reading.

Since Everett had no children, he left his small farm to me. I sold it and gave half the money to Henry. I met Rayford when he came home with Henry after the war. They stayed a couple of months. Everett was kind to Rayford, and I thought folks would be like-minded toward me when I agreed to marry Rayford and go to Pennsylvania with him. I was wrong, but our marriage continues to survive in spite of the prejudices that still linger. My father fought for the Confederacy; his for the Union. The war has been over for years, but both sides still carry a huge grudge. I've adapted to the culture of the north, and my children, Jenny and Samuel, are my life. I'm expecting number three around Christmastime, and I'm hoping it's another boy. Henry married a sweet girl, albeit a nervous woman who spends a lot of time either at the doctor's or else lying abed. They have no children, and maybe that's for the best with her constant illness. Looking back, I'm not sure that marrying Rayford was the smartest decision I ever made. He's a good, hardworking man, but he has a wandering eye when it comes to women. Mama told me when I got on the stagecoach to come here that I'd have to sleep in the bed I'd made. I wonder if the time will ever come when a woman will have the same rights as men.

Oh, Matilda, Lily thought, *the day did come, but human nature never changes.* Her mama saw something in Wyatt that Lily's blinded eyes couldn't. Vera told her the same thing about sleeping in her bed on the day she got married. Her mother said that Wyatt would break her heart because he had a wandering eye, too, and she was right. But she got two beautiful children out of the marriage, so it wasn't a complete failure.

Lily carefully closed the book and put it back. It was surreal how these women's lives, women that she'd never met before, could have such an impact on her. She crawled beneath the covers and turned off the light. Moonlight filtered through the lace curtains, leaving abstract shadows on the walls and ceiling. Sleep was a long time coming, and when it did arrive, it was filled with dreams of a grown-up Holly moving miles away and never coming home to see Lily.

Chapter Seven

*M*ack was glad to finish the first day back after Christmas break on Wednesday. He'd taught long enough to know that it took a couple of days for the kids to settle down after being away from the classroom for two weeks. With a long sigh of relief, he locked up the vo-ag building, got into his truck, and headed home. He turned the radio to his favorite country music station and listened to Blake Shelton sing "Who Are You When I'm Not Looking."

The lyrics made him wonder who Lily was when he wasn't around. Was she the stable mother he'd kind of gotten to know the past few days? He was still thinking about that when he parked in front of the house. The first snowflakes of the season drifted down from the gray skies as he made his way across the yard and onto the porch. The aroma of hot yeast bread and warmth surrounded him when he walked in. Now this was the life—coming home to the smell of good food and a warm house, even if the place was more than a hundred years old, with no closets and plenty of problems with the plumbing.

He hung his jacket on the hall tree in the foyer and kicked off his good boots. "Braden, I'm going out to feed the goats if you want to go with me," he yelled up the stairs.

The front door swung open behind him, and the kids rushed in. They dropped their backpacks on one of the ladder-back chairs in the foyer and hung their jackets beside his on the hall tree.

"I figured y'all would already be home," Mack said.

"We get on the bus first thing in the morning and off last in the afternoon," Holly sighed.

"I don't mind ridin' the bus all that time because I got all my homework done on the ride home," Braden said. "Did I hear you talkin' about feeding the goats?"

"I'm going to change into my work clothes and go out to take care of them. Want to go with me?" Mack asked.

"Sure thing, but only if I can wear Grandpa's coat. I don't even care if I look dorky in it. It'll keep me warm." Braden nodded. "I guess I'd better change, too, though. That old billy goat always wants me to pet him, and he stinks."

"Might be a good idea," Mack agreed. "Elvis is a big baby and loves attention. You want to go with us, Holly? You might like the new babies that were born a few days before y'all got here."

"They are so cute," Braden said as he ran up the stairs.

"No, thank you." Holly snarled at the idea. "Where's Mama?"

"I'm right here." Lily came out from the kitchen. "How was your first day?"

Holly shrugged. "Fine."

"Did anyone comment on your new earrings?" Lily asked.

"Rose and Ivy liked them, and . . ." Holly stopped before she finished and brushed past her mother. "And my history teacher says we have to write a paper on someone in our family. It can be on anyone, but it has to be fact, not fiction, so we can't just make up a character and pretend we're related to them. Rose tried to tell him that she was kin to Santa Anna, and he said she had to have documents to prove it."

The family journal instantly came to Lily's mind. "When is your paper due?"

"The last day before spring break," Holly said. "But I don't have any interesting people in my family, so what am I going to do?"

"I've got an idea. We'll talk about it tonight after supper," Lily told her.

"All right." Holly shrugged. "I'm going to have cookies and milk. I didn't like the cafeteria food today, so I only ate the dessert. What's for supper?"

"Potato chowder and hot rolls. Got homework?" Lily followed her.

"Nope," Holly answered. "But the sooner I can get on the history assignment, the better. I hate waiting until the last minute to do my projects."

Mack went to his room, changed into faded work jeans and an old T-shirt, and was on his way across the foyer to the kitchen when someone rapped on the door. He started that way, but Adam pushed inside without waiting.

Like always, he was dressed in a suit, tie, and loafers. Other than a few crow's-feet at the corners of his eyes, he didn't look a lot different than he did in high school. *One twin is good-looking; one is plain. One twin doesn't age; the other one looks every bit of his forty-one years,* Mack thought. But if the truth were told, Mack would bet dollars to goat droppings that he was more comfortable in his own skin.

"What brings you to the boonies?" he asked.

"Had some property to look at over this way again." Adam raised an eyebrow at the kids' coats when he added his trench coat to the mix. "Mama told me that Lily Miller has come back to Comfort and is living with you."

"More like I'm living with her—she owns the house," Mack answered. "What property are you looking at?"

"I'm ready," Braden yelled as he bounded down the stairs, but stopped in his tracks when he saw Adam.

Mack made introductions. "This is my twin brother, Adam. And this is Lily's son, Braden. We'll be a few minutes, Braden. Want to have some cookies and milk before we go?"

"Sure." Braden nodded and then turned his attention back to Adam. "Nice to meet you. For twins, y'all sure don't look alike."

"Thank God," Adam chuckled.

Lily came out of the kitchen again. "Hello, Adam. It's been a while, but you haven't changed a wink. I just made a fresh pot of coffee, and there's homemade cookies on the table. Y'all help yourselves."

"What? No hug? It's been twenty years since I've laid eyes on the beautiful Lily Miller, and I don't even get a hug?" Adam flirted.

"Sorry, I'm fresh out of hugs, and it's Lily Anderson now. I'll be back down here in a few minutes. I've got a phone call to make." Lily hurried off up the stairs.

Mack had never seen a woman brush Adam off like that. His poor brother checked his reflection in the mirror hanging above one of the chairs.

"Got a hair out of place?" Mack asked.

"Shut up," Adam growled. "I'm going to take her up on that coffee. It's cold out there, and it'll warm me up."

"Hey." Holly nodded to both of them as she passed through the foyer and went upstairs.

"That's my sister," Braden said. "Don't pay any attention to her. She's just in a mood. Let's go get some cookies. My mama makes the best cookies in the whole world. I hope they're peanut butter today. That's my favorite, especially dipped in good cold milk."

Mack followed Braden and Adam into the kitchen and went straight to the coffeepot. He poured two cups and carried them across the room. He set one down in front of his brother, who'd already taken a seat, and took a chair across the table from him. He added two spoonfuls of sugar to his mug and took a sip.

"Only sissies have to have sugar in their coffee," Adam said. "Or dip cookies in their milk."

"Guess I'm a sissy." Braden made a show of dipping a cookie in his glass of milk. "Me and Mack do this all the time, don't we, Mack?"

"Sure do." To prove the point, Mack dunked a cookie right down into his cup.

"Never," Adam answered. "I hate crumbs floating in my coffee."

"The best part is when you get a spoon and eat all those soaked-up crumbs from the bottom," Braden said. "Sometimes I let half a cookie just drop off in my cup so I'll have even more."

Mack bit back a smile when Adam shivered at the thought. Adam could never stand for dirt to be under his fingernails, among other things.

"So how are things between you and Charlene?" Mack asked.

"Right now I'm living in a hotel. We haven't filed papers yet," Adam replied. "Mama is mad at me. When Dad is lucid, he won't talk to me, and when he's not, he thinks I'm a teenager and is constantly giving me advice. And to top it all off, my secretary quit."

It was hard for Mack to be sympathetic when his brother had brought all of it on himself.

~

Lily had been restless all day. She'd gone up to her bedroom so she could call Sally and talk to her in private. Leaving Adam like that might be rude, but she'd never liked him, anyway, so a phone call seemed like a damn good excuse not to have to be around him. Fate had to have had a part in all this. It simply could not have happened by chance.

She called Sally and was about to hang up after six rings, but Sally finally answered. "Hello," she huffed.

"Are you all right?" Lily asked.

"I left my phone on the checkout counter, and I was all the way back in the furniture room," Sally said. "What's going on? Did the kids do all right on their first day of school? Damn, I've got to lose weight. I can't even catch my breath."

"Kids did fine. Her new friends, Rose and Ivy, loved her earrings." Lily took a deep breath and spit out, "If you were serious about that job offer, I can come to work Monday morning."

"Halle-damn-lujah!" Sally squealed. "You bet I'm serious. I'll get a set of keys made for you and bring them to church Sunday. This is wonderful, amazing, awesome, and all the other adjectives in the dictionary."

"I thought maybe I'd come in Friday morning so you can show me how to ring up sales," Lily said.

"I'd love that." Sally's breathing was almost back to normal. "Do you remember that old cash register over at the ice-cream shop? The one we used when we worked there in high school?"

"I'll never forget that thing. It was ancient," Lily answered.

"I bought it when they went to a new digital one. It'll be like riding a bicycle. You'll remember how to work it after the first sale," Sally said. "I can't even begin to tell you how excited I am. Destiny brought you home, Lily. I'm convinced of it."

"I so hope that you're right," Lily said. "I keep thinking that someone should pinch me to wake me up. Even with the kids squabbling all the time, I'm feeling like this was the right move. Thank you so much for the job."

"Hey, thank you. Got a customer. See you Friday, but we'll be talking before then." She ended the call.

Lily hugged herself and did a ten-second happy dance. Life had thrown her a curveball, but she felt like she'd hit one out of the park.

She started down the short hall to Holly's room to tell her the news but then thought better of it. She would wait and tell them all at once at the supper table that evening. She wanted to hold on to the excitement a little while longer, and Holly would probably figure out a way to throw ice water on the idea of her mother being a plain old salesclerk, and not something using her therapy degree.

Lily bit back a groan when she saw Adam's coat still hanging on the hall tree hook. "Dammit!" she swore under her breath, but she had to check on the soup and put the peach cobbler in the oven for supper, so she went on into the kitchen. She scanned the room, saw Braden sitting at the table, but no Mack.

"Where's—" she started to say.

Braden butted in before she could finish. "He's gone to change clothes so we can feed the goats."

Her skin began to crawl like a hundred little spiders had jumped off their mama's back onto her body. She turned to see that Adam was staring at her with a wicked gleam in his eyes. His gaze landed on her breasts first, and then traveled slowly down to her feet and only just back up enough to reach her breasts again. She did her best to ignore him and to not feel like she'd been violated. After all, Braden was right there in the room with them. If she said anything, it would complicate matters, but the tension was as thick as fog on a spring morning.

"Those cookies are amazing," Adam said.

"Thank you." Lily went to the stove and turned on the oven. "I made them by my mama's recipe."

"Well, they're great, and to repay you, I'd like to take you to dinner Friday night," Adam said.

Lily whipped around and glared at him. "Aren't you married?"

"Separated." Adam flashed a smile, showing off perfect teeth that were probably capped or were whitened on a regular basis.

Braden had just reached for another cookie, and his hand stopped in midair. He might only be twelve years old, but he wasn't stupid.

"Thanks, but no thanks," Lily said. "I never date married men, divorced men, or separated men. There's too much baggage there."

Braden heaved a sigh, picked up his cookie, and flashed a grin at his mother.

"Honey, I assure you, there's no ties left to that marriage. It's just a matter of filing the paperwork. Will you go out with me when the divorce is finalized?" Adam asked.

"Nope," she answered.

"Why not? You're divorced, so why are you so adamant about not dating divorced men?" Adam asked.

"If you can't make it work three times, what makes you think you can make it work with me?"

"Hey, I'm not proposing." Adam threw up both palms in a defensive gesture. "I just wanted to take you out and show you a good time. What's going on here? Are you and Mack—"

"Nope, they ain't," Braden piped up. "And if I was Mama, I wouldn't go out with you, either. You're kind of mean."

Adam stood up so fast that his chair flipped over backward. The noise sounded like a blast from a gun and brought Holly tearing down the stairs.

"Mama, what's going on?" Holly rushed into the kitchen.

"Nothin'," Braden answered for Lily. "Adam got mad and knocked his chair over."

"I'm not angry. I just need to be on my way. Knocking the chair over was an accident," Adam said. "See all y'all next time I'm in town." He left without picking up the chair.

Braden got up and righted the chair himself. "You can go on back to your room, sis. Nobody was trying to kill us. Adam was flirtin' with Mama, and he wanted to take her out to dinner, but she said no, and I told him he was mean. He was hateful to Mack, and I don't like him."

"Me, neither," Holly said.

Well, praise the Lord and pass the biscuits, Lily thought. Her children had agreed on something, even if it was only a dislike for Adam.

"I'm bored," Holly groaned. "Rose and Ivy can't talk tonight. They have tutoring on Wednesdays."

"You can go with us to feed the goats," Mack suggested as he entered the room.

"I'm not *that* bored," Holly declared.

Mack winked at Lily, and a warm flush crept up into her cheeks. It was a crazy thing that Adam could flirt blatantly, and it just made her angry, but Mack could close an eyelid and smile and she blushed like a schoolgirl.

"Then stop whining about being bored." Braden took his grandfather's coat off the hook and put it on. Frank Miller, Lily's father, had been a big man, about the size that Mack had been in his youth, but maybe thirty pounds heavier when he died. His coat came down to Braden's knees, and Lily had to roll up the sleeves several times.

"You're not my boss, and I can be bored if I want," Holly yelled at him.

"My English teacher said that bored people are boring people," Braden told his sister, and then turned to his mother. "The coat might be big, but it's warmer than a hoodie. And look, Mama, there's work gloves in the pockets."

"Your grandfather would be glad to see you wearing his coat and going out to feed the animals. He kept a few head of cattle right up to the day he died." She kissed Braden on the forehead. "Don't forget your stocking hat. Your ears will freeze off."

He wiped away the kiss and made a face. "I'm not a kid, Mama. I'm twelve years old." His voice cracked for the first time since they'd come home to Comfort.

"Let's go get the chores done." Mack opened the door and let Braden go out before him, and then he looked over his shoulder. "We really need to get him a coat that fits."

"Maybe so." Lily watched from the kitchen window as they walked side by side out across the yard. She shuddered to think of the path her children were on a week ago. Suddenly she realized that Mack had said *we*, not *you*, need to get him a coat, and it didn't seem strange to her ears.

~

Lily served a two-layer chocolate cake with fudge icing that evening for supper—both Braden's and Holly's favorite.

"It's not my birthday or Holly's." Braden stared at the cake. She usually didn't make it except for their birthdays.

"I'm celebrating something for *me* today," Lily said.

"Oh, yeah?" Holly held out her plate for the first slice. "What's that?"

"I got a new job," Lily said. "Starting Monday, I'll be working at Sally's shop."

"Congratulations," Mack said.

"Why would you do this to me?" Holly raised her voice and covered her face with both hands. "I've got this history paper and you said you had an idea and now you're going to be gone all day and I guess I'm supposed to babysit Braden after school and on Saturdays and"—she removed her hands and sucked in more air—"and I bet you'll even expect to load me up with chores."

"The world does not revolve around you," Lily said in her best no-nonsense tone. "If you like food and electricity, then I have to work, but it won't affect you all that much. I'll leave when you kids get on the bus and be home just before you are in the evenings."

"But that means no matter how good me and Braden are, we will never get to go home to Austin, doesn't it?" Holly persisted.

Lily cut two more pieces of cake and handed them off to Braden and Mack. She'd expected more whining from Braden than Holly. "If things work out with this job, we probably will give up our apartment in Austin when the lease runs out."

"Then why should I be good?" Holly asked. "I'm doomed to live here until I graduate, with no closet, sharing a bathroom with a boy, and—"

"That closet thing can be remedied over spring break," Mack said. "If your mama says it's okay, I can build a closet in your room."

"And what do I have to do to get that? Kiss your feet, Mama?" Holly snapped.

"You have to watch your attitude and your tone," Lily told her.

"I'm not sure a closet is worth all that," Holly smarted off.

"It's your choice, but if you continue to be disrespectful, then you can do the supper dishes for a whole week," Lily said.

"I don't care if you work for Sally," Braden said. "I like it that you'll be home when we get here, Mama, because I don't want Holly to ever be my boss. Will we still have cookies for an after-school snack?"

"Yes, but they probably won't be fresh out of the oven every day." She sliced off a fourth piece of cake for herself.

"I can dip them in hot chocolate or even coffee," Braden said.

Holly shot a mean look his way. "Don't you want to go home to Austin?"

"Not really," Braden said. "I kind of like this place, and we can't have a goat in the apartment. We can't even have a cat or a dog."

Holly kept her eyes on her plate, finished her cake, pushed back her chair, and stood up. "I'm going to my room."

"Not before you clear your spot and rinse your dishes," Lily told her.

Holly huffed through the whole process and then stormed off to her room, making sure she stomped on every wooden step up the staircase.

"I've still got a little bit of math homework. May I be excused?" Braden asked.

"Yes, and if you need help, bring it down here," Lily said.

He carried his dirty dishes to the sink. "Will you be home on Saturday?"

"We haven't worked out all the details, but if I'm not, I'll leave a list of chores for you and your sister to do," Lily said.

"Man, this moving sure changed things," he said as he left the kitchen.

"At least one of them isn't pouting about the move anymore," Lily sighed.

"Holly will get over it," Mack said. "Mind if I cut myself another piece of that cake?"

"Not at all." Lily slid the plate closer to him. "I feel sorry for her one minute and want to ground her for eternity the next. I'm sure when I was fourteen, I gave my mother grief."

"It's called paying for your raising." Mack cut a huge wedge of cake and put it on his plate.

"If my mother was alive, I would apologize for every time I hurt her feelings." Lily left the table and put away the leftovers and loaded the dishwasher.

"Speaking of that." Mack finished off his cake and took his dirty plate to the sink. "Have you been out to your folks' graves?"

Lily shook her head. "I've kind of buried my head in the sand when it comes to that. If I didn't come home to this house, and if I didn't go out to the cemetery, Mama is just gone on a little vacation." She wasn't ready to face the sight of her mother's name, birth, and death dates on a tombstone. Just seeing it would make it so final, and she needed just a little more time.

"When you get ready to go, I'll be glad to take you," Mack said.

"I appreciate that. I've got some last-minute things to work on, so I'm going up to my room." She escaped before the tears started streaming down her face. What kind of daughter was she, anyway? Her mother had been gone for five years, and she hadn't even put flowers on her grave.

Her feet felt like lead as she climbed the narrow staircase. She vowed that she would take flowers, maybe red roses, to her mother's grave before the weekend was over, and she would definitely go alone. Mack didn't need to see her all vulnerable and weepy. She grabbed a tissue from her nightstand and wiped her eyes. Then she took out the journal and carried it to Holly's room.

"What did I do wrong now?" Holly's tone was cold.

"Do you have a blank notebook?" Lily asked.

"You always buy too many, so yes, I've got one," Holly said. "What's that got to do with you going to work with Sally?"

"I thought we'd get started on that history project," Lily said. "This journal was started over a hundred and fifty years ago. Your grandmother's several-times-back great-grandmother wrote in it first, and it can be your proof of documentation for your project. I suggest that you write your paper like a journal and not only tell about what we read from your ancestors but also write about your feelings on each entry in the journal. What do you think?"

"Can I take that thing to school on the day we hand in our papers so that the teacher will know I'm not just making up a story?" she asked.

"I've got a better idea," Lily said. "We can take a picture of each page and print it out, and then you can glue it right into the notebook. That would be a way of doing graphics, right?"

Holly's eyes were twinkling with excitement, but knowing her, Lily didn't expect much—not yet. "I guess we can read the first of it, and then I'll make up my mind. Did Granny Vera write in it?"

"Yes, she did," Lily answered, "at the very end. There's lots of blank pages left for me to write in, and even for you someday."

"For real?" Holly showed more interest. "You mean someday this will be mine to keep?"

"Yes, and you can do with it whatever you want." Lily nodded. "You can put it in a museum or keep it and write in it, then pass it down to your daughter."

Holly brought two clean composition books from her backpack. "All right, let's look at the first page."

"Why two?" Lily asked.

"One to take notes in, one to actually write the assignment in," Holly explained. "Too bad I don't have a computer, so I could type all the information into it."

"It'll be far more effective this way." Lily opened the journal and read aloud what Ophelia had written in the first entry.

Holly sat in stunned silence, her mouth slightly open and her eyes wide. "Why couldn't Ophelia take care of things? You did after Daddy left. I can't believe my kinfolk had slaves. That's so wrong. A million kids in our schools are black."

Holly's question was valid for a fourteen-year-old kid just learning about the horrors of the Civil War. Lily thought about them all for a few seconds while she kind of basked in the comment that Holly had made about her taking care of things. The child would never know how much that simple sentence meant to Lily.

"It was a different time," Lily finally said. "Women couldn't vote. People weren't allowed to be a lot of things. The first female doctor graduated from medical school only a few years before that war broke out, and there were no woman lawyers until after the war."

"Why?" Holly was aghast.

"Because women hadn't fought yet for those rights. They were considered weak, and the men had to take care of them," Lily explained.

"God, I'm glad I didn't live back then," Holly said with high drama. "I can't imagine living like Ophelia did. I'm going to research"—she sighed so loud that she almost snorted—"but I can't because I don't have a computer."

"There's a whole set of encyclopedias on the bookcase in the living room, and you can always use your free time at school to look things up in the library," Lily said.

"Whatapedias?" Holly asked.

"Very funny. Go down there and look it up, and I'll take a picture of this page. We'll talk about the next entry another day, and you can

Carolyn Brown

see how things go from then until your Granny Vera wrote in it her last time," Lily said.

"Thanks, Mama," Holly said, and opened her notebook.

Lily closed the book and carried it over to her room. She went to the window and watched the snow. The big flakes swirled in circles as they tried to float to the ground. The weatherman said that the temperature tomorrow would be in the forties and there would be sunshine, so whatever stuck would melt before noon. *How many times had Ophelia stood in a window and watched a rare snowfall when Henry was off fighting for the Union?* she wondered.

If only she'd taken care of her mother's things earlier, she would have already read all of the journal. Now she felt like she should hold off and let Holly catch up so they could talk about each entry together. She wandered down the stairs toward the kitchen to get a scoop of ice cream.

"Busted!" Mack came out of the living room with a dirty bowl in his hands. "I always figure if no one catches me having a second helping of dessert late in the evening, then it doesn't have fat grams or calories. I got another slice of your cake and topped it with a spoonful of ice cream."

Lily passed him on her way to the kitchen. "I was about to get some ice cream."

"Put a little sliver of cake underneath it," Mack suggested. "I was going to put something in the DVD player. Want to watch a movie?"

"Sure," Lily said. "What are we watching?"

"I was thinking about *Lethal Weapon*, the television show, but you can choose whatever you want. I'm afraid there's not many chick flicks in my collection." He followed her to the kitchen, rinsed his bowl, and put it in the sink.

"I saw a couple of episodes of that show." She got out what was left from a cobbler she'd made a couple of days ago, and the ice cream. "I wouldn't mind watching it." She carried her bowl into the living room and settled into her mother's recliner.

Mack put the DVD into the player and sat down in her dad's chair. They were two episodes into the season when she finally asked.

"Why didn't you ever get married, Mack?"

He hit the pause button on the remote. "I don't talk about it, but if you really want to know, it's because of my brother."

"What did Adam do?" Lily's curiosity was piqued.

"It was my last semester in college, and I was going to ask my girlfriend, Brenda, to marry me. We'd more or less been living together that last year, and I was in love with her. So I brought her home to meet the folks over spring break. Mama said the first one of us boys to get married could have the engagement ring that had been passed down through the family for five generations. That didn't matter so much to me. I figured Brenda would be just as happy with a different diamond ring, and I'd already been looking at one. Anyway, to make a long story short . . ." He stared into space for a long time.

"If it's painful, you don't have to tell me," she said.

"I want to so you'll understand how it is between me and Adam," Mack said. "He'll be coming around every so often. I don't want you to think I'm a bastard because of my indifference to him. I love him, but I don't like him so much. But back to my reasons. Brenda and I went back to college after three nights here in Comfort. She was acting kind of weird, and after we left, she told me that the second night we were here, she had slept with Adam out in the hay barn. They were married as soon as school was out, and of course, Adam got the family heirloom."

"And it didn't last, did it?"

Mack shook his head. "Five years later, I fell in love with Natalie, but you can bet your sweet soul I wasn't bringing her around Adam. By then I was teaching in Hondo, and Natalie and I were living together. Mama and Dad came to visit one weekend, and I figure she'd mentioned Natalie to Adam. He showed up at the house one Sunday afternoon with the excuse that he hadn't seen me since Christmas. History repeated itself. He left Brenda for Natalie."

"Good Lord!" Lily gasped. "What's the matter with him?"

Mack shrugged. "I've talked to Drew about it several times. He says that Adam can't stand to see me happy."

"And his last wife, Charlene?"

"That's on him. She was Natalie's third cousin. He met her at the wedding, and he divorced Natalie six months after they were married. He and Charlene got married a few months after that," Mack said. "He's always been the good-lookin' twin, the one that could get any woman he wanted. I'll never understand why he had to take away my happiness."

"How can you even stand to be in the same room with him?" Lily asked.

"He's my brother, and he has a problem. I can't fix it, but I can't seem to cut ties with him, either," Mack replied.

"My sister and I got along well before she died, but then we were both really young. Sometimes I wonder if we'd have bickered like Braden and Holly if she'd lived longer than eight years. I was only five that year and just remember being lost without her. I admire you for continuing to be a brother to him after the way—" She stopped and stammered, "Do you think he was flirting with me because he thinks we are . . ."

"Probably, but then, you are a beautiful woman, Lily, and more likely, he simply couldn't help himself," Mack said.

"Well, I don't like him, never have, not even in high school. I'm sorry to say that about your brother, but I don't," she said.

"I don't like him most of the time, either, but I love him because he's my brother. When I was so mad at him for what he did with Brenda and then again with Natalie, it brought on a guilt trip because we're supposed to love our siblings. I've come to realize that you can love someone but not like them," Mack said.

"Was Adam like that as a little boy? Did he always want your toys?" Lily immediately felt like a therapist again.

"Oh, yeah"—Mack nodded—"and our mother's attention. He had to be number one, no matter what it took. He couldn't stand it because I was close to Dad. He thought he'd won another feather for his cap when our folks moved to San Antonio to be close to Dad's Alzheimer's doctor. I guess Adam thought since Dad wasn't in the goat business anymore that he would finally be number one with him, too." Mack paused. "I don't know why I'm telling you all this. You'll think I'm a big pushover."

Lily's heart went out to Mack. "I don't think that at all, but why didn't you stand up to him?"

"I got tired of the constant fighting. Besides, what did a toy matter? It wasn't until Brenda and Natalie that I realized he had this uncontrollable urge to take everything from me. The crazy thing was that I thought he deserved it. After all, he was the pretty one. He was the athletic son and the charismatic twin," Mack answered. "When he took away not one but two of my girlfriends, that's when I stopped giving in. It's when I figured out that in my own right I'm equal to him, and I got comfortable in my own skin. It's been tough on him ever since."

"Sounds to me like Adam has NPD, but until he realizes that *he* has a problem and gets some help, it's not going to go away," Lily said.

"I'd forgotten that you were a therapist." Mack grinned and asked, "What exactly does that mean?"

"School counselor to begin with, and then a therapist. I'm not a psychologist or psychiatrist," she replied, "and NPD stands for narcissistic personality disorder. It means that he's got exaggerated feelings of self-importance, a need for self-admiration, and a lack of empathy. People with that problem spend too much time worrying about success in everything, as well as their personal appearance. They tend to take advantage of the people around them. The problem usually starts early in childhood. He should've had some kind of therapy when he was a little boy."

"How do I help him now?" Mack asked.

Lily just shook her head. Mack was truly a good brother if he'd taken that kind of abuse all those years and still wanted to help his twin.

"He'd have to agree to therapy and be willing to admit he had a problem, and then he could work on making changes," Lily answered.

"I don't see that happening. What causes this disorder anyway?" Mack asked.

Lily shrugged. "I only had two students with those symptoms that I thought should be sent for a full evaluation. One came from an affluent family and had siblings. The other came from a poorer home and was an only child. They displayed the same traits. So all I can tell you is that you'll have to ask someone far smarter than me what causes it."

"Oh, well." Mack picked up the remote. "Like you said, until *he* realizes he has a problem, it's not going to get fixed, anyway."

"That's right," Lily agreed.

Mack started the next episode of *Lethal Weapon*, and Lily watched it with brand-new insight. One of the main characters, Martin Riggs, was flawed because of his wife's death. Mack Cooper had problems because of his brother's narcissistic attitude. It was easy to see why Mack would relate to Riggs. Lily wanted to hug Mack, but he sure wouldn't like that, she was certain.

When the episode ended, she yawned. "I've had enough for tonight. I'm going up to bed. Good night, Mack."

"'Night to you, and thanks for listening." He got out of his chair and rolled his neck to get the kinks out.

"Anytime," she said on her way out the door.

Once she'd had a bath and was dressed for bed, she got out the journal again. She read the entry about Henry's attitude when he had come home from the war. "He was like Adam," she whispered. "He felt entitled and special."

She turned the page to reread the entry dated December 1865:

Matilda left this morning on a stagecoach. I already miss her and she's only been gone a few hours. I feel like she's making a mistake, but she's adamant that she loves the man. She's going to marry a Yankee, the friend that Henry brought home last summer. They've been writing since he and Henry left, and Henry's been sending Rayford's letters to her with his. What did I do wrong with my children? Everett tries to comfort me, but I feel like a complete failure. I may never see my daughter again. My son says he has no intentions of ever coming back to the cursed south again. A part of me admires him for his conviction; the other part wants to shake him until his teeth rattle even though he's a grown man.

Determined that she and Holly should share the new entries, Lily closed the journal and didn't read on.

Chapter Eight

Mack used his planning period on Thursday morning to look up NPD, and was amazed to find that the symptoms fit Adam so well. He and his brother were twins, so it stood to reason that they would be drawn to the same type of woman. But if Adam really had NPD, then why hadn't Mack developed that condition, also?

Lunchtime was right after his planning period, and a 4-H meeting had been scheduled for noon that day. He had to hustle to get over to the library at the middle school for the meeting. Today, they would be discussing the upcoming junior livestock exhibition, and the kids would be taking the forms home to fill out concerning what animals they would show that spring.

He was surprised to see Braden enter the room with Isaac Torres, who'd won first place the year before with his Angus steer. Isaac came from a fairly affluent family, one with a pretty nice-size spread out west of town. However, he was an overweight kid, kind of shy, and didn't have many friends, despite his family's wealth.

"Hey, Mack," Braden said, and then his face turned scarlet red. "I mean, Mr. Cooper."

"It's all right." Mack grinned. "The kids in 4-H and FFA usually just call me Mr. Mack. Are you interested in 4-H?"

"Maybe," Braden replied. "Isaac said I could come to the meeting with him and see what it's all about."

"Well, then, thank you, Isaac, for inviting a new person to the club," Mack said.

Isaac ducked his head and blushed right along with Braden. "He said that he likes your goats. I thought he might like 4-H. Maybe next year he can show a goat."

"That would be great," Mack said as several more members brought their lunch into the library and took a seat. "Looks like we're all here. This is an informal meeting today. We're here mainly to talk about the spring livestock show here in Comfort and to make sure you have the forms to fill out. They're right here on the desk. You need a separate one for each category you plan to enter. Say hey to Braden Anderson while you're at it. He's just moved here from Austin, and he might be joining 4-H."

Everyone turned to look at Braden. Some nodded. Some said hello. Since he was sitting with Isaac, one of the geeks in the middle school, no one said much to him. At the end of the period, Isaac hurried to the bathroom, and Braden stopped by the desk where Mack was still sitting.

"Isaac is my new friend. Why do the other kids treat him like something is wrong with him? He's super smart and he's really fun to talk to," Braden whispered.

"Yes, he is, and he's a hard worker, too," Mack told him. "He really takes time to train his show animals, and that's why he does so well. I'm glad he's your new friend."

"But why do the kids treat him like they do?" Braden pressed for an answer.

"Number one." Mack held up a finger. "He's smart, and that makes them feel inferior." Another finger went up. "Two, he's a little overweight and kind of shy, so they put him down to make themselves feel all important." A third finger popped up. "And three, they're jealous."

"Well, that's just mean." Braden slung his backpack over his shoulders. "I don't care what they think. Me and him have fun together, and he's my friend."

"I'm glad you feel that way," Mack said. "Someday maybe the other kids will come around and see what you do. You better get on to class now before you're tardy."

"Thanks, Mack, and I'm going to talk to Mama about joining 4-H. Next year maybe I can get a goat and show it, like Isaac says." Braden threw the brown bag that he'd brought his lunch in that day into the trash, and waved as he left the room.

"How about that?" Mack said as he picked up what was left of the forms and headed out of the building. The halls were quiet, but in a few minutes the bell would ring, and all that would change. He paused at the door for a moment. Several times his life had changed drastically in the few seconds that a bell could have rung. Things in his world had been as quiet as the hallways—then Lily and the kids moved into the house, and bingo, everything had done a turnaround.

When he pushed the doors open to go outside, he noticed Braden and Isaac over in a corner. Both of them waved at him. That alone was geeky—students ignored teachers for the most part, and they sure didn't smile and wave.

He crossed the parking lot, got behind the wheel, and headed out of town toward the high school. He remembered asking his father pretty much the same questions that Braden had asked him that day. Only Mack's were about why the kids at school treated Adam like a celebrity. Mack made better grades and worked harder. Orville Cooper had been as honest with him as Mack had been with Braden.

Mack wished he'd taken better advantage of time with his father. Orville had Alzheimer's, and there were many days when he didn't even know Mack, and others when he thought his sons were still teenagers.

He parked in his spot at the high school, got out of the vehicle, and hunched his wide shoulders against the bitter-cold January wind. When he finally made it to his room, he realized he had a few minutes left before the bell rang for his next class, so he took the time to call his mother.

"Hello." She was out of breath when she answered on the fourth ring. "Sorry it took so long. Your dad and I just got back from our walk. The doctors say it's good for him to get his exercise every day, but boy oh boy, is it ever cold today."

"How is he?" Mack asked.

"No better but no worse. Today is a good day. He knows me and talked about you and your goats. How are you doing with a family in the house with you?" Nora asked.

"It's going great so far. Mama, did you ever realize that Adam has a personality problem?" he asked.

"Of course I did, honey," she answered.

"Put it on speaker so I can hear," Orville yelled.

"We'll talk about Adam later," Nora whispered. "Okay, it's on speaker, and you have me and your dad here."

"I've only got a few minutes," Mack said. "Just thought I'd call and check on y'all. When are you going to come to Comfort and help me weed out my goatherd, Dad?"

"I was just there two days ago, and we took care of that then," Orville chuckled.

"That's right." But it had been six weeks since his folks had been to see him. "With school starting back, I forgot about that. Now you have to come and meet the family that's living with me."

"When the weather gets nicer, I'll do that," Orville said. "Have you seen Adam? Charlene comes to see us pretty often, but Adam hasn't been here in a year."

"I'll fuss at him next time I see him." Mack's voice almost cracked.

"You do that, and make him go feed the goats with you. He should get his hands dirty once in a while," Orville said.

"Darlin', Adam is the president of a bank," Nora reminded her husband in a soothing voice. "He hates any kind of outside work. Remember? He even has a gardener to take care of his yard."

"I'm hungry," Orville said. "I'm going to get some cookies and milk. You want some, Mack?"

"I'm good, Dad," Mack said. "Mama, I have to go now."

"Just one more thing before we hang up," she whispered. "I'm taking it off speaker now. I knew Adam had problems when y'all were little, but I didn't want to believe it. After that thing with Brenda"— she paused for a full twenty seconds—"I didn't know what to do, so I ignored it and hoped it would go away."

"It's not your fault, Mama. Look, the bell is ringing, so I've got to go. We'll talk later." Mack ended the call. Ignoring problems didn't make them go away, but at this late date, what good would it do to talk about the issues concerning his brother? His father used to say that a person should let sleeping dogs lie, so unless his mother brought it up again, that's what he planned to do.

He caught a glimpse of Holly in the hallway with Rose and Ivy. He thought it might embarrass her for him to speak to her, so he just eased on past and hurried to the vo-ag building.

Some of his students were working on rabbit hutches. Others were helping Barry, Drew's son, refinish a stock trailer for his State Fair of Texas project. It had come into the shop looking like crap, but it would be downright beautiful when they got it finished. As he went from project to project, giving encouragement here and there, his mind kept going back to how comfortable he'd been with Lily the night before. Talking to her had brought Adam's problems out into the open and helped Mack realize that there was little he could do to help his brother. It had also solidified the fact that he was no longer the brother who had to walk in Adam's shadow, and that Mack was at last comfortable with his life, just the way it was.

~

Lily put a pan of brownies in the oven so they'd have an after-school snack. While the treats were baking, guilt jumped out of nowhere and settled on her shoulders like a heavy, wet blanket. She could list the reasons why she felt that way. First was that she hadn't visited her parents often enough, then after her father had died suddenly, that she hadn't gone to see her mother more. Now she would be working full-time away from home, which meant there wouldn't be after-school snacks straight from the oven for her children.

Guilt trips never take you anywhere. Her mother's old adage came to mind.

"Amen," she said as she set out glasses for milk.

The kids came through the front door. She could hear their backpacks hitting the chairs and their arguing as they hung up their coats. Then they both tried to come through the door at the same time. Holly hip-checked Braden to the side and made it to the kitchen first.

"I smell brownies." Braden evened the match by getting to the table first. "I made a new friend at school today, and his name is Isaac Torres, and can I join 4-H so I can maybe show a goat next year and"— he stopped for a breath, then went on—"can I go to Isaac's house on Saturday and hang out with him?"

"I'll think about it." Lily poured milk for each of them.

"Rose and Ivy invited me to go to choir practice on Friday nights." Holly helped herself to the first brownie. "They said their mama would pick me up and bring me home. It's at the church, and it's from seven to nine. I promise to get all my homework done before I go."

"She just wants to go because Clay will be there. That's the preacher's son, and she's got a crush on him," Braden tattled.

"Do not," Holly argued.

"Do, too," Braden shot back.

"Hello," Mack called from the back door. "Is that chocolate I smell?"

"Brownies," Braden yelled. "You better hurry before Holly eats them all."

"You're the pig when it comes to brownies," Holly accused.

Braden snorted just like a hog.

"You're disgusting." Holly took another brownie from the pan.

The comment Holly had made back in Austin about Braden being Lily's precious angel son had been weighing heavily on her mind all day in addition to all the other bits of guilt. She wondered if she was enabling Braden to be a little narcissistic, but after listening to them argue, she decided that she was raising two healthy kids. They might be as different as night and day, but they were not suffering from NPD.

"Coffee is in the pot. Sweet tea's in the fridge," Lily told Mack. "Where are your glasses? I just realized that you haven't worn them in several days."

"I only wear them when I have to," he said. "Most of the time I wear contacts, but I had an allergy flare-up and had to use my glasses for a while."

He brushed past her on the way to get a cup of coffee, and there were those sparks again, only this time they were even hotter than before. An image flashed through her mind—she was cuddling up with him on the sofa, and he was tipping her chin up with his calloused hand to kiss her.

"Should I pour a cup for you?" Mack asked.

His deep voice jerked Lily back to reality. "Yes, please, and thank you." She hoped he attributed her burning cheeks to the heat in the kitchen.

It seemed like the kids swallowed their brownies whole and hurried up the stairs to do their homework, or in Braden's case, to change into different clothing so he could go to the goat pens with Mack.

"You also run the 4-H, right?" Lily asked when she and Mack were alone.

"I do." Mack nodded. "Braden came to the 4-H meeting today with his new friend. Isaac Torres is a good kid. He's a little shy, but he's super smart. He's always on the superintendent's honor roll."

"Then it's all right for Braden to—" Lily started and then stopped. "Is he Levi Torres's son? The Torres Ranch folks? Didn't you and Levi graduate the same year?"

"We did, and yes, Isaac is his son. Levi married a girl he met in college. She's from down around Houston and grew up on a ranch like Levi did," Mack answered.

"Levi was smart and shy, too," Lily remembered, and stopped herself before she added, "A lot like you."

"You're the mother, but I think Braden and Isaac will be good for each other." Mack reached for a brownie.

"Why's that?"

"Braden is outgoing, and he'll help Isaac in that department. From what I see in Braden, he needs someone to challenge him intellectually, so Isaac will be a help to him that way. Same way that Holly is good for Rose and Ivy. Their parents are strict with them, so you don't have to worry about her smoking pot. Yet they could sure use someone like Holly to give them a little push when it comes to grades."

"Holly wants to go to Friday-night choir practice with the girls, and Braden wants to know if he can go to the ranch and hang out with Isaac on Saturday. What do you think?" Lily hadn't asked for anyone's input where her kids were concerned in years, but she really needed Mack's opinion.

"If they were my kids, I wouldn't have a problem with either the choir or the ranch," he said.

"Thank you." It was beginning to look like she'd made the right decision in her fit of anger over their behavior.

"I talked to my mother and dad today," Mack said.

"How are they doing?" Lily carried her coffee to the table and sat down on the other side from Mack.

"Dad's not good," Mack replied. "He's getting more confused about time than ever. They haven't been here since the end of November, but he thought it was two days ago, and he told me to make Adam help me with the goats. Mama's got her hands full with him, but she's doing okay."

Lily reached across the table and laid a hand on his. "I'm so sorry. That has to be the worst disease ever."

"Thank you." Mack patted her hand with his free one. "I asked Mama if she realized Adam had a problem, and she said yes. She thought he'd outgrow it, and then felt like it was too late to do anything about it when he broke up my engagement with Brenda."

"Parents don't like to admit their kids have issues," Lily said.

"You didn't mind admitting your kids had problems. You took steps to keep them from getting into more trouble than they were already in. Even though they whined and threw hissy fits, you were a solid, good mother and did what was best for them."

Lily could have kissed him for that bit of encouragement, but Braden came bursting into the room at that very moment. She jerked her hand free from Mack's and said, "I didn't even hear you coming down the stairs. You usually make enough noise that the neighbors think it's thundering."

He held up a foot. "I only got on my socks. I thought I'd wear Grandpa's boots as well as his coat."

"You wear a size eight. Your grandfather wore an eleven," Lily told him.

He jerked an extra pair of socks from his hip pocket. "I'll stuff the toes."

"We really should make time to get that kid a pair of rubber boots and a work coat," Mack said.

"Yes!" Braden pumped his fist in the air. "Can we get them before I go visit Isaac on his ranch?"

Mack glanced over at Lily. "We could take him to the feed store tomorrow evening. They don't close until six, and they carry coats and boots."

"Please, Mama," Braden begged.

"I suppose," she agreed. "If you're really going to be in 4-H and show goats, you should have a warm coat and boots that will keep your feet dry."

Braden ran to her side and wrapped his arms around her. "Thank you, Mama. Can we go get them right after school, and can Mack go with us?"

"Be glad to," Mack offered.

"Don't see why not," Lily said at the same time.

"See why not what?" Holly poked her head around the door.

"I get to go to the feed store and get boots and a coat," Braden sing-songed.

"If he gets to do that, can I go to Sally's store again?" Holly asked.

"Why don't you and I go to Sally's, and these two guys can go to the feed store?" Lily asked.

"Fine by me," Braden said. "A girl don't belong in a feed store, anyway."

"Hey, now, they have all kinds of western clothes for girls in there," Mack said.

"Then I want to go there instead of to Sally's. Rose and Ivy have western belts that they wear with their jeans. Can I have one of those?" Holly asked.

"We can look at them." Not long ago, Lily had been arguing with these two about moving to Comfort, and now they argued about rubber boots and a western belt. She almost pinched herself to see if she was dreaming.

Later that evening, after Lily had taken a bath and washed her hair, she went to her room and got the journal. She adjusted the lamp so she could see better, then like a kid with a dollar in a candy store, she couldn't help herself from peeking at the next entry in the journal. She knew that she probably shouldn't keep reading the journal without sharing it with Holly, but she was drawn to it that evening.

December 1870: My precious son was stillborn a month ago. He was a month early and so very small. He was a perfect baby, but he never took a breath. I don't know if I will ever get over the feeling that it's my fault. What did I do wrong? Rayford doesn't seem to care that we buried our baby, or maybe he doesn't know how to show it. I'd like to think that's the reason he's so indifferent, but in my heart, I'm sure it's because he has a new woman. I refuse to be like Henry's wife, so I put on a front and keep going.

Lily tore a page off a notepad on the nightstand to use as a bookmark, closed the journal, and let what she'd read sink deep into her soul. She'd had to put on a brave front when Wyatt left. She hadn't lost a baby, but she had just lost her mother—and a marriage. Grief was the same, no matter what caused it. She could relate to the way that Matilda held on to her dignity through it all, and wondered if Rayford had ever changed. She was tempted to keep reading, but if she did, she knew she wouldn't stop until she'd read the whole journal, and she needed to get some sleep.

"Wyatt and Rayford should be thrown in a tow sack with a few big rocks and shoved off into the Guadalupe River. They were born more than a century apart, but they prove that men have always been the same," she muttered.

Is Mack Cooper like those two men? The question stabbed her in the heart.

"No," she declared. "He's not, and any woman would be lucky to have him in their life. If he falls in love a third time, I'll take on Adam single-handedly, so he can't come between Mack and his new lady."

A shot of jealousy went through Lily at the very thought of Mack with another woman. She tried to brush it off as caring for him like she would a brother, but down deep she knew better.

Chapter Nine

*F*or the past fourteen years, Lily hadn't paid much attention to what was hanging in her closet. She worked in black slacks, a white shirt, and a black jacket when she was a counselor. If she didn't have clients that day, she wore pajama pants and an oversize T-shirt. She had church clothes, a couple of basic dresses for funerals, and a few fancy things that she'd worn to the church Christmas parties.

It seemed fitting to start to work on a Monday. Begin the new week with a new job. So, what to wear when you work in a vintage shop? She finally decided on jeans and a bright red sweater. She swept her hair back up into a ponytail and put on a pair of gold hoop earrings. Maybe, she thought, she'd buy a pair of Granny Hayes's special earrings to wear next week when she got her first paycheck. She and Holly could share them—unless her daughter decided over the weekend that she needed horseshoes or fancy cowboy boots dangling from her ears. Teenagers so easily swayed from one thing to the other, but Lily had faith that her daughter would find her own style—whatever it might be.

It was just after nine when she walked into the store, and the place was crawling with customers. Sally was at the cash register ringing up sales, so Lily stashed her coat and purse under the counter. She went to the nearest lady and asked if she could help her.

"I'm just admiring all the gorgeous glassware," the lady said. "I collect it and have it sitting everywhere—one of those swan dishes is in my bathroom right now with little guest soaps in it."

"I'm sure it's lovely," Lily said. "What brings you to the store?"

"We're on a little road trip," the elderly lady said. "Our Sunday-school class does this every January."

A different lady held up a hobnail milk glass vase. "Look at this, Nadine. Isn't it pretty?"

"It would look real sweet sitting on your piano with a little bouquet of flowers in it," Nadine said.

Lily made the rounds, but it was a slow process. Every one of them wanted to talk. When Nadine finally said, "If we're going to make all the stores in Comfort by noon, we'd better be paying for our purchases and getting—" She sucked in a lungful of air. "Oh. My. Goodness! I must have one of these shawls. Virgie, come look at this. You should get the yellow one for Easter."

By ten thirty they'd nearly all trickled out. Sally dropped into a chair behind the counter and said, "Thank God you came in when you did. I couldn't keep up with the lot of them. I don't think a senior citizens' Sunday-school class would rob me blind, but if they did, I wouldn't have known until inventory time."

"Want something to drink? I can go across the street and get us something," Lily offered.

"No need." Sally shook her head. "That old Philco refrigerator in the back room still runs beautifully. It's stocked with drinks and stuff to make sandwiches. I'll take a diet root beer if you're going that way. Oh, and there's candy bars in the basket on top of the fridge."

"Snickers?" Lily asked.

"Is there any other kind?" Sally chuckled.

Lily got two candy bars, a diet root beer, and a bottle of sweet tea from the fridge and carried it all to the front. "How often does that happen?"

"In the summer, it's a daily thing. In the spring, maybe three times a month, yet not so much this time of year." Sally pulled the tab from her can of soda and took a long drink. "I sold two thousand dollars' worth of stuff this morning, so I'm not complaining, and now you can see how bad I need help. Sit down." She pointed to the other chair. "Tell me about life with Mack so far."

"How well do you know Adam?" Lily asked.

"Good God, please tell me you aren't interested in him," Sally said. "He's trouble in a thousand-dollar suit."

"I'm not one bit interested in him." Lily went on to tell her about Adam flirting with her.

"Just more proof that he's an asshole," Sally declared. "When we were sophomores and he was a senior, he sweet-talked me under the bleachers after a football game one Friday night. I was all excited. I mean, after all, I was a chubby sixteen-year-old, and the quarterback of the football team was interested in me. Right up until he told me that we were going to have sex. I told him no, and he called me every name he could think of. He stormed off, and I half expected him to tell all his friends that I'd put out, but he didn't."

"Probably because he didn't want to admit someone had told him no," Lily said. "If a person could buy him for what he's worth and sell him for what he thinks he's worth, they'd make a fortune."

Sally almost choked on a sip of soda. "Amen, sister."

Lily went on. "Are you aware that he broke up Mack and his almost-fiancée, married her, and then turned around and did the same thing a few years later?"

"I heard something about that at the time. Granny Hayes told me that Mack brought a girl home to meet his folks, and Adam took the woman away from him. She didn't mention it happening a second

time, but hey, if those women really loved Mack, a pompous fool like
Adam . . ." Sally ripped the paper from her candy bar, took a bite, and
groaned, "Well, crap! Here comes Ruth-Ann Winkler. She's still the
biggest gossip in town. Be careful what you say."

"I think I may just go to the next room and straighten the clothes
racks," Lily whispered.

Sally laid the rest of her candy bar to the side and stood up when
the bell above the door jingled. "Well, hello, Ruth-Ann. What brings
you to town on a school day?"

"I'm taking a late lunch. I saw Holly Anderson wearing the cutest
pair of earrings. She said she got them here, so I thought I'd come take a
look." Ruth-Ann looked around as if she were trying to find the jewelry.

"Over at the end of the counter." Sally pointed.

"They *are* pretty." Ruth-Ann picked up a pair and held them up to
her ears. "Handmade?"

Lily peeked around the corner. Ruth-Ann's back was to her, but she
could see Sally very well.

"Yes, they are." Sally nodded and slid a sly wink toward Lily when
Ruth-Ann wasn't looking at her.

"I heard that Lily Anderson is going to work for you," Ruth-Ann
said.

Rumors in small towns always ran rampant, but Ruth-Ann was
baiting her hook to go fishing for the really good stuff. Evidently it was
true that a leopard couldn't change its spots, or a gossip her daily need
for something to spread.

"Starting today." Another nod from Sally, but no wink this time.

"I also heard that she and Mack have had a thing going for years,
even in high school. Think that's true?" Ruth-Ann lowered her voice
like she was telling a secret and laid two pairs of earrings on the counter.
"I'll take both of these."

Lily almost marched out there and told the woman to mind her
own business, but she held her peace and just listened.

"I wouldn't know," Sally answered. "You'd have to ask her."

Great answer, Lily thought. *And when you get up the nerve to ask me, I'll tell you that what goes on in my house stays in my house.*

"Oh, I couldn't." Ruth-Ann threw a hand over her mouth. "That would be like gossip, and I never do that. It's unprofessional. I always thought she might have had a little side fling with Adam. He used to look at her like he knew something the rest of us didn't."

Great balls of fire! She was really fishing now. Lily had never given Adam Cooper the time of day.

"Oh, yeah? I never noticed." Sally rang up the earrings and said, "Thirteen ninety-five."

Ruth-Ann handed over her credit card. "In my professional opinion, I think that they're two consenting adults. In my parenting opinion, I would hope they aren't sleeping together when the kids are in the house."

Lily knotted her hands into fists. If something like that got out, Mack could lose his job.

"Good God!" Sally ran the card and handed her a receipt to sign. "She's only been home a short while. Do you really think she and Mack would get a relationship going that included sex that fast?"

"One never knows this day and age," Ruth-Ann said. "Got to be going. See you later. Maybe I'll stop in next week when Lily is here."

"I'm sure she'll be so tickled to see you," Sally said.

As soon as the woman had closed the door, Lily came back to the checkout counter. She sank down in a folding chair and sighed. "I shouldn't have moved in with Mack. I should have given him notice to move out of the house before I came back. If he loses his job, it'll be my fault."

"He's not going to lose his job. He's got tenure, for one thing, and it's not 1895, girl. For a third thing"—Sally held up three fingers—"he's a damn good vo-ag teacher, and he's really built up the program. I'm surprised that you didn't march out here and tell her to go to hell."

"I wanted to, but"—Lily finally grinned—"why spoil a good source of what people are saying or thinking about me with one little temper fit. A gossip is a good way to find out things. I may hide every time she comes into the shop. Now, how about showing me how to run that cash register?"

"Soon as I finish my candy bar." Sally picked up her candy bar and took another bite.

~

Lily didn't leave until almost four that afternoon. She had just walked in the door when the school bus pulled up and let Holly and Braden out. They rushed into the house, both of them talking at once about going to the feed store again—this time for more than goat feed.

"Do I need to change clothes?" Holly asked.

It had been so long since Holly had asked for her mother's opinion that Lily was taken aback for several seconds.

"No, I think you look just fine," Lily answered.

"When is Mack coming home? He'll be here before the store closes, right?" Braden tossed his backpack on the chair and headed for the kitchen. "Do I have time for cookies and chocolate milk? I don't even care if they're bought cookies. I'm hungry. They had spaghetti at school today, and believe me, Mama, their spaghetti does not taste like yours."

"I had the salad bar, and it was fine," Holly said.

"I'm not a rabbit," Braden said.

"Well, you look like one when you make that face," Holly told him. "I hear a truck. You better scarf them cookies down if you want to go get boots and a coat."

"I'll eat later," Braden said.

"Hey, everyone is home!" Mack said as he came through the kitchen door. "Y'all ready to go get some shopping done? I thought maybe we would have burgers for supper. We could all go in my truck. There's plenty of room. Would that be okay, Lily?"

"Sounds fine to me." She thought of what Ruth-Ann had said about her sleeping with Mack, and her cheeks burned. She'd blushed more since coming back to Comfort than she had in five years.

"Then let's load up and get going," Mack said.

"Shotgun!" Braden yelled.

"We don't mind riding in the back seat, do we, Holly?" Lily asked.

"I'd rather ride in the back with you than up front with that spoiled brat." Holly pointed at her brother.

"Hey, I'm not spoiled." Braden grinned. "You can't spoil the favorite child."

"Dream on, little brother." Holly did one of her famous head wiggles. "*I'm* the favorite since we moved to Comfort, and you don't get to ever be favorite again."

Lily immediately thought of Adam. How many times had he lorded it over Mack with similar words? "Hey, now," she said, "you're both my favorite. Braden is my favorite son, and Holly, you're my favorite daughter."

"But I'm your *favorite* favorite, right?" Holly pressed.

"Tell you what." Lily pointed at her daughter. "You can each be the favorite three days a week, and Sunday is my day to not have a favorite kid."

"Today is mine, right?" Holly kept it going.

"Nope," Lily said. "It's like this. You each get three days, but they can change according to your behavior. It's up to me to decide which kid gets that day, and right now I haven't decided who's the favorite today."

Braden answered by sticking his tongue out at his sister and running out the back door toward Mack's truck. Holly ran after him, yelling that if she beat him, she was going to ride shotgun.

"Ain't life grand with kids in the house?" Mack asked. "And FYI, I liked your answer a lot. I wish Mama would have told me and Adam something like that when we were kids."

"Thank you, but I'm not sure Adam could have handled it," she said.

He put a hand on her lower back and ushered her out to his truck. "You got that right. He'd have gone into a depression for sure, but it would have been good for him."

"Probably so." She nodded.

He opened the truck door for her, waited until she was seated comfortably, and then closed it. She could hear him whistling all the way around the front side of the truck to the driver's seat. He started the engine, and the radio came on right then to Blake Shelton singing, "Goodbye Time."

Lily had so many goodbyes to say that she didn't know where to start. She'd gone through all the stages of grief for the deaths of her parents and the divorce—all except for the acceptance part at the very end. Yet it was definitely time for her to say goodbye to all of it so that she could begin to look forward to a future that looked brighter than she'd ever imagined it might be.

Chapter Ten

Surprisingly enough, the kids didn't fuss about getting up for church that morning. They'd carried on the previous week like they had to get a shot at the doctor's office. However, that morning, they were both up and ready to go by the time Mack pulled the truck around to the front doors.

The church lot was full that morning, and Mack had to park all the way out at the edge of the street. When they made it inside, Mack, Holly, and Braden left Lily in the sanctuary with Sally, and the three of them hurried on back to their Sunday-school class. Braden helped Clay set up the chairs, and Holly went right to the Sanchez twins to whisper and giggle before class began.

Once Sunday school was over, Mack noticed that several people craned their necks as he entered the sanctuary with Holly and Braden by his side. Mack couldn't hear the whispers, but the buzz told him that folks had something to say about his new living arrangements. He'd learned long ago, after the first fiasco with Adam, to let rumors slide off his back like water off a duck. He just hoped that what people said didn't affect Lily or the kids.

They had to sit in the second pew and were so cramped that Mack's shoulder and hip pressed right up against Lily's. Not that he minded, but it sure raised the temperature in the church by several degrees. His tie started to throttle him, and his pulse raced. He reached for the last hymnal at the same time Lily did. His hand closed over hers, and the sparks almost scorched the book.

"We'll share," he whispered.

She gave him a brief nod. Should he have offered to share with Braden, who was sitting on his other side? They sang a congregational hymn, and then the preacher started his sermon. Mack tuned him out and thought about how nice it would be to have a woman like Lily in his life—someone who would be willing to listen to him, and even more so one that couldn't be swayed by Adam's charms.

Mack had really enjoyed the routine that they'd all settled into the past couple of weeks. Mornings were hectic for the most part, with all of them getting ready for school or work, but in the evenings the kids spent time in their rooms pretty often, and he and Lily had wound up relaxing in the living room by themselves.

Could it be possible that he was ready to move on again? He probably shouldn't be thinking of the Blake Shelton song he'd heard on the radio on the way to the feed store a few days before. He should have come to the realization long ago that Brenda and Natalie were as much to blame as Adam. If they'd really loved him, even just as another person, Adam wouldn't have been able to seduce either of them. It was time to say a final goodbye to all the anger in his soul and let it go for good. The words of the hymn they'd sung that morning replaced Shelton's song—one line said that we cannot see beyond the moment. With that in mind, he should make the most of every second he was given. A loud clap of thunder rattled the church windows, and Grandpa Wilson, who'd been snoring in the pew right behind Mack, sat up straight.

"God spoke pretty loud right then," Drew chuckled. "Evidently, he wants all of y'all to hear my final words, and that is God has something for all of us if we're patient. Now if Grandpa Wilson will deliver the benediction, we'll try to get y'all home before the rain starts."

The elderly gentleman rose to his feet and mumbled a short prayer, and then the rain started coming down in sheets. A strong north wind accompanied it, blowing it fiercely against the stained-glass windows and slamming it against the roof with so much force that it sounded like hail.

Most of the folks ran from the church to their vehicles without even stopping to shake the preacher's hand on the way out. When Mack's group reached the back pew, he noticed that Granny Hayes had stayed seated. An old black felt hat with a peacock feather stuck in the band was crammed down on her head. Two long gray braids fell to her waist, and her face was weathered and wrinkled.

"Could I take you home, Miz Hayes?" Mack asked. "It would be quite a ride out to your place in this weather for Dusty."

"Or you could have Sunday dinner with us," Lily said. "We've got a nice big roast in the oven at home, and a cherry pie for dessert."

"Dusty don't like storms. I reckon he's already broke his tether and is halfway home by now." Granny Hayes looked past Lily and Mack and focused on Holly. "That's a pair of my earrings you're wearing."

"Yes, ma'am." Holly's face lit up in a grin. "They're my favorite pair. I wish I knew how to make more."

Granny Hayes stood up. "I'll let you take me home, and I thank you for the offer of dinner, but I've got dinner in the oven." She glanced at the earrings again. "What's your name?"

"Holly Anderson. Vera Miller was my grandma," Holly answered.

Mack was shocked that Granny Hayes talked to Holly at all. He'd never seen her pay a bit of attention—good or bad—to any of the kids in the church.

~

Lily marveled that Holly had mentioned her grandmother, and wondered why she did that. Maybe she wanted the elderly woman to know that she wasn't a stranger in Comfort. Holly and Braden both continued to surprise Lily more and more every day.

"Vera was a good woman. You look like she did when she was your age. Holly, would you like to have dinner with me, and afterward I could teach you how to make earrings if you're interested in learning?" Granny Hayes asked.

"Yes, ma'am, if it's all right with my mama, and I really do want to know how to make them and to make the shawls, too." Holly looked up at Lily. "Please?"

"Thank you for the offer, Miz Hayes," Lily said. "When y'all get done, you just give me a call, and I'll come get her."

"I don't have a telephone or any of these newfangled gadgets. You can come get her at three thirty. That's when I take my Sunday nap," Granny Hayes said. "Don't honk the horn. It spooks Dusty. We'll be waiting on the porch."

"We'll remember that." Lily could understand someone Granny Hayes's age not having a cell phone, but she didn't know a single soul this day and age that didn't at least still have a landline. How did a person live without a connection of any kind to the outside world?

Very simply. Vera was back in her head.

Lily thought about how much simpler her life had been since she'd taken away all her kids' devices, and nodded in agreement with her mother's voice.

"I'll go get the truck and drive it up close to the door," Mack offered.

"I'm going with you," Braden said, and followed right behind him.

Lily extended a hand to the elderly woman. Granny Hayes put her veined and bony hand in hers and said, "Thank you. Old bones like mine don't like the cold weather or the wet, neither one, and when it's both, they really do fuss."

"You're very welcome," Lily said. In spite of the layers of clothing, Granny Hayes felt so light that pulling her to her feet was like picking up a bag of marshmallows.

"It's a real chore on Sunday to ride into town for church," Granny Hayes said as she moved toward the door. "But the Good Book says that I should give my best to the Master, so I try to do just that."

"We'd be glad to come get you on Sunday mornings and take you home." Lily followed behind her.

"I appreciate that offer. Sally has said the same thing, but the truth is, Dusty kind of likes to come hear the singin'," she told them, "and the ride quiets my soul and gets me ready to listen to what Preacher Drew has to say to us."

"Well, anytime you change your mind, we'll be glad to come and get you," Lily said.

Granny Hayes nodded and pulled her scarf up around her ears. When they were outside, Lily rushed around her and intended to open the truck door for her, but Mack beat her to it. Rain was dripping off the brim of his hat, but he had a smile on his face when he motioned for Granny Hayes to get into his truck. With the agility of a teenager, she hopped into the back seat and slid over to the middle. Lily got in right beside her. Holly ran around the truck and was already seated on the other side of Granny Hayes, buckled in, and had the door closed before Mack got behind the wheel.

"Don't you wish you had got some rubber boots like mine?" Braden asked from the front seat.

"What good are they doing you?" Holly shot back. "They're at home in the foyer, not on your feet."

Granny Hayes chuckled. "I had a brother once, and he was a smarty-pants at times, too. But then in them days, I was just as bad as him."

In her youth, Lily had seen the woman smile a few times, but she'd never heard her laugh. What made the old soul so solemn? she wondered. She'd have to remember to ask Sally about that when she went to work the next day.

Even in the rain and having to go the last mile on a dirt road, it took less than ten minutes to get from the church to Granny Hayes's old log cabin. Chickens roosted on the porch, but they'd pecked the yard dry long since, and the rain had turned it into a giant mud puddle. A couple of ducks huddled against the door, and the mule, Dusty, had indeed come home to his lean-to shed not far from the house.

Mack pulled up right next to the porch, and chickens scattered every which way, but the ducks didn't budge. Holly took a deep breath, got out, and ran through the puddles to the porch. Granny Hayes slid across the place where Holly had been sitting, hiked up her skirt to reveal black rubber boots, and trudged through the mud to the house.

"Go on in, child. I don't believe in locked doors," Granny Hayes called out.

Holly slung open the door and disappeared into the house. Lily slid over to the other side of the back seat and tried to catch a glimpse of what was inside the cabin, but all she saw before the door slammed shut was a big yellow cat.

"Don't worry." Mack locked gazes with her in the rearview mirror.

"Do you know anyone else who's ever been inside that cabin?" Lily was now alone in the back seat of the truck.

"Nope, but then I've never heard her laugh before, either. Maybe the old gal is mellowing." He drove out of the yard and headed back toward town.

"Comfort ain't the boonies," Braden said with a shudder from the front seat. "But *this* is, for sure. That lady reminds me of Granny Clampett in *The Beverly Hillbillies*."

"You're too young to have seen that movie," Mack said.

"My mother loved that crazy show," Lily said. "She bought all the episodes on DVD when they came out. They're probably still in the house somewhere. She showed the kids the movie the last time they stayed with her. Holly wanted to adopt a raccoon for a pet when she got home. I'm surprised that Braden remembers it. He couldn't have been more than six years old."

"It was dorky," Braden laughed, "but I kind of liked it. Can we watch the movie again?"

"Sure," Lily agreed. "Want to get it out of the buffet and watch it after dinner today?"

"That would be fun," Braden said.

~

Mack thought it was the perfect Sunday afternoon—an old movie, Braden laughing until he had to hold his sides, and Lily on the other end of the sofa from him. It was all surreal, but he loved every minute. Right up until Adam breezed into the house without knocking. His brother removed his leather jacket and tossed it on the empty recliner, then sat down between him and Lily.

"I might have expected you to be watching some silly show like this." Adam's tone was downright cold.

Braden piped up from the other recliner. "I asked to watch it. Granny Hayes reminded me of Granny Clampett, and I remembered this movie. It's so funny. You should've been here from the beginning. It's almost over now."

"No, thank you." Adam scooted a little closer to Lily. "Got any coffee?"

"I'll go make a fresh pot." Lily jumped up and headed for the kitchen.

"While she does that, I'll make a trip to the little boy's room," Adam said.

"It's just the bathroom. We don't have separate restrooms in the house, only at school," Braden told him, and then laughed at the next scene in the film.

Mack wished he'd been more like Braden when he was a kid. If he had been, maybe Adam wouldn't be such a jerk now. The show ended, and Mack stood up and stretched. "Want some hot chocolate? I can make the packaged stuff. It's not as good as what your mama makes, but it's not bad with a topper of whipped cream."

"Yep, and thank you." Braden nodded.

Mack heard scuffling before he reached the kitchen and hurried a little. He made it to the archway just in time to see Lily's open hand connect with Adam's cheek. Adam's right hand closed into a fist, and he started to draw it back to retaliate, but Mack took several fast steps forward and grabbed his brother's arm.

"You don't really want to do that," Mack whispered.

"Sorry, it was instinct." Adam growled. "But she led me on, and then when I tried to kiss her, she slapped me."

"Tell the truth." Lily glared at him.

"That's what happened," Adam declared.

"No, it's not. You came up behind me, wrapped your arms around my waist, and pressed your body against my back. Then you kissed me on the neck. I told you to quit, and you said that you were better than Mack, and once I had a taste of what you had to offer, I'd kick him out," Lily said.

Adam flashed one of his brilliant smiles at his brother. "She's lyin'. You'd do well to get out of this place before she ruins your reputation and you get fired at school."

"I believe her." Mack could feel the coldness in his own voice. "It's time for you to go. It would be best if you didn't come back."

"Come on, brother." Adam's smile faded. "I've changed since Brenda and Natalie."

"Don't let the door hit you in the ass," Mack said.

"Mama isn't going to like this." Adam's mouth tightened into a firm line.

"After what you've done to Charlene, she might not believe your story," Mack said.

Adam glared at him for several seconds, then stomped out of the room like a petulant child. Mack heard the front door slam and his brother's cute little sports car roar out of the driveway.

"I'm sorry," he said.

"It wasn't your fault," Lily told him. "But thank you."

"Hey, is that hot chocolate ready?" Braden yelled from the living room. "And did y'all realize it's time to go get Holly? I'm going to ask her if she wants to watch *The Beverly Hillbillies* with me again when she gets home."

Mack had never wanted to hug anyone in his life as much as he wanted to hug Lily at that moment. She would never know how much it meant to him to see a woman, especially one he'd begun to like, fend off Adam's advances.

Mack checked the time on his phone. "I should get there at exactly the right time. Want to go with me?"

"I'll stay here and make hot chocolate while you're gone," Lily offered. "It should be ready when you get home."

In less than half an hour, Holly came bursting through the back door. Her long blonde hair was in two braids, and she was wearing a pair of new earrings and a crocheted scarf around her neck that was the same color blue as her eyes.

"Mama, can I have a kitten? Granny Hayes has this big, yellow mama cat that's got three babies, and she says I can have my pick of them if you say it's all right." She touched her ears. "We made these earrings together, and she says we can make another pair next week if I can go home with her after church. I'll wash dishes every night if you'll say yes."

"I guess you had a good time, then?" Lily poured up four cups of hot chocolate.

"Yes! Yes! Yes!" Holly exclaimed. "I got to sit in front of her fireplace and hold all the baby kittens, and she told me stories while she was teaching me how to make earrings. Did you know that Sally buys her the basic supplies, but Granny uses feathers from her own chickens and ducks to make the earrings? She dyes them different colors, and she's got a whole bunch right there in her cabin."

"Let me help you take those mugs to the table." Mack entered the room right behind Holly.

He was so close to Lily that his warm breath sent shivers down her spine. She managed to nod but was afraid to speak for fear her voice would sound breathless.

Holly removed her coat and hung it on the back of a kitchen chair, then sat down. "And she's going to teach me to crochet so I can make scarves, and she says that when I get really good at it, maybe Sally will sell them in her store."

"We watched *The Beverly Hillbillies*," Braden said.

"Rats!" Holly frowned. "Can we watch it again tonight? And Mama? What about that kitten?"

"If she gets one, I get one, too," Braden said.

"Not if Granny Hayes doesn't want to give you one. She likes me. I don't know if she likes you." Holly caught sight of the leftover blackberry cobbler still sitting on the cabinet. "Can I have some of that with ice cream on it?"

"Sure, but you have to get it yourself. I'm already sitting down." Lily wasn't sure if she chose that moment to stop waiting on her daughter to teach her to be independent, or if maybe she was a little jealous of all the love that Granny Hayes was getting that afternoon.

"Yes, ma'am." Holly jumped up. "Anyone else want some?"

"Not me," Mack said.

"Not me," Braden echoed. "What did you have for dinner? Did you have to kill a chicken for that woman to cook before you could eat?"

"She made an oven stew and sliced a loaf of bread that she made yesterday. We had a peach upside-down cake for dessert. It was really good, and I ate two bowls, but I love Mama's cobbler," Holly said.

"You don't have to butter me up," Lily told her. "I'll think about the kitten business and give you an answer when they're old enough to leave their mama."

"Thank you." Holly nodded.

Everyone settled down to drink their hot chocolate. After they'd finished, Braden started *The Beverly Hillbillies* movie again.

When the goats had been tended to that evening and supper was over, the kids went to their rooms to do the last bit of their homework. Mack brought out his briefcase, took out a sheaf of papers, and laid them on the kitchen table.

"Anything I can help you with?" Lily asked.

"No, but thanks," he replied. "It's just the forms for the youth livestock show. I always go over them to be sure the kids have gotten them all done right. That way they don't get disqualified."

"Then I'll see you at breakfast," she said. "I'm going up to help Holly with her history project before bedtime."

Mack laid his pen down and looked up at her. "I don't want to influence you, but I don't mind cats or dogs. I thought about getting one or the other, but I didn't want to ask you if it was all right. I mean, after all, you've given me the use of your home, even with all the furniture. It seemed a little much to ask if I could bring pets in the house, too."

"I always had cats when I was growing up," Lily told him. "There's at least three buried out there under the pecan tree in the backyard. Smokey, Fuzzy, and Amos were their names. Amos died after I went to college, and Daddy buried him for me. The thing is, what if this job doesn't work out? What if we all do have to move back to Austin at the end of the school year? We can't have pets in our apartment in the city, and it would devastate the kids to have to leave them behind."

"I've been meanin' to talk to you about that." Mack looked uncomfortable. "If that should happen, will you sell me this place? And if you do decide to move back, and the kids can't have their pets in the city, I'll be glad to adopt them."

"I guess we'll have to see what the future holds, but if I decide to sell the property, you'll definitely have first chance at it." She laid a hand on his shoulder. "And thanks for the offer to take on whatever pets the kids might have. I appreciate that."

She removed her hand and headed out of the room. When she got to the staircase, she looked at it to see if it was as red as it felt. It wasn't, so she held it to her face and was surprised to find that it was actually quite cool and not on fire at all.

She checked on Braden and found him reading another Harry Potter book. "You need to get your bath, brush your teeth, and be ready for sleep at nine thirty. You can read until ten; then it's lights out."

"I used to get to watch videos on my tablet until midnight," he grumbled.

"That was before you got into trouble." She closed the door, got the journal from her bedroom, and went across the hall to Holly's room.

Her daughter was busy flipping through hangers on her clothes rack. "Would you like to have a closet?"

"Yes, I would, but it's all right if Mack can't build it until after spring break. Granny Hayes has a rack just like this. She said that she was born in that cabin, and she'll die in it, and that she likes being able to see all her clothes without having to open a door," Holly answered. "I'm trying to find something to match my new earrings for tomorrow. What do you think of this?" She held up a blue shirt.

Lily was taken aback at being asked for her opinion. "Looks great. Wear your denim jacket with it and you'll be beautiful."

"Nope." Holly held up her pink jacket. "I made the earrings with pink and blue feathers so it would look good with this combination. I just don't know if this shade of blue matches the earrings right."

So much for getting excited about her opinion, Lily thought. "It looks great. Lights out at nine thirty, but we've got time to work on your history project if you want to."

"Yes!" Holly pumped her fist in the air. "I got all my notes written up, and I'm ready for the next entry. I hope it's about Matilda, still. I like her, but I wish she'd leave her husband, like you did Daddy. I love him because he's my dad, but sometimes I don't like him so much now that I'm old enough to know what he did. Are all men like that, Mama?"

"No, honey, they aren't," Lily answered as she opened the journal. "There are good men out there in the world. When you get ready to date or get married, I hope you find a really good one."

"I will, Mama." Holly laid a hand on Lily's shoulder.

Lily sat still, hoping that maybe it would turn into a hug, but Holly removed it and picked up her notebook.

"And if he's a cheater like Rayford and Daddy, then I'll shoot him," Holly said in a matter-of-fact tone.

"That would just put you in prison," Lily told her.

"Nope, it wouldn't. Mack will help me bury the body where no one will ever find it. Now, read me the next entry, Mama," Holly said.

"This is new territory for me, too. I haven't read this part because I wanted to share it with you." Lily opened the journal and began to read to Holly, just like she did when her daughter was a little girl.

Matilda Smith Medford Massey, May 1875: What a difference five years makes in the life of a woman. I was so depressed after I lost my son that I vowed I'd never write in this journal again. I still remember the feel of his tiny body. Rayford left me for one of his women—who knows which one. To tell the truth, I was relieved to have him out of my life, but I have to admit that he did have the decency to leave the area and move to Maine. The kids and I moved in with Henry and his wife, poor Pansy, who died the next year. We decided to go back home to Vicksburg and see if we still had rights to our land. We did, and the house was still standing. As I stood there looking at the place, the yard in shambles, Mama's rosebushes hidden by weeds, tears ran down my face. We had a house, but the home we'd grown up in wasn't there. That might not make sense, but it's the way I felt. No matter, we were glad to find it still there and know that it belonged to us. There was no furniture left, so we slept on the floor for a week until we could get some ticking sewn into mattresses and stuffed with hay. Tears turned into joy with each tiny step forward we took. I'll never forget that first night that we went to sleep on something other than the hard floor. I thought I could never be happier than that moment, but I was so wrong. This journal and a trunk full of our clothing is all we brought to our old plantation with us. I almost left the journal behind because I didn't want to read any more about Mama's heartbreaks, but I just couldn't.

We could not farm the whole plantation, but Henry had enough money saved that we could hire a few hands, and we had a pretty decent, even if small, cotton crop. I was so proud when we brought it all in and had made a good profit. Henry had sworn he'd never come home to the South, but we both needed a change, and we got it. Henry remarried to a woman who's a little older than him. She grounds him and is an excellent manager, and I remarried a wonderful man with the farm next to ours. My third child was born in March, and I'm so happy. Money can't buy happiness. Only love can *do that. Jenny is now nine years old, Samuel is seven, and the new little girl, Lily, is healthy. God has given me a second chance. I'm so grateful.*

"Did Grandma name you Lily after that little girl?" Holly asked.

"I believe she did." Lily vaguely remembered her mother telling her that she was named for an old ancestor.

"It's kind of strange reading about our relatives like this, isn't it, Mama?" Holly asked. "But I'm glad we got to read that Matilda's awful husband finally left her. Why did she wait for him to leave, though? Why didn't she kick his sorry ass—I mean butt—out the door when she found out about him cheating on her? I'm so glad I didn't live in those days. I couldn't put up with that."

"Hypothetical question," Lily said. "What are you going to do if you're dating a boy and he's going behind your back, say with Rose or Ivy, and kissing them when you're not there?"

Holly snapped her fingers and did her head wiggle. "Goodbye, sucker. Don't come around me anymore, and then I'd tell whatever friend he was kissing that they weren't my friend either for doing that behind my back." Then she got serious. "Was Victoria your friend before"—Holly's brows drew down in a frown—"you know, before Daddy left?"

"No, she wasn't, and honey, I didn't know your dad was seeing her until he packed his things and left." Lily didn't ever want her daughter to think that she knew and put up with that kind of behavior. She wanted her to be strong and stand up for herself.

Chapter Eleven

*L*ily opened the shop on Monday morning, turned on the lights in all three rooms, and then shoved her purse and jacket under the counter. Being there alone for the first time was a little eerie, but Sally had called that morning and said that she was going to an estate sale in Boerne. She wouldn't be in until noon.

Lily started in the furniture room at the back of the store and made her way to the front, straightening things as she went. She'd just finished the job when the bell above the door jingled and Polly waved at her.

"I brought a thermos of hot coffee and doughnuts," Polly said.

Lily turned and headed toward the break room. "I'll get the cups and a roll of paper towels."

Polly set the thermos and a box with a dozen doughnuts on the counter. Then she took off her coat and scarf, tossed them on the counter, and sat down in a metal chair. "Sally keeps sweet tea and soft drinks in the back room, and she's got a little hot pot so you can make hot tea or instant coffee, but I can't stand that instant crap, so when I pop in, I bring my own."

"Here we go." Lily brought in two mugs, filled them with coffee, and then opened the lid on the box of doughnuts. She took out one with maple frosting and sat down beside Polly.

"Sally kind of caught us up on everything last night when I called her." Polly chose a doughnut with chocolate sprinkles.

"Where have you been?" Lily sipped at her coffee.

"Me and your mama always had this dream that someday we'd go on one of those over-fifty cruises," Polly said between bites. "We kept putting it off for years, and then your mama passed. But I got this last-minute deal in the mail a few weeks ago, and two of my cousins said they'd go with me. Seemed like an omen. We just packed our bags and drove down to Galveston, got on the ship, and went. Who knows how long any of us will be aboveground? I've decided to start spending my savings and do everything I can while I'm still able." Polly reached for her second doughnut. "It was amazing. Vera would have loved it."

"Why did you wait so long? Why didn't you and Mama do the cruise while she was alive?" Lily asked.

"Vera wouldn't leave your daddy, and he wouldn't go because he got sick if he even went out on a fishing boat. And then she was so depressed after he passed away that I was lucky to talk her into going out to dinner once a week. Then she passed, and losing my best friend put me in a depression. I thought that I couldn't go without her, so I kept putting it off." Then Polly leaned forward and whispered, "But I kind of took her with me in spirit. I've got an old black-and-white photograph of the two of us when we were little girls, so I took it along. Everywhere I went, whether it was to a musical production, to watch a movie, or just to have our meals, I took the picture with me and set it up so she'd be right there with me. My cousins thought it was weird, but I didn't give a damn."

It took two sips of coffee for Lily to swallow the lump in her throat. "She never mentioned a cruise to me."

Polly laid a hand on her knee. "Honey, that was our own dream—something we saved our dimes and nickels for. I'm surprised you haven't found her stash somewhere in the house. When we got fifty dollars in change saved up, we'd cash it in for a bill." Polly shared the last of the coffee between the mugs. "It took us years to get that first fifty dollars. I made each of us a little light-blue velvet bag to keep our fifties in. I have enough left in my bags to go on another cruise in the summer. This time I'm going to Alaska. Want to go along?"

"Thank you, but I won't have enough vacation time by then," Lily answered.

Polly opened her purse and brought out a small album. "I had two of these made. One for me, and one for you. I tried to get the picture with Vera in each one."

"Thank you." Lily managed to keep her tears at bay as she flipped through the pictures. She wished she'd known that her mother was saving change for such a thing—she'd have given her rolls of nickels and dimes for Christmas and Mother's Day. "This is amazing. I'll treasure it forever." Lily held the album to her chest.

"All right, enough sentimental crap," Polly sighed. "I'm about to start crying, so tell us about you and Mack and the kids to get me pepped up."

"Well," Lily said, "Braden is interested in the goats, and Granny Hayes invited Holly to have Sunday dinner with her and showed her how to make earrings."

"Holy shit!" Polly gasped. "No one other than Sally has even been close to that cabin. What did Holly do to get an invitation?"

"Other than the fact she was wearing a pair of the earrings that Granny Hayes makes, and maybe looks a little like my mama, I have no idea," Lily answered. "She and Holly were visiting about the earrings while Mack brought the truck around after church yesterday. It was storming, so we offered to take her home."

"Her old mule broke his tether and went home at the first clap of thunder, right?" Polly said.

"Yes, ma'am." Lily took a second doughnut from the box.

"Well, that just blows my mind away," Polly said. "Not that old Dusty took off for home, but that she asked Holly to eat with her. Was Holly bored?"

"Oh, no!" Lily shook her head. "She came home all fired up about the whole afternoon. She asked if she could have one of Granny Hayes's kittens, and she wore her hair in braids to school today."

"Sweet Jesus!" Polly whispered. "Has that old gal cast a spell on your daughter?"

"I don't think so," Lily giggled. "I'm just glad she's making friends with an older person. She can learn so much if she just listens to what Granny Hayes has to say."

Polly shook her head. "And I thought she and *Sally* had a strange friendship. It's time for me to go if I want to get home before it starts raining again. The weatherman says we're in for a frog strangler right after lunch."

"Thanks for stopping by and for bringing doughnuts," Lily said.

"This is my first usual stop Monday morning. Have to catch up on everything with Sally. Your mama and I used to have coffee out at her place every Monday morning. When she passed and Sally put in the store, I started coming here. It helped, and now that you're here"—Polly gave her a quick hug—"it's almost like Vera is back with me. If I don't see you before then, I'll be back next week." She put on her jacket and picked up the thermos. "If you need anything or even want to talk, just give me a call."

"I appreciate that, and thanks for everything." Lily stood up, gave Polly another hug, and walked her to the door.

She had a couple of browsers in the middle of the morning, and then a very serious buyer right after that. She felt better after she'd rung up a $500 sale for a few pieces of antique crystal. At noon, she was about to have another doughnut when Teena breezed into the shop.

"You might not recognize me because I haven't been much of a friend since you came home," she teased as she took off a long black leather coat, "but I'm Teena."

"I guess I haven't been such a good friend, either, because I haven't called you. Everything has been crazy what with getting the kids settled in and school, and the fancy new job." Lily giggled and took Teena's coat, hung it on a rack just inside the door, and motioned toward the doughnuts. "We've got instant coffee if you want some."

"No thanks on the coffee. I like sweet tea better. I just talked to Sally. She said to tell you she's bringing pizza for dinner today." Teena crossed the floor in a few long strides—Lily had always envied Teena's long legs—and hopped up on the counter. "It's been hectic at home and at the real estate business. I haven't even been to church in two weeks because I had property to show on Sunday morning, so let's catch up. What's this I hear about you and Mack dating?"

"We've got to start getting together at least once a month like we did when I was in Austin." Lily sidestepped the question about Mack.

Teena shook her head. "We don't have to do that. I'm in and out of this place a couple of times a week. Sometimes I bring lunch with me; sometimes Sally has it delivered. We'll be seeing each other more now that you're here every day and my crazy world has settled down. Kudos on the new job. Sally's needed help for quite a while now."

The bell above the door jingled, and both women looked that way. Lily even inhaled deeply to see if she could catch a whiff of pizza, but it wasn't Sally.

"Lily Anderson?" the young lady asked.

"That would be me." Lily stepped forward.

"This is for you." The woman put a bud vase with a yellow rose, a pink rose, and a white daisy arranged with greenery and a pink bow in her hands. "Y'all have a great day now."

Lily set the vase on the counter, removed the card, and read out loud, "Congratulations on completing your first week at the new job—Holly, Braden, and Mack."

She hadn't received flowers in years, not even on her last anniversary with Wyatt. He'd gotten her a box of candy, but he'd had to work late that night—supposedly. She had found out a few weeks later that he'd taken Victoria to a fancy restaurant in San Antonio and then to a five-star hotel for a round of sex before he came home to her and the kids.

"Flowers?" Teena raised an eyebrow.

Lily handed the card to her. "Pretty sweet of them, isn't it?"

"Yes, it is, but then Mack is a sweet guy," Teena answered. "You should give him a chance. I hear that y'all have been sitting beside each other in church the past couple of Sundays and that Braden adores him. You know that sitting together in church and sharing a hymnal causes folks to wonder what's going on behind closed doors."

"Who sent me flowers?" Sally pushed her way into the store with a huge pizza box in her hands. "I got the deal that has pizza, breadsticks, and cinnamon sticks all in one big package." She set it down on the counter beside Teena. "I'll get the sodas from the fridge, and we can dive right in." She headed to the back room.

"The flowers are from Mack and the kids, and they're for Lily," Teena yelled toward the back of the store.

"I already knew that," Sally hollered back. "Polly heard about it from Dorothy down at the flower shop. I saw her at the pizza place."

"I'd forgotten that Dorothy is Polly's daughter," Lily said.

Sally set three bottles of soda on the counter. "Coming home is like riding a bicycle. Even if you haven't ridden in five years, it don't take you long to remember all the parts."

"Amen to that," Lily said.

~

Lily had talked more and used more words that day than she'd used in years, maybe even a decade. The afternoon was so busy that she seldom had time to sit down after lunch. Folks dropped into the shop to buy or just to look around, but they all wanted to talk. She was glad to get home to a few minutes of blessed silence that afternoon. She plopped down on the sofa, kicked off her shoes, and leaned her head back. She must've fallen asleep, because she didn't even hear the school bus when it let the kids off. The front door opened, and she sat up so fast that the whole room took a couple of spins. She tried to get her bearings, but Holly and Braden had stormed into the room before she was fully awake.

"Did you like the flowers? I picked out the daisy because you're always doodling them," Braden said.

"They're on the kitchen table if you want to see them," Lily said.

"I wanted the pink rose since pink is my favorite color," Holly said.

"It was so sweet of y'all to think of me." Lily followed them to the kitchen, leaned forward, and smelled the bouquet. "They're beautiful."

Braden threw his arms around his mother and said, "It was Mack's idea, but we each got to pick out one of the flowers."

"Well, you all did really good, and that makes them even more special." Lily hugged him back and wished that Holly would make it a three-way hug.

"So how did things go today?" Holly asked as she sat down beside Lily. "Did you sell any of Granny Hayes's earrings?"

"Not today." Lily took a chance and draped her arm around Holly's shoulders. "But I did sell two scarves and a shawl."

Holly clapped her hands and jumped up. "I can't wait for her to teach me how to crochet."

"How did your day go? Did Rose and Ivy like your braids?" Lily wanted her to sit back down, but she didn't.

"No, they thought they were ugly and made me look like a little girl. But Faith loved them. I even braided her hair during lunch period. We're going to wear them again tomorrow, and she's got a pair of earrings like mine, so she's going to wear them, too. What's for after-school snack today?" Holly asked.

"The cookie jar and the fruit bowl are both full," Lily answered. "Who's Faith?"

"She's my new friend. Faith Torres—Isaac's big sister. And she's real smart, like Isaac. She's doing her history paper on her mama's great-great-grandmother who came over here from Ireland," Holly answered.

"So she's Irish?" Lily asked.

"I guess a little bit, but she's mainly Mexican like Rose and Ivy. There's lots of Hispanic kids in the school, just like in Austin. Faith is real sweet, and I like her a lot," Holly answered. "I think I'll have a banana and some milk. Can I take it to my room and do some of my homework while I eat? I sure can't do it with Braden around. He wants to argue about everything."

One baby step forward, Lily thought. At least she asked before she went running off to her room, and she had talked to her about her new friend.

"Sure." Lily nodded. "Is she your age?" Lily wanted her to stick around and talk some more.

"She's a junior—she's already got her driver's license," Holly replied, and was gone before Lily could ask anything else.

She heard the back door open and could hear Braden saying something about the flowers. Then he raced up the stairs. She started to get up and head that way when Mack came into the living room and sank down in the recliner in front of her. "It's sure enough been a Monday. How did your day go?"

"It went fast, and I got a lovely bouquet. Thank you," Lily answered. "They're beautiful. It's been years since I had flowers. How did you know that yellow roses are my favorite?"

"I didn't, and this is going to sound corny"—he almost blushed—"but the yellow reminded me of all the sunshine you've brought into my life these past days."

Lily felt her own blush rising, but she couldn't do anything to stop it. "That's so sweet."

Mack shrugged. "It's the truth, and you should have flowers often."

"Thank you for saying that. Now tell me about your day." Lily steered the conversation down another path.

"I broke up a fight between two girls," Mack said. "Girls are meaner than boys, and they fight dirty. Then I had to take a student to the office for smoking pot behind the ag building. He's got four weeks of in-school suspension, ISS. To top it all off, I caught another kid in my classroom with one of those vapor cigarette devices. That got him a week in ISS."

"I guess kids are the same no matter where you live," Lily groaned. "I was hoping that those things wouldn't even be here in Comfort."

"Honey, that sort of thing is everywhere, but we have fewer students, so we can control it a little better than they can in the big schools," he said. "I'm getting an afternoon snack—an apple and a glass of sweet tea. Can I bring you something?"

"Just tea. I've been nibbling all day," she answered.

"Prop your feet up and rest a few minutes," Mack told her.

Lily swung her feet around so that she was stretched out with her back against the arm of the sofa. When Mack returned, he brought a tray with two glasses of tea and a plate with an apple and four cookies on it. He sat back down on the recliner and picked up the apple first.

"What do you know about Faith Torres?" Lily asked.

"She's a straight-A student, but like her brother, she's not popular. She's tall, has dark hair, and wears glasses. She drives a flatbed pickup truck and brings her brother to school every day. She may be the brightest kid to ever come through Comfort High and will probably be the valedictorian of her senior class," he said. "Why are you asking?"

"Rose and Ivy thought Holly's braids were ugly today and made her look like a little girl. It must've offended Holly. She told me that Faith is her new friend."

"Kids go from one group to another all the time." Mack took a drink of his tea. "Faith is a really good kid. I guess she's what you and I would have called a nerd in our day."

"Nerd is better than pot smoker." Lily reached for her tea at the same time Mack was setting his glass back down. Their hands touched again. Her breath caught in her chest, and her pulse jacked up several notches.

"I'm going to ask you a dumb question," he drawled. "Do you feel chemistry between us?"

Her chest tightened. Of course she felt something between them, but she damn sure didn't want to talk about it like they were discussing the price of goat feed. And yet . . . they were adults, not hormonal teenagers who jumped into the fire with both feet when they felt something for another person. How many times had she told her clients in therapy sessions to talk things out?

"Why is that dumb?" she asked.

"It kind of sounded dumb in my head, and even more so when I said it," he said.

"Yes, I do feel something between us." She nodded. "I've wondered if it's because I haven't dated all that much. How about you?"

"No dates in three years. Nothing serious since Natalie," he admitted.

"Do you think it's because we hav-haven't," she stammered.

"No, I think there's definitely an attraction between us, and I'll tell you right now, up front, you deserve better than me," he said.

Lily frowned so hard that her eyes became mere slits. "Why would you say a stupid thing like that?"

"I'm a high school vo-ag teacher, and I'll never be rich. Hell, I'm forty-one, and I don't even own a house. I've just got a pickup that's paid for and a herd of goats," he said.

"Why, Mack Cooper, are you thinkin' marriage?" she joked. "You haven't even kissed me yet."

"I'm just thinking that we shouldn't start anything without being completely honest, and, honey, I can remedy that kissing part anytime." His green eyes twinkled.

Lily felt heat rising to her cheeks when she thought of kissing him. How in the devil would it even work if they did decide to go out, or got into a relationship beyond friendship? They lived in the same house with Holly and Braden underfoot all the time. "I've got two kids," she blurted out.

"I've got forty goats." He grinned.

"Did you say it's time to go feed the goats?" Braden came across the room and leaned his arms on the back of the sofa.

Point proven, she thought.

"Yep, it is," Mack answered. "I reckon we both need to get changed so we don't ruin our good clothes."

"I'll be down in five minutes." Braden ran up the stairs.

Mack crossed the room and bent to brush a sweet kiss across her lips. The tenderness of his mouth barely touching hers and his drawl combined to send a heat flash through her whole body. If that brief contact created such an effect, a relationship might burn down the house.

～

Lily feared that supper would be awkward, but it wasn't at all. The kids bantered as they ate their chicken and dumplings and fought over who got the last piece of chocolate cake. When they'd finished with the cleanup, Mack got out a whole stack of papers to grade, and the kids disappeared to their rooms.

She thought about sticking around or watching an old movie, but she was afraid that Mack might think she was angling for another kiss, so she went upstairs to her room and took the journal over to Holly's room. She rapped on the doorframe and asked, "You ready for the next chapter?"

"You mean entry?" Holly asked.

"Either one." Lily held the book up so she could see it.

"Yep, but, Mama"—Holly put away the book she'd been reading and got out her notebooks—"I wish it was more like a diary where they wrote in it every day. I like the way my paper is coming together. I even let my history teacher look at what I'd done, and he said it was excellent work."

Matilda Smith Medford Massey, June 1886: Jenny was married today. I'm sure that it won't be remembered like the event when the president of the United States married his lady in the White House earlier this month. But to me, it was much bigger since I was right there in our little church with her. I've always regretted not having my mother at my wedding, especially the second one, since it was on our plantation. We'll miss Jenny, but she's only five miles away, so we can see her every month or so. I'm hoping that her husband is as good to her as William is to me, and that she never has to deal with a cheating man like her father. If she does, I plan to shoot him and drag his body out into the woods to feed him to the coyotes. My mama would have done that for me if she'd known what I was living through in those days.

"Yes!" Holly did a fist pump. "I just knew Matilda had some balls . . . I mean, guts. Will Jenny be the one that gets women the right to vote?"

"I don't know," Lily said. "We'll have to keep reading to find out."

"I wonder what her wedding looked like." Holly's eyes went all dreamy. "I want a big white dress with a train that reaches all the way to the back of the church, and a cake that's got calla lilies on the top of it. What did your wedding dress look like, Mama? Do you still have a picture of you in it?"

Lily almost wished that she hadn't thrown the last remaining picture of her in the dress away. "I got married in my mother's dress. Her wedding picture is on the mantel in the living room, so take a look at that."

"But Grandma was tall and you're short," Holly said.

"Mama shortened it, removed the sleeves, and cut away that high collar, so use your imagination when you look at it," Lily said.

She closed the journal. "I'm glad that Matilda was happy and that Jenny is living close to her mama."

"Me, too." Holly didn't look up from her notes.

"Good night." Lily started to kiss her on the forehead but thought that might be pushing it.

She wandered halfway down the staircase to where Vera's senior picture from high school still hung. For the first time, she realized the wisdom God had in taking Vera on to heaven to be with her sweet husband when He did. Her mother had been an easygoing woman, but when she was riled, no one, not even the devil himself, would cross her. Had Vera Miller known what Wyatt was doing, the torment that he put Lily through when she was grieving for her mother—well, Vera was a damn good shot with a pistol, and she had taught Lily to shoot when she was just a little girl. Had she been preparing Lily for the future? Had she disappointed her mother when she didn't shoot Wyatt?

Chapter Twelve

$\mathcal{L}$ ily could hardly believe that it was only three days until the first of February that Tuesday afternoon when she looked at the calendar. She was still staring at it, wondering where the time had gone, and thinking about how much happier she was in Comfort, when Holly stomped into the house. She didn't hang up her coat or drop her backpack on the chair, but stormed right up to her room. Braden hit the kitchen in a run, went right to the refrigerator, and got out a root beer.

"Holly's being a pain in my"—he hesitated—"in my neck. She's mad at someone, and she won't talk. She sat in the back seat of the bus and ignored Rose and Ivy."

"You don't have any idea what she's angry about?" Lily handed him a banana.

He laid it on the table and opened the cookie jar. "Kids were whispering on the bus about how she and Rose and Ivy were yelling at each other at lunch hour. Something about a *quincy*. What is that, Mama?"

"Where is everyone?" Mack called out from the foyer.

"In the kitchen," Braden yelled.

Lily rushed into the foyer and met Mack coming her way. "What is a *quincy*, and why would Rose and Ivy argue with Holly over it?"

"I heard the twins and their friends talking about celebrating their fifteenth birthday in a couple of weeks with a quinceañera. That's kind of like a debutante party. In the old days, it meant they were old enough for marriage, but these days, it's changed to a time when they can date. The girls get all dressed up, and there's something to do with a waltz," Mack explained. "Didn't they invite Holly to it?"

"I have no idea," Lily replied. "I know what those events are but didn't associate it with the word *quincy*. Holly's never been to one."

"Mama!" Holly's tone left no doubt that she'd been crying.

"I'll be right there," Lily yelled up the staircase. "Thank you," she mouthed to Mack.

The door to Holly's room was open. Holly was sitting cross-legged in the middle of her bed. Her arms were wrapped around a teddy bear almost as big as she was, and she was sobbing into his shoulder. Lily's first instinct was to rush in and gather her weeping child into her arms. Instead, she gave Holly her space and asked, "Need someone to talk to?"

"Oh, Mama!" Holly tossed the stuffed animal aside and opened her arms.

Lily didn't waste any time getting across the room, sitting down on the bed, and taking Holly in her arms. "What can I do to help?" She patted her daughter's back.

"I can't be friends with Rose and Ivy anymore." Holly continued to sob into her mother's shoulder.

"Why?" Lily asked.

"Be . . ." Holly hiccuped. "Cause . . ." Another hiccup. "They'll kill me."

Fourteen-year-old drama was a bitch on steroids. Holly's pain was very real to her, even if someday she would look back and realize that what seemed so important now wasn't even a speed bump in her life.

"Oh, honey, they won't really kill you." Lily handed her a box of tissues from the little table beside her bed. "They may not ever like you, but that's about it."

Holly pushed back from Lily, pulled three tissues out, and blew her nose. "They might as well kill me. They said they'd tell stuff at school, and everyone will think I'm a slut. But if I did what they wanted me to, I'd really be one."

Lily felt as if cold water had just been poured down her back. Finally, she asked, "And what do they want you to do?"

"Sneak out of choir practice and get laid tomorrow night so I won't be a virgin, and we can talk about sex since we'll all three know what it's about," Holly whispered, and then her voice got stronger. "But I told them no, and they said if I didn't, they wouldn't invite me to their quinceañera party, and they'd tell the other girls that I had to move here because I was a junkie slut. I asked Faith if she was going to the party, and she said that she wouldn't be invited because everyone thinks she's a nerd. She said that when she turned fifteen, she told her parents she didn't want a party because she wasn't ready to date. So since she didn't have one that they could come to, then they wouldn't invite her even if she was popular. Please don't tell Rose and Ivy's mama. That would just make things worse," Holly begged.

"From what I understand, they aren't supposed to be dating until they're fifteen," Lily said. "Do you think they're just pulling your leg?"

Holly shook her head. "They don't ever go to choir practice. They sneak out and go to the river with their boyfriends, who work on a ranch in Sitterdale."

"You mean Sisterdale?" Lily asked.

"Maybe." Holly nodded. "They were so mad at me that they started talking to each other in Spanish, and I couldn't understand it. They aren't druggies, Mama. They like vodka instead. They said their mama can't smell that on their breath when they get home."

"Who else goes with them?" Lily asked. "Someone has to drive them or come get them."

"A bunch of kids from the school go there on Wednesday and Friday nights. Someone picks Rose and Ivy up around the corner from the church and brings them back two hours later. I'm not ready to have sex, Mama," Holly sobbed. "And I didn't even know about the parties until this week. I promise I haven't been to one."

"I'm glad you've made that decision." Lily hugged her again. "Maybe Faith and you have more in common than you and the twins."

Holly nodded. "Does that make me a freak?"

"No, it makes you smart," Lily reassured her. "It tells me that you're growing up and won't let your friends decide what you should and shouldn't do. I'm proud of you for telling them no."

"For real? You're not still mad at me for the joint?" Holly asked.

"Yes, I'm proud of you, but I'm still a little mad at you, too. I wish you'd had the nerve to stand up to whoever gave you that marijuana like you did with Rose and Ivy," Lily told her.

"I'm not going to choir practice anymore," she said. "I'm going to stay home and talk to Faith on the phone. She don't go to choir practice because she says she can't carry a tune in a milk bucket."

"That's your choice," Lily said. "Are you ready to come downstairs and have a snack?"

"Are Braden and Mack out of the house?" Holly asked. "My face is a mess, and I don't want my brother smarting off about it."

"Hey, Mama," Braden yelled from the bottom of the stairs, "is it all right if I go to the store with Mack? We need to get a load of goat feed."

"Of course, and tell Mack to pick up a gallon of milk on the way home," Lily answered and turned back to face Holly. "Give them a minute, and then we'll go on down."

"You won't tell Rose and Ivy's mother, promise?" Holly's eyes widened.

"You've got my word, and thanks for telling me what happened," Lily said.

"Rose called Faith a smart-ass bitch." Holly slid off the bed. "I had my fists doubled up to hit her when Faith pulled me away. She told me that getting ISS or getting expelled wasn't worth it, and besides, it would be like getting into the gutter with them. But, Mama, the teachers all think they're good girls."

"The truth has a way of surfacing," Lily assured her. "Let's go make a banana pudding for tonight's dessert."

"Banana pudding is only for special days," Holly said. "Like Easter and Fourth of July."

"Today is a special day." Lily draped her arm around Holly's shoulders.

"I'm not going to argue. Banana pudding is my favorite." Holly took a step back and followed her down to the kitchen.

Lily's feet felt like they were floating on air rather than going down the stairs. It was wonderful—no, it went beyond that into fantastic—for Holly to ask her opinion about things these days.

~

After supper, Mack turned on the television and found a channel showing reruns of *NCIS*. He twisted the top off a bottle of beer and tipped it up for a long gulp. When he came up for air, Lily had slipped into the living room and was sitting on the other end of the sofa.

"Well, hello," he said. "Did you figure out what was upsetting Holly?"

She nodded and proceeded to tell him the whole story. "But we can't tell anyone, or else it'll all come back on Holly and make things worse."

"Wouldn't dream of it," Mack chuckled.

"What's so funny?" Lily's tone was downright chilly.

"The cops used to make a run to the river about once a month on a Saturday night. They'd round up the underage drinkers, and their parents would have to come get them at the jail. I'm friends with one of the deputies, and he was bragging last week that their busts had cleaned up the situation," Mack explained.

The smile on Lily's face started small, but soon she giggled. "The kids just changed it to Wednesday and Friday nights and used choir practice for an excuse to get out of the house. Wonder what they do on Saturday night?"

"Stay home. Get sober. Go to church on Sunday to make their parents think they have wings and a halo." Mack offered her his beer.

To his surprise, she took it from his hands, took a drink, and handed it back. "Thanks. I rarely have a beer, but I do enjoy one now and then."

"What's your favorite drink? Piña colada? Daiquiri?"

"I'm not a mixed-drink or wine person. I like a beer sometimes, or a shot of whiskey on special occasions, but that's only once or twice a year, if that often," she told him.

"There's a bottle of Knob Creek smoked maple in the cabinet. It was there when I moved in, and I've had a shot on the past five New Year's Eves," he admitted.

"That was Mama's favorite. Daddy would hold up his beer bottle on New Year's Eve, and Mama would touch her shot glass to it," Lily told him. "When I got married, Mama and I had a shot just before I walked down the aisle. It might be the same bottle since she only had a drink once a year."

"Well, then, I'd say it's very well aged." Mack took a drink from the bottle and offered her another one. He loved spending time with her and listening to her husky voice confide in him. He felt as if he was really part of a family.

She shook her head. "Fourteen is way too young to be drinking or having sex."

"We have a sophomore who had a baby last year when she was just a freshman, and there are also two seniors who will be mothers before they graduate. It can't be blamed on race, color, creed, or social standing. They come from all walks of life," Mack said. "You're a good mother. Holly talked to you rather than listening to her friends."

"Most days I feel like the meanest mama in the whole state." She pulled a quilt down from the back of the sofa, stretched her legs out, and wrapped the quilt around her body.

"You shouldn't." Mack tucked the quilt around her feet. "You've been tough on them for a reason, and it's plain as the horns on a billy goat that it's paying off."

"I appreciate you saying that," she said, and pointed toward the television. "I haven't seen this episode. Ziva is still on the show. I missed her when she left."

"If you leave this summer, I'll miss you, Lily." His drawl seemed even deeper than usual.

She looked up into his eyes. "I promised the kids that if they stayed out of trouble, we'd go back to Austin."

"I understand that, but what if they decided they wanted to stay here?" he asked.

"Then I'd sure be willing to give up the Austin apartment," she replied.

~

Lily woke to the sound of the *NCIS* theme song playing at the end of the episode. She could hardly believe that it was ten o'clock, or that her feet were now in Mack's lap. She started to pull them away, but he threw back the quilt and began to give her a foot massage. She all but purred when his big calloused hands gently worked on her toes and then worked their way up to her ankles. He finished her left foot, covered it back up, and started on the right one.

"Why are you teaching school? You could make a million dollars a year doing this," she moaned.

"I'd rather be teaching wild kids than putting up with most women." His green eyes locked with her brown ones. "You are special, Lily."

"I sure feel like it right now," she said. "I could lie here all night if you'd keep that up, but we've got to get up in the morning. But five more minutes, please."

"For five more minutes. Then I get to walk you to the end of the staircase and have a good-night kiss," he said.

Lily thought that she might just drag him up the stairs, throw him down on her bed, and make wild, passionate love with him until morning if he'd massage her feet for ten more minutes, but she didn't say that. She simply nodded, and wondered if the second kiss would affect her as much as the first one had.

When the five minutes had passed, she stood up, folded the quilt, and laid it on the back of the sofa. Mack tucked her hand in his and led her to the bottom of the stairs. She expected a quick kiss, but he looked deeply into her eyes, ran the palm of his hand down her cheek, and traced her lips with his fingertips.

"You are so beautiful," he murmured.

She moistened her lips with the tip of her tongue just as his mouth closed over hers. It started out as a sweet kiss, but then his tongue touched her lower lip, asking permission to enter. She opened up to him and the kiss deepened into more. Her knees went weak so she wrapped her arms around his neck. When the kiss ended, she leaned into him and laid her cheek on his chest. His heart was beating as wildly as her own—the two of them keeping time together.

"Wow!" he muttered. "How about another foot rub?"

She tiptoed and kissed him on the cheek. "That might lead to more than kisses."

"I'm willing if you are."

"Don't tempt me," she said. "Good night, Mack." She took a step back and started up the stairs.

"Good night, Lily." His deep drawl followed her up to her room. She closed the door behind her and fell backward onto the bed. The springs squeaked and the slats creaked, but she didn't care. All her hormones screamed for more than just a long, passionate kiss. Every nerve tingled, and it would take more than sucking on a lemon to wipe the smile off her face.

Lily picked up the journal and went over to Holly's room. She rapped on the door, and Holly yelled, "Come on in."

"Want to see what happens next?"

"Sure," Holly said. "It'll take my mind off Rose and Ivy."

Lily opened the journal and began to read.

Jenny Medford O'Riley, May 1889:

"No!" Holly put up a palm. "Matilda can't be dead. What happened to her son and to her new daughter, Lily?"

"I don't know, but let's keep reading," Lily said.

Mama gave me this journal when I left Georgia. She said it was possible that she'd never see me again and that I should write in it sometimes, like she and her mother had done in the past, so it could be passed down through the ages, and our future daughters would know us better. I've read about the grandmother I never met, and Mama's struggles. So now it's my turn to write about my life. My daughter, Rachel, is two years old. I'm twenty-three, as is my husband, Danny O'Riley. We left our home and came west when we heard about the government giving away land here in Indian Territory. We were able to stake out our hundred and sixty acres last month. We're living in a tent right now, but by winter, we will have enough logs cut to build us a fine cabin. At that time we will have shown improvement on the land, and it will be ours. The work is hard and we've struggled sometimes to have food on the table, but our love will carry us through these next years. When we're old and gray, we'll tell our grandchildren the stories of how we survived our first winter in Oklahoma. Although it's late for a garden, I've put one in. We have a stream not far from our tent. The water there is good for the garden, but not fit to drink, and it's backbreaking work to carry full buckets to my garden, but I'm determined that we'll have harvest food for the winter from it. There are days when I'm lonely for female companionship, and I miss my mama so much, but no one said life is easy, and at the end of the day, Danny and I have each other.

"Wow!" Holly said. "I can't imagine life with no water in the house."

"Like she said, it was hard. Imagine living where you only got to see other girls maybe once every few weeks when you could go to church," Lily said.

"That would be worse than having to live by a man's rules." Holly yawned. "I don't even want to imagine having to live like that."

"It's past your bedtime." Lily picked up the journal and headed to her room.

"'Night, Mama," Holly whispered.

"Good night to you, darlin' girl." Lily felt like dancing across the hall to her bedroom. That was the first time Holly had told her good night without prompting in months.

As she got ready for bed that night, Lily kept going over the last words she'd read at the end of the day. Jenny and Danny had each other. Lily had her kids, and tonight she'd had an amazing kiss from Mack, but she wanted more than that. She wanted a relationship so that at the end of the day, she could go to sleep cuddled up next to her husband.

When she woke up in the morning, she wanted to have more than just pillows in bed with her. *Why now?* she asked herself. She'd been content with her lot for five years, and now she wanted someone in her life.

Your life has taken a turn for the better. Her mother's voice in her head was so clear that she almost dropped the journal.

"I hope so, Mama," she whispered as she put the journal back into its place in the secretary. When she tried to close the flap, it wouldn't lock in place. She lowered it again, removed the journal, and felt all the way to the back side of the shelf. Her hand closed around something soft and furry, and she jerked her hand back like she'd been shocked. If that was a dead mouse in there, she was marching down the stairs to get Mack. There were two things she hated in the world—and dead or alive, a mouse was both of them.

Lily laid the journal on the bed and got a small flashlight from the drawer of her nightstand. Her hands shook as she adjusted the beam toward what she figured was a shriveled-up rodent. She thought of what Polly had said about saving nickels and dimes and turning them into bills when she saw the light-blue velvet bag.

She was surprised to see how solidly the bag was stuffed, and that it was heavy. When she undid the drawstring and wiggled the roll of bills out, she couldn't believe that it was as big as her fist. A note was wrapped around the roll. Lily slipped the rubber band off, and the fifty-dollar bills spread out in her hands. She unfolded the note to read:

My dear Lily,

If you find this and are reading this, then I'm with your father in eternity. Polly will explain about the money. Take it and go on the vacation I never got to go on. Your dad hated the idea of being out in the water so far that he couldn't see land. Going to Germany on a boat when he was in the army made him never want to do it again. Now that he's gone, the desire to travel has left me. I just want to stay right here in this house where all his memories are. I hope someday Wyatt learns to appreciate you and the kids. If not, then shoot the sorry bastard. I never have liked him.

Love,
Mama

With tears rolling down her cheeks, Lily counted the money. Seven thousand dollars—enough to take her and the kids on a cruise—and Mack, if he wanted to go. But the note meant more to her than all the money in Texas.

Chapter Thirteen

*L*ily tried to sort through all the emotions of the day before as she drove to work, but it was totally impossible. She was glad to see Sally's little red sports car parked right in front of the store when she drove up. Maybe her friend could help her figure out everything that was going on in her life. Then she noticed Teena's business SUV parked right behind Sally's car and almost squealed. She could talk to both of her friends at once.

"Yesterday was a roller coaster of nerves," she told them as she took her coat off. "I'm so glad y'all are both here already. I feel like if I don't talk to someone I'm going to explode."

"Me, too," Teena said from behind the counter, where she was pacing from one end of the space to the other and back again.

Sally came from the back with a quart of ice cream. She set it down with such force that the three spoons she'd stuck in it rattled together. "Must be the phase of the moon." She dug into the mint chocolate chip ice cream. "I guess we all had a helluva night. Who's going first?"

Teena held up a hand. "I will. Ryder's girlfriend is pregnant. He says he's dropping out of college and marrying her, and he wants me to give him a job in the real estate business."

Lily stashed her coat and purse under the counter and plopped down in a chair. "He and Creed are only eighteen, right? He can't be ready for marriage. Who is this girlfriend?"

"The twins were nineteen in November." Teena handed a spoon to Lily, and then she dipped into the ice cream. "His girlfriend graduated a year before him. She works at a nursing home and is going to school nights to finish her LPN degree. She'll be finished in May. The baby is due in July. I'm going to be a freakin' grandmother. I'm too young for that."

"Evidently not," Sally said. "When's the wedding?"

"They're going to the courthouse this weekend, and he's moving into her apartment with her. He says if he can work at the business with me, he'll start at the bottom and take night classes to get his license." Teena moaned. "I wanted my kids to do better than that, but what can I do?"

"You can be a good grandmother and support them, even though it'll mean growing a new tongue every other day," Sally suggested. "And be a good mother-in-law, too. Being a mean one won't help the situation at all. *I'm* living proof of that."

Lily used her spoon to point at Sally. "You've never been a grandmother or a mother-in-law."

"But I've had a mother-in-law that kept throwing little digs until she convinced her son I wasn't good enough for him," Sally reminded her.

Lily's good news didn't seem as important as it had when she got to the shop, not when Teena was dealing with so much. She thought of those little soon-to-be-fifteen-year-old twin girls having sex and hoped they were using protection. How old were the boys they were out partying with? Did they have enough sense to at least bring condoms?

"Well, my news isn't that big," Sally sighed. "I went on a date last night with this guy I met on a dating site, and it was a disaster. His picture and profile said he was forty years old and a banker."

"And?" Teena stopped pacing and sat down in a chair.

"He might have been forty at one time, and he was a retired banker, but he has kids as old as me and several grandchildren." Sally groaned. "I barely made it through thirty minutes of drinks before I fled. That's what I get for trusting a dating site."

Lily giggled first, then Teena got tickled, and soon they were all laughing. When things settled down, Lily dabbed at her eyes with a tissue she pulled from a box on the counter. "I tried one of those dating sites once, too. I went to the restaurant where we were to have dinner, saw the rose on the table—that was to be my sign—and walked right past him to the exit."

"Why?" Sally asked.

Lily shrugged. "He looked too much like Wyatt. I went straight home, paid the sitter, and made popcorn for the kids. We watched a movie. Never tried it again."

"So we both had crappy nights." Teena focused on Lily. "What happened that you needed to talk?"

"Holly talked to me." Lily told them and went on with the story.

"I remember all of us being fourteen and not talking to our mothers," Sally sighed. "It must be horrible to be the mother and going through that."

"I have boys," Teena said. "They're inclined to either tell too much or not enough. It's totally different than raising girls, or so I'm told. I'm glad she's confiding in you, and really glad that my new daughter-in-law is at least nineteen years old and not fourteen. Messin' around with a girl that age could land my boys in jail."

Lily nodded. "And Mack kissed me."

Teena grinned and Sally nodded.

"That's all I get?" Lily asked. "Just a grin and a nod?"

"Come on. We've been expecting it," Teena told her. "We just knew if you ever came home even for a weekend visit that the two of you would hit it off."

"It was just a kiss, and that doesn't mean wedding bells," Lily told them.

Sally opened her mouth to say something but didn't get the first word out before the jingling bell above the door announced a customer.

"Good morning, Ruth-Ann!" Sally called out. "What brings you out in the middle of the week?"

Ruth-Ann came straight to the counter. "I had to run some school errands for Mr. Stewart and thought I'd stop in to buy more of Granny Hayes's cute little earrings. They're the big thing at school right now." She adjusted the mirror beside the display so she could see herself, and held one up to her ear.

She held up another earring. "I like these better. I heard that Holly had a falling-out with the Sanchez twins, and that Holly is now best friends with Faith Torres." Ruth-Ann laid two pairs of earrings on the counter and fumbled in her purse for her credit card. "I would never have put those two together. I guess opposites really do attract."

"I guess they do." Lily exhaled slowly.

"Is Holly devastated that she won't get to go to the quinceañera party?" Ruth-Ann asked.

"Not in the least." Lily rang up the sale and ran the credit card. "And I'm really glad, since I don't have to buy a fancy dress for her to wear."

"I went to one for Janie Green when I was fifteen," Ruth-Ann sighed. "It was even better than our high school proms or the school Christmas party we throw for the teachers every year."

Teena headed for the door. "I'm showing a house at nine, so I have to be going. See y'all later."

The minute Teena was out the door, Ruth-Ann leaned across the counter and whispered, "I also heard that Ryder Smith is getting married real soon because his girlfriend is pregnant. Do y'all know the date?"

Lily shrugged as she handed Ruth-Ann the sales slip to sign. "Thank you. I know Granny Hayes will be tickled that her earrings are selling so well."

"They're really cute." Ruth-Ann headed toward the door, then turned back. "We really must do lunch or go shopping sometime, Lily."

Lily nodded but didn't commit to anything. She eased down into the chair that Teena had vacated, and sighed. "I told Mack about the kids in confidence."

Sally patted her on the shoulder. "Don't worry. Mack does not spread gossip. Ruth-Ann probably heard about the parties from a student in the hallway. Kids tend to think that teachers can't hear their whispers." She picked up her coat. "I'm going to an estate sale in Fredericksburg this morning. The advertisement said that it would open at ten and that there would be lots of crystal glassware. This younger generation doesn't know what they're passing up when their grannies offer to give them their priceless collections of pretty dishes."

She hadn't been gone but a few minutes when Lily's second customer of the day arrived. By noon, she'd had a total of five. Two of them were small-time buyers and spent less than twenty dollars each. The other three made up for it. They came in together and said they had a shop in San Antonio that sold only items made in Texas. Lily showed them Granny Hayes's shawls, scarves, and earrings, and they bought the entire stock for resale in their business.

When they'd left, Mack arrived with a brown bag in his hands. "I brought food," he said. "Burgers and fries and root beer. Hope you haven't eaten already." He pulled two cans from the pockets of his denim coat.

"No, but I'm hungry." She opened the bag as soon as he set it down. "Ruth-Ann came by this morning."

"I already heard." He got out the burgers and fries and set them on the counter. "That's one of the reasons I'm here. Did she say anything about those river parties?"

"Nope." Lily unwrapped a burger and took a bite.

"That's good. The kids are all whispering about it in the hallways. I was afraid that you'd think I'd betrayed your confidence, and I'd never do that." He unwrapped his burger. "I also wanted to see you."

"Thank you for that. Why didn't you bring enough food for Sally?"

"Because she's over in Sisterdale at a sale and won't be back until after lunch," he replied.

"Fredericksburg," Lily corrected him.

"She went there first, but now she's in Sisterdale. There's an antique dresser over there that she's interested in buying. She sent a picture of it to the English teacher who is all excited about it and was showing off the picture of it in the teacher's lounge. Sally is buying it for her," Mack explained. "And Rose and Ivy have bragged too many times to too many people about those parties on Friday nights, but the older kids are moving the party out to Grandpa Opperman's vacant barn. Don't tell me that kids aren't smart these days."

"Devious and stupid is more like it." Lily was glad that Holly wasn't going to the party. "Grandpa Opperman has a shotgun and a temper."

"He died last year. His place has been cleaned out, and it's up for sale. Adam thought I should buy it, but it's too big for what I need." Mack squirted ketchup over his fries. "You'd think that kids couldn't get into too much trouble in only a couple of hours."

"I imagine it'll go down something like this," Lily told him. "Susie will tell her parents they're spending the night with Grace. Grace will say she's staying with Amber. Then Amber will say that she's staying with Susie. The story will be that the mothers will take the girls home early on Saturday morning, and some kid who's old enough to drive will really be the one to drop them off. Boys will do the same thing, and if no one gets caught, then the parents are never the wiser."

"Man, I'm glad I'm not that age anymore," Mack said. "You're right. They are devious little snots. How'd you get so smart about all this?"

"Duh!" Lily popped her palm against her forehead. "Smoking pot in the library bathroom not even a month ago. I'm surprised that Holly's not mixed up in the middle of it all."

"Maybe," Mack chuckled, "no laptop, phone, or any electronic device has taught her a lesson. I've got to get back to school now. I've got an FFA adviser meeting after school. The teachers from several surrounding schools are gathering, so I won't be home until after dark. I'll miss having supper with y'all tonight." He dropped a kiss on her forehead and headed for the door.

Dammit! She wished that she could tell him that she was already putting deep roots down in Comfort and never wanted to go back to Austin. But a promise was a promise, and she'd given the kids her word.

"I can pray that they'll change their minds, though, can't I?" she muttered.

~

Lily made a right turn into the lane, and the school bus pulled in right behind her. The kids beat her into the house and were already in the kitchen by the time she'd gotten her coat hung up and her purse set on the bottom step of the staircase.

"Are, too!" She heard Braden already arguing with his sister.

"Am not!" Holly's voice had gone all high and squeaky.

Lily crossed the foyer and went into the kitchen. She checked on the pork roast she'd put in the slow cooker that morning. "Are what?"

"Holly's friends, Rose and Ivy, are going to a party tonight in some old barn. Isaac said that they want her to go with them. I told her to be careful because rats live in old barns, and she's scared of little bitty mice, so she'd probably faint if a rat started chasing her," Braden said.

"How'd you find out about that?" Lily asked.

"Isaac told me. Some of the high school boys work out on the ranch for his daddy, and they were bragging about outsmartin' the police.

They didn't know that Isaac was in the tack room," Braden said, and then grinned. "I guess I could go with her—so if there is a rat, I could chase it away."

"How would little old bitty you take care of a dam—darn—rat?" Holly shivered. "And I'm not going anywhere tonight but up to my room to work on my math. If I have trouble, Faith said I can call her and she'll walk me through the problem."

"*You* are mean," Braden smarted off.

"*You* are obnoxious," Holly told him.

"Both of you eat a cookie, and don't talk with food in your mouths," Lily told them.

"Mack should be home by now, right?" Braden asked.

"He had an after-school meeting," Lily answered. "He won't be here until late."

"I can take care of the feeding," Braden said. "You want to help me, Holly?"

"Only if Mama goes with us," Holly answered.

"Why?" Braden frowned.

"Because if there's a mouse out there, you'll get it by the tail and chase me with it," Holly replied.

"Get finished with your snack, and we'll take care of the evening chores together." Lily figured it would be well worth her time to get Holly interested in the goats.

Of course, Holly had to change her clothes, braid her hair, put on fresh lipstick, and get out her oldest boots. Not even the goats were going to see her looking like a bag lady. Lily put on a pair of jeans, a flannel shirt, and her dad's old work coat. It didn't fit her much better than it had Braden.

"I'll show y'all how it's done." Braden puffed up with pride on the way from the house to the barn. "It's not hard, and you're goin' to love the new babies, Holly. They're even cuter than a cat."

"Not possible," Holly declared.

The feeding chore only took half an hour at the most, but they spent another hour in the pen, petting and loving on the new babies. Holly was the child who begged for five more minutes when they had to go back to the house, and who pouted when she had to leave behind her favorite little black-and-white kid that was only a couple of days old.

After supper, Holly and Braden hurried to the living room to watch an old movie. They'd argued all during the meal about a funny scene. Holly said that one thing happened in it; Braden swore that it didn't. That would keep them busy for a couple of hours, Lily thought. She went upstairs to take a long, soaking bath.

She adjusted the water, got it just to the right warmth, and then dropped all her clothes on the floor. Her phone pinged with a text from Sally. Her boss wouldn't be in the shop until after ten the next morning. Then there was one from Mack saying that his meeting was running longer than he'd thought.

She sent a smiley-face emoji back to Sally and a message to Mack telling him that they'd taken care of the chores. She immediately got a heart emoji back from him. She laid the phone on the ladder-back chair beside her towel, added some scented oil to the bath, and sank down into the warm water.

When the water had gone lukewarm, she got out and wrapped a towel around her body, made sure the coast was clear, and padded down the hall to her bedroom. Once she was there, she dressed in flannel pajama pants and a faded T-shirt left over from Christmas several years before.

Both kids had finished their homework, and everything was quiet downstairs, which meant that the controversial scene in the movie had not played yet. After all the bickering that usually went on, Lily appreciated the moment. She took out the journal, peeked inside the velvet pouch with all the money, and sighed. She'd have to figure out where to go on a cruise when summer arrived. The Caribbean? Or maybe Alaska?

She tucked the money back into the secretary and was about to go over to Holly's room when her daughter came in with her two notebooks. "The movie is boring, but I was right about that scene. Can we read some more about Jenny now?" She crawled up in the middle of Lily's bed and opened her notebook.

"Sure, we can." Lily joined her on the bed, opened the journal, and began to read:

Jenny Medford O'Riley, March 1908: Oklahoma is a state as of last November, but that hasn't changed the way we live here in Dodsworth. I got a letter from Mama a few days ago, and I've read it dozens of times. My tears have made the ink run in places, especially when she told me my brother had died, leaving behind a wife and two children. I have such fond memories of the times I spent with Samuel when we were young. I hope that my daughter, Rachel, and her brothers have memories like that. Rachel is now twenty-one, married, and has a daughter and a son of her own. It's hard to think that so much time has passed, but months and years stand still for no one. I'm glad that Rachel is happy. She was such a rebellious child, and I wanted to pull my hair out before I got her raised. We have settled into life here in Oklahoma, but I do miss Mama. She's getting on up in years now, and I do wish I could see her once more before her time comes to an end.

"Mama, if I live a long way from you when I leave home, will you write me real letters that I can keep and read over and over?" Holly asked.

"Of course I will, but where are you planning on living?" Lily answered.

"Well." Holly hesitated. "Faith is probably going to the Air Force Academy when she graduates next year, and I might do that, too, when

I get out of school. The counselor is looking into what all she has to do to get into the academy. It sounds like a good program."

"If that's what you want to do, I'll support you in your decision," Lily promised, all the time hoping that she'd change her mind by the time she graduated.

"Thanks, Mama." Holly gave Lily a brief hug. "I'm not going to think of Jenny dying, even though I know she will before we finish the journal. It makes me real sad to think that I'd ever lose you, so you have to live forever."

Lily had to work hard to keep the tears at bay, but the moment passed quickly when Holly jumped up and grabbed her notebooks. "I've got to go get some of this written down while it's fresh in my mind."

Lily remembered the day that Sally had called to tell her that her mother had passed away. Jenny had had poor means of transportation and miles between where she lived and her mother, Matilda. Lily had only the excuse of being busy, and she had regretted not having visited her mother more often in the past five years.

Chapter Fourteen

"Holly! Holly! Come quick! Hurry!" Braden yelled at his sister as he hit the back door with a thump after school the next day and rushed inside with a newborn baby goat in his arms. "I need help, Holly! We got to keep her alive."

Holly had been in the living room watching television, but she didn't waste time getting past her mother in the kitchen. "Good Lord, Braden. I thought Mama was dying."

"Not Mama," Braden huffed. "*This* baby's mama died, and we got to keep her warm or she won't make it. Get some old towels. Mack said to rub her fur until she's dry, and then we'll see if one of the other nannies will take her."

Lily opened a bottom cabinet drawer where her mother always kept scrub rags and tossed a fistful into the utility room. Braden and Holly each grabbed an old towel and started rubbing the newborn baby. They were talking to the animal as if it were a human baby, and they weren't arguing. Lily watched them, amazed. Who would have ever thought her kids would bond over a goat?

When Mack finally came into the house, the baby was on her feet and throwing a fit. Evidently, she was hungry and wanting either a bottle or a mama that had more to offer than dry towels.

"I've put two nannies that gave birth today into stalls," Mack said. "We can take her out to see if either one of them will take her as their own."

"Can't we keep her in the house?" Holly asked. "I'll give up my cat from Granny Hayes if we can."

"She'll be healthier if we put her on a nanny, but she can be your goat. You can name her and spoil her every day," Mack said. "Since Braden carried her to the house, *you* can take her to the barn."

"Her name is Star, because that white spot on her head looks like a star." Holly wrapped her in a clean towel and scooped her up in her arms.

Mack winked at Lily, who was still in shock that Holly would even touch a goat. Life had sure taken a big turnaround since the first of the month. Lily fully expected Braden to hate the name or else put up an argument that the goat was his, but he just followed his sister out the back door with Mack right behind them.

The table was set for supper, and the food was ready to be put into bowls by the time they got back from the barn. Lily remembered a few times when her father had brought a calf into the utility room to warm it up and then took it out to put it on a cow that had just given birth. Sometimes it worked, sometimes not. If it didn't, then they had to bottle-feed the little critter until it was big enough to eat feed. She crossed her fingers that didn't happen. Holly would not like getting up thirty minutes early every morning to go feed Star, or traipsing out to the barn every evening, whether it was snowing or raining, to take care of the goat again.

What will be, will be, Lily remembered her mother saying, and everything happens for the best.

Braden came through the door first. "Guess what, Mama? One of the nannies took Star right in and let her eat, and she's a prize-winning mama goat, and her own baby is a boy, and Mack says he can be my goat to show next year at the livestock show!" He stopped long enough to draw in a long breath. "And I named him War Lord."

"So does that mean you don't want to go back to Austin?" Lily dipped the mashed potatoes out of a pan and into a bowl.

"Hell—I mean, heck, yes." Braden grinned. "Why would I want to leave War Lord? He'd miss me awful bad."

Lily could hardly believe his answer. A month ago, he'd been so against the move that she feared he'd never forgive her. She glanced over at Holly and raised an eyebrow.

"The jury is still out," Holly said. "I've got to go wash up."

"Me, too." Braden rushed out of the kitchen ahead of her. "I bet I beat you to the bathroom."

"Don't you dare lock the door," Holly yelled.

"If these old walls could talk, I wonder how many stories they could tell." Mack stopped at the kitchen sink to wash his hands. "Kids running through the place, first kisses on the porch swing, tears and giggles."

Lily thought of the journal in her bedroom. Life going past at lightning speed. Happiness. Wars. Changing times. Like the house, the old journal had its stories to tell, but unlike the silent walls, the book told its tales, even if they weren't long.

"What would the walls tell me about your life here the past five years?" she asked Mack.

He raised one shoulder in half a shrug. "It could be written on a postage stamp. Work, home, old movies, more work. I'm a boring fellow for the most part."

"That's a matter of opinion." Lily lifted the hot rolls out into a basket.

"And yours is . . ." He paused for her answer as he dried his hands. Then he wrapped his arms around her waist, pulling her back to his chest.

"That you're kind and sweet and that I love living with you." She smiled.

The pounding of two kids' feet on the wooden stairs broke up the moment. Mack gave her a slow wink and picked up a bowl of potatoes to take to the table. Holly pulled out a chair and sat down in it. "Since Star is my goat, do I get to go feed her every evening?"

Braden pulled out his chair and took a seat. "Feeding is my job."

"Hey, now." Mack pulled out his own chair and sat down. "We can use all the help we can get, but for the next few weeks, Star won't get fed except by her new mama. You can sure go out to the stall and love on her until about Sunday. Then I'll turn her mama loose in the pasture with all the other goats and their babies." He bowed his head and led everyone in a blessing for the meal.

"Will she forget me?" Holly's chin quivered.

"Never. She'll always be your special pet, and will probably come running to you when she hears your voice. Especially if you take time to pet her every day until Sunday."

"I will," Holly said seriously.

"No, you won't," Braden argued. "You'll get tired of her in two days." He turned to Mack. "When she does, can I have her?"

"No, I won't," Holly said. "And you can't have her. Eat your supper and hush."

"You're not the boss of me," Braden said.

The house phone rang, and everyone froze for a couple of seconds, and then Holly jumped up and ran to answer it. "It's probably Faith. She said she'd call, and we're having supper late and . . ." She grabbed the phone on the third ring. "Hello, Faith. I was going to call you in a few minutes. Oh." She stopped. "Hi, Daddy. Guess what? I got my very own goat today, and her name is Star, and she's going to be my special pet."

The kids hadn't heard a word from him since the move, so why was he calling now? Lily began to worry. Had he been thinking about the kids moving in with him? Would they leave her if he gave them the chance?

"Sorry, Daddy, I have to be here over the weekend to pet my new goat, or she won't know me when she goes out to pasture," Holly said. Then there was a long silence while she listened to him. "Well, if it's only one night, and I can pet her before we leave and you'll have us back home before four on Saturday, that would be all right, I guess. But you better talk to Mama before you reserve a hotel room for us." She laid the phone down on the counter and went back to the table.

"It's Daddy, and he wants to talk to you," she told Lily, and then nudged Braden with her elbow. "I told him we could only be gone from tomorrow evening until Saturday. If you don't back me up, I'm going to strangle you."

"I don't want to go at all," Braden said. "I'd rather be here."

Lily took her time pushing away from the table and going to the phone. "Hello, Wyatt," she said. "We haven't heard from you in a month. Did you lose the number to the house here in Comfort?"

"I've been too busy to call, but I want the kids for the weekend. I'll pick them up tomorrow and bring them home Sunday evening. Have them ready at four," he said.

She turned toward the table. "Sure you don't want to stay over until Sunday?"

Both kids shook their heads.

"The kids have projects they're working on, so they'll have to be home Saturday evening fairly early," she said in a businesslike tone.

"Victoria and I want to take them to a couple of museums on Saturday, and then to the Alamo on Sunday. From what Holly just told me, they could use some culture," he almost growled.

She relayed the message to the kids.

Braden pretended to gag.

Holly shook her head. "I'm not even going if Victoria is going to be there."

Braden raised his hand in agreement.

"They'll go, but for one day only," Lily said. "How about if you go to the Alamo and then to the shopping mall?"

"No museums," Braden said.

"Only if we get to go to the mall." Holly got up for the second time and held out her hand for the phone. "It's me again, Daddy. Here's the deal. We'll go if you pick us up tomorrow, and we can go to the Alamo and the shopping mall Saturday. We want to eat at the barbecue place in the food court, not some fancy place with cloth napkins, and then we want to be home before four so we can take care of our goats. Deal?"

She listened for a few minutes and then hung up. "We got the deal, brother, and to make it sweeter, Victoria doesn't want to go to either place. She's spending the day in a spa."

Braden held up his hand for a high five, and Holly slapped it. Then they went back to their food as if nothing had happened.

Lily couldn't help but wonder how Wyatt must have felt. This was the first time the kids hadn't fallen all over themselves to get to spend time with him. He must've thought they would jump at the chance for a weekend away from the boonies. Well, now maybe he would think again.

~

"Thank God for goats," Lily muttered.

"What was that?" Mack unloaded the dishwasher so they could put the supper dishes inside.

Lily repeated what she'd said, continuing, "This is the first time that Holly or Braden haven't gotten excited to get to spend time with their dad. It's about time that he realizes they're growing up and away from him. It breaks my heart the way he throws a relationship with them away for Victoria."

"Why does he do that?" Mack asked.

"She's very wealthy, and she doesn't like children. She's about ten years older than Wyatt. I don't know if she loves *him* or the fact that he's so pretty and looks good in a five-thousand-dollar suit. Of course, I also don't know if he loves her or the lifestyle she affords him. He has always liked being a big shot," Lily told him.

"Is she the reason he doesn't get the kids every other weekend and a month in the summer?" Mack asked.

Lily shrugged. "He gave me sole custody in the divorce and said that he'd spend time with them when he could. It's been six months since he's even seen them."

"Not even at Christmas?" Mack's face was a study in pure shock.

"He sent a few expensive gifts, but not even at Christmas," Lily replied. "They called him and wanted to move in with him when I told them we were moving to Comfort. He said no way, and I kind of felt sorry for the kids even though I was upset with them," she explained.

"Man, he's a fool." Mack slowly shook his head. "He has no idea the fun he's missing."

"Hey," Braden yelled, bounding down the stairs and into the living room. "Me and Holly want to know if y'all old people want to watch a movie with us. I brought the whole Harry Potter series with me, but we ain't got a TV in either of our rooms."

"They want to spend time with us? It's a miracle," Lily whispered.

"Well, let's don't waste a single minute." Mack grinned and led her from the kitchen to the living room with his hand on her lower back.

Even through her shirt, she could feel the heat starting at the place where his hand was touching her and going all the way through her body. Holly met them in the foyer and raced ahead to argue with her brother about who got to sit in the recliner.

For the first time, Lily was glad they were arguing and didn't notice that she was practically blushing.

"First come, first served," Braden taunted his sister.

"Oh, yeah." Holly wiggled her way into the chair beside him and put her arm around his shoulders. "You're my itsy-bitsy brother, so we can share the chair."

"Yuck!" Braden jumped up, grabbed a quilt and throw pillow from the sofa, and stretched out on the floor. "Want me to put the first one in the DVD player, Mama?" He pointed toward the television.

"I'll do it." Mack started toward the television. "I've never seen Harry Potter or read the books. Which is better? Movies or books?"

"Books," both kids said at the same time.

"Then I'll have to read them later after we see the movies." Mack put the first one into the player and handed the remote to Braden.

Lily sat on the sofa, and Mack sat on the other end. Lily found herself wishing that Mack was beside her with his arm draped around her shoulders, but getting to spend time with her kids, even if it was watching Harry Potter, was pretty danged special, too.

As soon as the movie ended, Mack asked, "So is going to Universal Studios and seeing the Harry Potter place on your list of things to see someday?"

"Naw," Braden said. "I'd rather go to the beach and just do nothing but play in the sand and collect seashells."

"Me, too. Braden can find seashells while I work on getting a tan." Holly yawned and headed out of the room. "I'm going to bed."

"I'm going to read for half an hour after I get my bath," Braden said. "I still think the books are better, but every time I see the movies, I can see the characters better."

Mack stood up and held out a hand to Lily. "Walk you to your bedroom door?"

"No, but you can walk me to the bottom of the stairs. That would be really nice." She laced her fingers in his.

He stopped just before they made it to the bottom of the steps, wrapped Lily up in his arms, and hugged her tightly. "I like the way you fit in my arms."

"So do I," she said. "But, Mack, you might want to think long and hard about things. We could go back to Austin at the end of the school year. Braden is the only one who's said he wants to stay here. Holly says the jury is still out."

He tipped up her chin with his knuckles and kissed her. When it ended, she leaned into his broad chest. It felt good to have a man's strong arms around her and to hear him say nice things about her. But—there always seemed to be a *but* in her life—she couldn't start something and then walk away from it in a few months. It wouldn't be fair to him, and it would break her heart, too.

He turned around and headed the short distance to his bedroom, and she went on up the steps, taking them one at a time, and wishing the whole time that she could go back and follow him into his bedroom. Her breath was still coming in short bursts when she reached her bedroom and got the journal out of the secretary. She started toward Holly's room with it, only to meet her in the hallway.

"Can we read some more?" Holly asked. "I've got thirty minutes before bedtime, and I'd like to work on my project."

"Great minds think alike." Lily turned around and led the way back to her room.

"Oh, yeah." Holly grinned and crawled up in the middle of Lily's bed. "It seems strange, Mama, to read about these women that were kin to us, and the time from one chapter to the next being so far apart. It seems even weirder that we've been here in Comfort as long as we have, and it only seems like a day or two."

"It does, doesn't it?" Lily thought of her and Mack. They were adults living in the same house, but it could so easily turn into more than that, given time. Would she ever write in the journal that she'd gotten married a second time? Would it be Mack, or was he just showing her that there were still a few good men out there in the world?

"Are you going to read or not?" Holly asked impatiently.

Lily glanced down at the book and read:

Jenny Medford O'Riley, May 1917:

Holly let out a long sigh of relief. "I'm glad that she's still alive. I like her."

Lily went on:

All we've heard for three years is war, war, and more war. The newspapers are full of it. Rather than crops and cattle, our men talk about it constantly. I can't believe they were so happy when the United States declared war. It's like they're little boys in a candy store. I swear if my Danny wasn't too old, he would rush down into town and enlist. Two of my sons have already joined the army, and two more are about to join. I know now how Grandmother Ophelia must have felt when her husband went to war. Rachel says that if they'd take women, she'd join up tomorrow. I can't ever imagine a day when women will be in the military. Right now Rachel is working for women's rights. Although they aren't accepted so well in a man's world, we do now have women lawyers and doctors, so we've come a long way—and some states are allowing women to vote. My stepfather died last year, and with Samuel gone and Lily moved off to Savannah, Mama was all alone, so she's come to live with us. I love having her here, and she really enjoys having her great-grandchildren around her. She's seventy-one years old now, but she's still in good health.

Lily closed the book and looked straight at Holly. "Are you going to vote when you're eighteen?"

"Of course I am. Faith and I take our lunch to the library most days and do research. Tomorrow I'm going to look up World War I and women's voting so I can write a little about it in my journal." Holly slung her legs off the bed. She didn't hug Lily that night, but she did stop at the door and say, "Thanks, Mama, for sharing this with me. I'm glad that our Matilda is living with Jenny now. That's where she belongs, since she's old."

"Me, too." A sudden cloud of guilt floated down to surround Lily like a thick fog. When her father died, she should have insisted that her mother live with her in Austin. They'd had plenty of room in the house she and Wyatt had lived in, so there was no reason Vera couldn't have stayed with them. Lord only knew, she would have loved to cook for the family, and it would have given her something to live for.

"I could never leave your father's memory, not even for a week," her mother had said when Lily asked her about moving to Austin. "Besides, this is where we've always had the holidays, and I've already got the decorations up."

That's what she had said, but now Lily wondered if a little more begging could have convinced her to move in with her and Wyatt.

"I could have tried," Lily said out loud as she gathered up her things to take to the bathroom. "But I was so wrapped up in my own life that I didn't. And I haven't even been to her grave since I got back. Some daughter I am."

When she'd finished taking her bath, she opened the door to find Braden waiting with his clean pajamas in his hands, sitting on the floor, his back against the wall. He was small for his age, but a pretty boy, Lily thought, with his big brown eyes and dark hair. She could feel that he wanted to talk about something, so she sat down beside him.

"Got something on your mind?"

He nodded.

"Want to talk about it?" she asked.

"Why can't Daddy be more like Mack?" Braden asked. "Daddy is always looking at his gold watch when we're with him, like we're not even there, or he's texting or talking to Victoria. Mack don't even *wear* a watch."

"Your dad has always worked on a busy schedule, and his job has a lot of pressure involved, and he kind of always brought it home. Now that he does a lot of work on the road, I expect it's even harder on him to forget about his work." Lily tried to explain without saying that Wyatt was a jackass. "Mack has a different kind of job and doesn't get in such a hurry."

"Well, I wish you would have married Mack instead of Daddy." Braden hopped up and disappeared into the bathroom.

Lily got up and slowly went to her bedroom. She wondered what her life would have been like if Mack had asked her for a date when they were young, and she'd gone out with him.

Chapter Fifteen

How on earth could it be Friday already—where had the whole month of January gone? Lily wondered as she went to work that morning. The month had gone by so fast, and she had enjoyed her work so much more than she had listening to people's problems all day. She hummed a country song all the way to work. She couldn't remember the name of the tune until she parked her car at the back of the shop between Teena's van and Sally's cute little sports car. Getting out, she sang the lyrics she could remember to "Hush, Hush" by the Pistol Annies. The group had a brunette and two blondes—just like Teena, Sally, and herself—and the song reminded her of small towns with their church potluck dinners, rumors, and gossip. She'd forgotten how much she missed living here until she'd gotten back into the middle of it all.

She used her key and went through the back door. At first she thought what she was hearing was giggling, but then she realized that someone was weeping. She removed her coat as she picked up her pace until she was practically jogging through the clothing room to the front office. Surely no one had died or Sally would have called her.

"What's going on?" Lily threw her coat and purse on the counter.

Tears streamed down Sally's face. "Ryder's girlfriend, Macy, had a miscarriage last night."

"I caused it," Teena wailed. "I didn't want him to be married and be a father at nineteen."

Lily crossed the room and hugged Teena. "I'm so sorry, but this is not your fault. If we had that kind of suggestive power, then Wyatt would have dropped dead years ago, and Victoria would have lost all her money. They would both be living in a cardboard box in an alley behind a beer joint."

"See, I told you that you didn't cause it," Sally said.

"Stop crying and go see Macy. Where is she right now? At her apartment?" Lily asked.

Teena nodded. "At her place, and Ryder is with her."

"That's even better. Go see both of them. This was Ryder's child as much as hers. He has to be strong for her, but he needs your strength," Lily said.

"Did you go with them to the ER?" Sally held the trash can out for Teena to throw in a fistful of tissues.

"Ryder didn't call me until an hour ago, and he'd already taken Macy home." Teena pulled more tissues from the box. "I came straight here. I didn't want to be a grandmother, and now I feel like I've lost a part of me. It's confusing as hell . . . and crazy! But you're right, Lily. I need to go see them both, but not with my face a mess."

Lily handed her the whole box of tissues. "Don't do one thing to your face. Go just as you are, and let them see that you're grieving with them. Remember how you felt when you lost that baby when the twins were a year old."

"You were on a guilt trip then, too," Sally reminded her. "You were devastated when you learned you were pregnant again, and then when you had the miscarriage, you thought it was your fault."

"What's that got to do with now?" Teena asked.

"You're reliving the guilt," Lily answered.

Teena took the box of tissues from Lily. "Should I take anything? Flowers? Food? I don't know what to do."

"Just take that box and give them both a hug," Lily said. "The rest will take care of itself."

Teena stood to her feet, put on her coat, and picked up her purse. "I've taken the day off work. I'll be back after a while."

"We'll be right here," Sally said.

"Thanks"—Teena took a step toward the door and then turned around to get the tissues—"for everything. I'm so glad that we're back together."

"Me, too," Lily said, and she meant it.

Sally slumped down in one of the chairs behind the counter. "I feel drained and so sorry for her. I wonder if Ryder and Macy will still get married, or if they'll grow apart now when he goes back to school."

Lily dropped into the other chair. "How long have they been dating?"

"Since they were in the ninth grade," Sally answered.

Lily vaguely remembered Teena being concerned about Ryder getting too serious about a girl when he was a sophomore—it must've been Macy. That's what happened when Lily only saw her friends for a couple of hours once a month. She heard the stories, forgot them in the midst of all her own problems, and never got the full emotional impact of being a true friend.

The last customer Sally and Lily wanted to see that morning was Ruth-Ann, but the doorbell jingled, and there she was.

Sally sighed.

Lily groaned.

"Did y'all hear that Macy Jones had a miscarriage last night?" Ruth-Ann went to the counter and frowned. "Where are the new earrings?"

"We heard." Sally nodded.

"Of course you did. Teena and y'all two were joined at the hip in high school." She pointed to the empty space.

"A customer bought all of them, plus all the crocheted scarves and shawls," Lily told her. *Joined at the hip?*

Maybe not in the past several years, but lately they were getting that old closeness back again.

"So is Ryder still going to marry Macy?" Ruth-Ann asked.

"You'll have to ask him about that," Lily answered. "I heard that you collect milk glass. Have you seen these new pieces that Sally picked up at the estate sale she was at earlier this week? They're really rare and the price is great." She got up and moved over to the display.

"I don't have time to look at those today. I only had a minute on my way to the post office to mail stuff for school. Ta-ta." She waved.

"You're brilliant," Sally giggled. "That woman has never bought a single piece of glassware from me, but she hits all the garage sales looking for good buys."

"Can't change a zebra's stripes," Lily said. "And thinking about Granny Hayes, what can you tell me about her past? She's always been Comfort's odd little person, but none of us ever knew why she lived the way she did."

"I asked her how long she'd lived in that cabin, and she told me since she was born," Sally said. "When the community wanted to put up a historical marker out there, she told them no. When they persisted, she told them to go to hell. When they did it anyway, she took it down and used the metal for the bottom of a feed bin for her old mule."

"But the cabin has to be a hundred years old," Lily said. "Why wouldn't she want it memorialized?"

"She said it would bring people out there to her place. She didn't want strangers coming around, and if they did, she was a real good aim with her shotgun. That's when the 'No Trespassing' signs went up," Sally said. "But it got me interested in her story, so I went to the old newspaper files at the library. Her mother and father were some of the first folks of German descent that settled here. She was the youngest of six kids, and her father was a farmer. The older five children were boys, and they went to school. But evidently, those folks had different ideas about girls because Johanna Hayes Mayer was never listed on the school rolls."

"So that's her name?" Lily asked. "If she was never listed on the rolls, how'd you find out her name? And I wonder how come we've always called her Granny Hayes instead of Granny Mayer."

"First of all, I found the record of that historical plaque, got her parents' names from it, and then went digging for birth certificates," Sally answered. "She was born in 1921, so she's ninety-eight years old. Her mother was forty-four, and the youngest of her sons was eighteen years old when Granny Hayes came along. All of the boys were grown and had left home by then. I asked Drew to check the church rolls, and he found that Granny didn't start attending until she was past sixty. But I don't remember a time when she wasn't there, or when folks didn't call her Granny Hayes. I pried a little one afternoon when I took her an order of yarn and asked her why she didn't go by Granny Mayer. She got real quiet and said that her father was a hard old German. Her mother's maiden name had been Hayes, and she liked being Irish more than German. That's all she'd say."

"Holy smoke!" Lily gasped. "I thought she might be in her eighties, but ninety-eight? Man, she sure don't act that old. You should have seen the way she got in and out of that pickup truck."

"I want to grow up and have her kind of strength and energy. Can you imagine riding a mule five miles to church?" Sally asked.

"I wonder if any of those brothers settled around here?" Lily shook her head. "Whoa! Hermann Mayer is the name on the historical marker out at the end of the lane from my house. It says the place was the homestead of Hermann and Lucille Mayer from their marriage in 1890 until their deaths. They were active in community affairs and raised a son, Frederick Mayer, who occupied the house when his parents were gone. The homestead includes the house, a barn, a smokehouse, and it's a significant part of the German-Texas heritage of the state. I wonder if he's one of the sons."

"That wasn't one of the sons' names. I can't remember them all, but Hermann wasn't one of them. He might have been a brother or a cousin to Granny Hayes's folks, though." Sally rubbed her hands together. "I'll have to go back to the library and see what I can find out. Maybe that's why she likes Holly so much—maybe y'all share a little DNA."

"I was never interested in genealogy like Mama was, but this makes me want to find out more," Lily said.

Polly brought a blast of cold wind with her when she entered the front door of the shop. She usually arrived with a big smile on her face and a spring in her step, but today she was somber and serious. She set a box from the bakery on the table and opened it. "I brought cookies for when Teena gets back. She's on the way." Then she set her thermos beside the box. "Hot chocolate. I thought I'd come offer a little support with the food."

Teena came in through the back door. Polly opened her arms, and she walked right into them. "I miss my mama today, so thank you for coming."

"I know you do, darlin'," Polly said. "Losing a baby is a tough thing, no matter how old a woman is. How's Ryder and Macy?"

"They're both so sad." Teena took a step back and sighed. "I'm glad I went, Lily. It meant a lot to Ryder and to Macy. Poor girl hasn't had many breaks. Her little garage apartment is spotless, and she really loves my son. I've misjudged her, and I feel bad."

"God works in mysterious ways," Polly said. "It wasn't the best of situations, but He brought Lily back to Comfort where she belongs."

"That was marijuana, not God," Lily said.

"God uses whatever is at hand to work His miracles," Polly informed her. "Now let's have some cookies and chocolate. Food always helps."

~

That evening after work, Lily drove up to her house and slapped the steering wheel. *Dammit!* She had forgotten all about Wyatt coming at four to get the kids, and there he was in his $1,000 black coat, getting out of his low-slung sports car. A flashback of him coming into the house wearing a similar coat, only a much cheaper brand, came to her mind. He'd been driving an SUV in those days, and back then he'd been a father, even if it was, for the most part, in name only.

She got out of her car, and he held up a gloved hand in a wave. She ignored him and went on toward the house.

"Are the kids ready?" he yelled.

"I'll see," she answered without turning around. She could almost see her mother's disapproving expression. No southern lady treated anyone with such cold hatefulness, but she ignored the thought.

She had just opened the door when she heard the rumble of the school bus coming up the lane. That's when she turned and pointed, but Wyatt had already heard it and was looking that way. The kids got off the bus with Holly in the lead. Neither of them ran to hug him. Holly stopped and talked to her father and then came on toward the house.

"He wants to know if he can wait for us inside," she told Lily. "I said I'd ask you about that, and reminded him that he wasn't supposed to be here for another hour and that I had to take care of Star before I could leave."

"Of course he can wait inside." Lily just couldn't be hateful in front of Holly. "Are you packed and ready to go?"

Holly nodded and ran through the house, out the back door, and across the yard and pasture to the barn. Braden came in behind her with his father in tow, and followed his sister outside.

Wyatt nodded at Lily and said, "Cold out there today."

"Yes, it is. You can either sit right there"—she pointed to the empty ladder-back chairs—"or you can go to the barn with Braden." She glanced down at his expensive loafers. "Your choice."

Wyatt removed his topcoat, took a seat, and folded his coat on his lap. "Are you ever going to forgive me? Can't we be friends for the kids' sake?"

"I can be civil and let you come in out of the cold for the kids' sake. I will never be your friend." She went upstairs and left him alone in the foyer.

Her hands shook with anger as she got out the journal to calm herself.

Jenny Medford O'Riley, December 1919:

That surprised Lily since there hadn't been as many entries from one woman. There were usually several years between each recording, but this one was only two years after the last. She read through the page the first time, but Wyatt was still on her mind, and she was feeling a little guilty about reading it without Holly. She vowed that she'd backtrack when Holly got home and go over it again with her.

The flu epidemic made its way to Oklahoma. We lost Mama last week, and she's been on my mind ever since. I was young when my daddy left with that other woman. We never saw him again. I'm still a little bitter, but my precious mama used to tell me that there was no room in a heart for both love and hate. She said that hate would soon eat up its half of the heart and want more and more until soon there would be no love left for anyone. I'm in mourning still, but I'm so glad I got to be with her all the way to the end when she took that final step from this world into a better one. I only hope that the flu doesn't take any more of us. It seems like we do nothing but attend funerals these days.

"Okay, Mama." Lily closed the book. "You might not be here to tell me in person, but you spoke loud and clear."

She marched back downstairs. Wyatt was still sitting in the same place. He looked up at her with eyes the same clear-blue color as Holly's. "How much longer do you think they'll be? I was hoping that we could meet Victoria for dinner this evening."

Lily sat down on the bottom step. "Wyatt, they know that Victoria doesn't like them and hates being around them. They'd far rather spend time with you in a burger shop than eating in a fancy restaurant. They don't care about museums or the Alamo. They've been to those places on school trips at least a dozen times. What they'd rather do is play a board game with you, or watch one of Braden's collection of Harry Potter movies—again, *with you*. You could hole up in a hotel room, play games, watch movies, and order pizza brought to the room, and they'd be happy. And"—she inhaled deeply—"if you can put your phone away and not call or text Victoria every ten minutes, they'd appreciate that, too. They need your time and your love, not your money."

"Did they tell you to say that?" Wyatt asked.

She shook her head. "I'm trying to help you out. They'll come home tomorrow and probably not see you again for months. You might remember to call on weekends or you might not. They never know what to expect, and when they do spend time with you, it's like you're a tour guide, not a father. Get to know your kids, and make them want to see you or talk to you."

Wyatt narrowed his eyes at her. "You mean they don't want to see me now?"

That was typical Wyatt, always and forever twisting her words.

"When I caught Holly smoking weed and found out that Braden was sneaking out of the house to smoke cigarettes and drink, I took a step back for a couple of days and figured some things out. You weren't around. I seldom got out of the house, except for church on Sundays, and buried myself in my work. I told myself that by helping others I was doing a good thing, but I didn't spend nearly enough time with the kids. It wasn't a healthy environment for either of them. So I changed that, and they're so much better now. If you'll adjust what you do with them when you have them, it'll help you and them," she tried to explain.

"I tell you what, Lily." Wyatt's tone was downright chilly. "You do things your way and have goats and live in a miserable old house like this in the country. I'll do the cultural scene with them when I have time for them. And, darlin', I will *never* not answer a text or a call from my wife."

"You lost the right to call me *darlin'* a long time ago," Lily said as she left him sitting in the foyer and went to the kitchen. "I tried, Mama. I really did, but he only hears what he wants to hear," she muttered under her breath.

The kids arrived not long after she'd poured herself a glass of tea. They didn't burst inside arguing like always. Braden gave her a hug and said, "Can we call from the hotel when we get there?"

"Sure, you can. You can call however often you want. Just use the room phone," she said.

"I hate hotels," Holly declared. "I'm going to call and check on Star before I go to bed and before we check out in the morning. God, I hate that we have to go to the Alamo. I don't even like going to the mall with Daddy. A ten-year-old wouldn't be caught dead in what he wants to buy me."

"It's only twenty-four hours," Lily said. "Maybe things will be different this time."

"Yeah, right." Braden's shoulders were slumped as he left the room.

Holly gave Lily a quick hug. "If it's not any better this time, then I'm not going again. Not even God can make me." She flounced off to get her things.

"You kids ready?" Wyatt's voice carried to the kitchen.

"In five minutes," Holly answered.

"I'll go warm up the car."

"See you there," Holly said.

Mack came through the back door so quietly that she didn't even realize he was there until he slipped his arms around her waist and pulled her back against his body. "Are they gone yet?" he whispered.

The front door closed. There was the sound of the kids coming down the stairs, and Holly called out, "We're leavin', Mama. Talk to you later this evening."

"I thought they might tell you goodbye," she sighed.

"They did." Mack kissed her on the neck and took a step back. "We just spent half an hour or more out in the barn with the goats. I thought maybe it would be best if I made myself scarce this time. Next time he comes around, I'll introduce myself. Braden gave me a hug before he left, and Holly patted me on the arm. I'm making progress. Mama has invited us to eat with her and Dad tonight. It's only a forty-minute drive, but I told her that I'd have to ask you."

She turned around to face him. "Mack, are you sure you want to take me home to meet your parents? Things didn't go well when you took Brenda and Natalie home to meet the folks, did it?"

"I don't think I have anything to worry about. Besides, the third time's the charm. 'Course if you don't want to, that's fine. We can always grab a burger at Dairy Queen and drive down to the river and watch the fish flop out of the water." He grinned and then gave her a sweet kiss on the lips.

"Or I can make supper here," she suggested. "But I'd love to see Nora and Orville again. I haven't seen them since Mama's funeral, and Nora was so good to organize and help Polly in the kitchen."

Mack nodded and took his phone from his pocket. "I'll send her a text and tell her to expect us in about an hour."

"That leaves me fifteen minutes to get ready." Lily started to leave the room.

"I thought you *were* ready." He took her hand in his, brought it to his lips, and kissed her knuckles. "You look beautiful to me."

She pulled her blonde hair from the band holding her ponytail, ran her fingers through it, and shook it loose. "After a comment like that, what can I say except 'Let's go'?"

"Got your cell phone?" he asked.

"In my purse," she answered.

"I wrote my number down on a piece of paper for each of the kids, and they said they knew yours, so that's covered." He took her by the hand and led her to the foyer, helped her into her coat, and opened the door for her.

She picked up her purse and headed toward his truck that was parked right beside her car. Even though it was dusty, it sure looked better than that sleek little sports car Wyatt had been driving.

~

Taking her to his folks' house might not be called a date, but Mack chose to think of it as one, anyway. He started the engine and adjusted the heater so that she would be warm. When they passed the historical marker out at the end of the lane, he asked, "So you're the third generation to live in the house?"

"Sally and I were talking about that today. I think I might be the sixth." She explained what she and Sally had pieced together. "And we could be long-ago kin to Granny Hayes."

"Small world." He didn't want to talk about ancestors and relatives. He'd rather hear something about Lily. "Did you like growing up in the old stone place, or would you have rather lived in a modern one-story house?"

"It was home, so I never gave it much thought, except when tourists blocked the driveway or drove right up in the yard to take pictures of the place," she said. "How have you liked living there?"

"Loved it. The whole place, from the house to the barn to the old smokehouse, has got personality," Mack said. "It kind of reminds me of the place where I grew up. It wasn't on the historical registry, but it wasn't a newer, modern place, either. Personally, I think Mama would have been better to keep Dad in his familiar surroundings, but Adam was insistent that they move closer to Dad's doctors. Now he's even more disoriented than before, and he gets angry when he can't find things. Mama says the doctors say that's part of the disease and not to argue with him." His phone rang, and he fished it out of his hip pocket, laid it on the console, and put it on speaker. "Hello."

"Mack, this is Braden. We're in the car on the way to the hotel, and I forgot to tell you that I left my boots in the barn. If Star gets them, she'll chew them up."

"You're on speaker," Mack said. "Your mom is right here beside me. I'll take care of the boots."

"Gimme that phone," Holly shouted. "This is Holly, and I'm talking now. My goat won't eat his smelly old boots. His goat might, but my sweet girl doesn't like the taste of dirty feet."

"That's enough about boots," Wyatt said. "And I don't want to hear about goats while we're at dinner with Victoria."

Mack tried to keep the smile off his face, but it was impossible. He glanced over at Lily and chuckled. "I guess that means y'all better not talk about kissing Star on the nose, either."

"Or that you're getting a cat from Granny Hayes," Lily said.

Holly squealed so loud that Lily could just imagine the expression on Wyatt's face. "Mama said we can have a cat, Braden."

"I got the phone again," Braden said. "If she gets a kitten, does that mean I can have one, too?"

"I imagine one would get really lonely all by itself," Lily said.

"What are you going to do with goats and cats when you move back to Austin this summer?" Wyatt asked.

"We're going to take them with us," Holly said in a sticky-sweet voice. "And when we come to visit you, we'll bring them all along so you can get to know them."

"Bye, Mama. Thanks for taking care of my boots, Mack." Braden ended the call.

"I love those kids." Mack laughed out loud.

"They've sure done a turnaround since we moved back home," she said. "Thank you for helping with that."

"I didn't do anything." He shrugged. "They had some troubles, but they're both good kids, and they're smart. You can't fool a child, Lily. They know it when they're loved."

"I decided when we came to Comfort that I was going to *show* them that they were loved. I've told them for years, but I'm afraid that my actions were lacking. I let my work consume me, and then they spent too much time in their rooms or with unsavory friends."

"But you're taking steps to correct that, and it's working." After the phone call from the kids, Mack was more excited about his life at that very moment than he had been in too many years to count. He just hoped that Adam didn't choose this evening to make a surprise visit to his folks.

Chapter Sixteen

The sun had solidified into a huge orange ball sliding down on the far horizon when Mack parked his truck in front of a small brick home on the outskirts of San Antonio. The front yard was so small it could have been cut with manicure scissors, and from what Lily could see from the passenger seat, the fenced backyard couldn't have been much bigger.

"I would never have thought your parents would be happy with a place like this," she said.

"They aren't." Mack unfastened his seat belt and turned to face her. "Dad hated it at first, but now he doesn't remember living anywhere else until he comes to visit me, and then he thinks he's back on his own little goat farm. He doesn't know who Mama is some of the time, and he thinks Adam and I are still teenagers. He loves it when Mama brings him up to the farm, though. That's what we call your place. He'll sit for hours and hours and watch the baby goats romp around. It's the only time I've seen him really happy lately. Just be prepared. He may not know you at all." He got out of the truck and hurried around the front end to open the door for her.

"Thank you," she said, smiling.

His mother, Nora, met them at the door. A tall, rawboned woman with more salt than pepper in her hair, she looked just like she had the last time Lily had seen her. Tonight she wore jeans and a pretty light-green sweater that matched her eyes. She gave Mack the first hug, and then she hugged Lily and whispered, "Orville is having a good day. I'm so glad y'all came." Then she raised her voice. "I've got dinner ready to put on the table. I hope you still like fried chicken, Lily."

"Of course she does," Orville's gruff old voice said from the living room. "I remember she always loved your fried chicken at the church potlucks. Come on in here and let me look at you, Brenda."

She looked up at Mack, who shrugged. "Just play along with him."

The house was laid out with what real estate agents called a great room—dining room, living room, and kitchen all combined. Lily left Mack's side and went to give Orville a hug. He had always reminded her of a bulldog—a wide face with drooping jowls, broad shoulders, and big biceps. Mack had gotten the best features of both his parents—his height and those big, broad shoulders from Orville, and his face shape from his mother. Adam must have been a throwback to a past generation, Lily thought, because she couldn't see a blessed thing about him in either of his parents.

Orville hugged her and then took a step back and looked down at her with a frown. "Where's Adam? I thought he was coming with you. Why is Mack bringing you to dinner?"

"I just arrived at the same time he did, and we came in together," Lily told him.

"Did I hear my name?" Adam came into the room with a big smile on his face.

"There he is," Orville said. "I knew he'd be along soon if you were here. Nora, is supper ready? The kids are all here now. Brenda's here, too. Seems like forever since we've seen her."

"How'd you get here before me, darlin'?" Adam headed straight for Lily. "We always play along to keep from upsetting Dad," he whispered as he leaned in for a kiss.

"Touch me, and the only thing you'll be doing is staring at a hospital-room ceiling," she said in a soft voice.

Orville sat down at the head of the table and motioned for everyone to take their places. Mack seated Lily while Adam pulled out a chair for his mother. Then both boys sat down across the table from each other. Orville bowed his head and said a short grace and then looked over at Lily.

"I'm so glad all you kids"—he frowned and cocked his head to one side—"you're not Brenda. You're Vera Miller's daughter. I've got this forgetting problem lately so I can't remember your name." He picked up the platter of fried chicken, took two legs for himself, and passed it on to Adam.

"Thank you for having me." *And for recognizing me.* "My name is Lily. Mama passed away, and I'm living in her old house in Comfort."

"I'm sorry to hear that. Nora and Vera were good friends. You got kids?" Orville asked.

"Two," she answered. "A boy and a girl. Braden is twelve. Holly is fourteen."

"I fell in love with Nora when I was fourteen." Orville reached over and touched his wife's arm.

Even with the declaration of love, Lily could feel the tension in the room. Adam glared at Mack, who ignored him. Nora's eyes kept shifting between the three men, as if she knew one of them would explode at any time.

"This is wonderful fried chicken," Lily said. "Sometime you'll have to share your secret with me." She felt something touch her ankle.

"I'll be glad to," Nora said.

Adam was still shooting daggers at Mack, but his foot was sure enough sliding up the inside of Lily's leg, and it kept going when it reached her knee. There was no way it could be Mack, because he was sitting right beside her. She dropped her chicken on her plate, reached under the tablecloth, and picked up his foot. His expression went from amusement to pain when she bent his big toe backward until it popped.

"Do you use rice flour instead of wheat?" Lily hung on to the toe with both hands like a bulldog with a bone, but she never took her eyes off Nora.

"No, just plain old flour. It's technique, not recipe. The grease has to be just the right temperature, and oil doesn't work as well as shortening," Nora told her.

"I'll have to try that next time I fry a chicken." Lily shoved Adam's foot away from her like it was garbage. "Please excuse me. Where's the restroom?"

"First door on the left down the hall," Nora said.

Lily's heart pounded as she turned on the water and squirted liquid soap into her hands. She washed them three times, but they still didn't feel clean, so she did them one more time. When she'd dried them and went back to the table, Mack was telling his father about the new baby goats. She took her seat and pretended that nothing had happened.

Adam glared at her, but he kept his foot away from her leg. She had a feeling that if he could do it without getting his hands dirty, he'd throw the bowl of gravy at her.

"I never thought I'd see the day that my fourteen-year-old daughter, who has always been a girlie girl, would be so tickled with a baby goat." She entered the conversation as she passed the biscuits around the table again. "If I'd let her, she'd bring it into the house and let it sleep in her bed like a puppy."

"I got to meet this child," Orville said.

"And her brother, Braden, helps me feed every evening, Dad," Mack told him. "You really should come to the farm and see the new babies while they're still young. What do you say, Mama? Can y'all come next weekend?"

"Of course we can," Orville answered for her. "We'll come on Saturday and spend the day."

Nora caught Lily's eye and raised a brow.

"That would be wonderful," Lily said. "The kids would love to get to spend the day with y'all."

"Then Saturday it is," Nora said.

"Is tomorrow Saturday?" Orville asked.

"No, but it's real soon," Mack told him.

Out of her peripheral vision, Lily caught sight of Adam's scowl. Even at his age, he didn't like not being the center of attention or not being invited to a family gathering.

"You could come and bring Brenda," Orville told Adam.

"No, thanks." Adam's tone dripped icicles. "I've got better things to do than spend a day with goats."

Orville looked like he might cry until Nora patted him on the arm. "Maybe another day Adam can get away from his busy schedule."

Orville nodded, but his expression didn't change. Lily wished she'd broken every bone in Adam's foot for treating his father like that.

They'd just finished dessert—pecan pie with ice cream—when Lily's phone rang. She excused herself and rushed to the other end of the room where she'd set her purse and coat on a rocking chair. She answered just before it went to voice mail.

"Mama, can you come get us?" Holly asked.

Lily's blood felt like ice water in her veins. "Are you hurt? Has there been an accident?"

"No, we're both fine," she said. "But Daddy is mad at us, and he . . ." She started crying.

"Gimme that phone," Braden shouted.

Things had to be catastrophic for Holly to let him have it without an argument. "We told Daddy that we didn't want to go to a fancy dinner, that we'd rather have pizza or burgers, and that we didn't want to go to the Alamo tomorrow. He got mad at us and said if we wanted to be little rednecks, then he'd let us. We're in a hotel at"—he rattled off the address—"and he said to keep the doors locked other than opening it for the pizza guy. He wasn't going to miss having dinner with Victoria or doing stuff with her tomorrow just because of ungrateful kids. He said if we changed our mind, then he'd come get us and we could join them. He ordered pizza for us, but it was cold and burned when it got here, and I had to give them a dollar of my allowance money to pay the bill because Daddy didn't leave enough money."

"We just want to come home, Mama. This place is scary," Holly said.

"Remember our safe word?" Lily asked.

"Alligator," Braden said.

"Don't open the door until you hear that word. Mack and I will be there in a few minutes. We're already on the outskirts of San Antonio. Now repeat that hotel address to me one more time."

Lily was livid when she hung up the phone.

Mack was right behind her when she turned around. "Everything all right?"

She shook her head, almost afraid to open her mouth because of the language that would spew out. "We need to go get the kids right now. I hate to do this to your folks, but . . ." Tears of anger began to flow down her cheeks.

"You go get in the truck. I'll make it right with everyone and be out there in two minutes." He was already putting on his coat as he started back to the dining area.

She'd just gotten her seat belt fastened when Mack got behind the wheel. "Are they hurt? Was there an accident?" He started the engine and made a U-turn to head back toward the highway.

"Neither, but . . ." She told him what had happened and then gave him the hotel address.

"Good God, Lily, that's a hotel in the crappiest part of town. I wonder why he didn't at least put them up in one of the nicer places on the River Walk." He slapped the steering wheel. "What in the hell is he thinking?"

Lily held her hands tightly in her lap. "I don't know, but this is the last time he gets to take them anywhere. He gave up his rights to see them at all at divorce court, so if he wants to see them again, he can come to the house."

"I'd like to get ahold of his sorry ass tonight," Mack growled. "Those kids better be all right when we get there."

"They'll be fine. We have a safe word, and they won't let anyone into the room unless they hear it. How far is it from here?" Lily asked.

"Fifteen minutes at the speed limit, but we'll make it in ten," he answered.

Her thoughts went from strangling Wyatt to worrying that something horrible would happen before she got her kids out of that motel. Every minute lasted two hours, and it had only been three seconds short of eternity when Mack made a turn into the parking lot of a 1950s-style motel.

"Room 228," Lily said.

Mack pulled his truck right up in front of the door, and she bailed out before he turned off the engine. She rapped on the door with her knuckles and yelled, "Alligator."

Holly already had her suitcase in her hand when Braden threw open the door. A cockroach ran up the side of it, and she squealed loud enough that a man in the next room cracked open his door, too.

Mack had gotten out of the truck, and he quickly snapped pictures of the room and the roaches before he brushed the bug away, then stomped on it.

"Just a bug," he told the man.

"That ain't the first one," Braden said as he wheeled his suitcase outside. "Here's my key, Mama. Daddy kept the second one."

Lily took the old-fashioned key on a fob from him and marched up to the office. The door was locked, but there was a window to the left of it with a note: *No vacancies. Leave key in slot.* She dropped the room key in what looked like a mail slot and went back to the truck. Both kids were already strapped into the back seat.

"We were scared, Mama," Braden said. "We ain't never stayed in a place like that. Holly wouldn't even sit down."

"Not after a mouse ran across the bed. Mama, I'm never going with Daddy again. If he wants to talk to us, he can come to our house or call on the phone," Holly said.

This was the child who had wanted to go live with her father and who had hated her a few weeks ago? Lily started to remind her of that, but she was so grateful to have her kids back unhurt that she couldn't say a word.

Braden agreed with his sister. "Me, too. I chased the mouse, and it went through a hole in the wall. And then I heard a lady in the next room squeal. I guess she was afraid of them, too."

"I took a few pictures just in case he takes you back to court for visitation," Mack whispered to Lily.

"Thank you," she mouthed.

"You kids want something to eat?" Mack asked. "I see a sign for a McDonald's at the next exit."

"Yes," Holly said. "Daddy got us a pizza, but we didn't eat any of it. I'm starving."

"I am, too," Braden said.

Mack made the next turn and found the McDonald's. "Want to go in or order at the window?"

"Go in, please," Holly answered. "I need to go to the ladies' room and wash my hands. I didn't touch anything after I saw the mouse, but I feel dirty."

Braden unfastened his seat belt and got out of the truck. "That place wasn't even fit for us to turn our goats loose in. I'll go wash up, too."

"Come with me, Mama?" Holly asked.

"Sure, I will," Lily answered.

When they were alone in the restroom, Holly washed up and then held her hands under the hot-air dryer. "Do you think they're clean now, Mama, or should I wash them again?"

"I imagine that they're clean enough," Lily told her.

Holly nodded. "I tried to stay brave for Braden, but I've never been so scared in my whole life. Why would Daddy do that to us? We just wanted him to know that we didn't like fancy dinners, and we didn't want to go to the Alamo again. He called us ungrateful, but we weren't even mean and hateful like we were to you when you said we were moving to Comfort." Tears began to stream down her face. "I'm sorry, Mama. I'm sorry that I smoked pot. I'm sorry that I yelled at you. I'm sorry that I almost said I hated you."

Lily gathered her daughter into her arms. "It's all right. I forgive you. I'm just glad there was a phone in the room so you could call me."

"We had to charge the call to the room." Holly hiccuped.

"That's just fine." Lily held her close and patted her on the back. "I'm glad you called. When did your dad say he'd be back to get you?"

"If we didn't call him, then he said he'd be there by eleven tomorrow morning at checkout time, and he said that we *were* going to the Alamo, or he'd pay for us to stay in that place for another day, and he'd get us in time to get us back to Comfort to take care of our precious goats," Holly answered.

"Well, you did the right thing," Lily assured her. "Now let's go eat and then get on home."

"Can I please have a bath tonight after Braden has his turn in the bathroom?" Holly asked as they went back out into the restaurant. "I know my turn is in the morning, but I can't sleep if I don't have one. I feel dirty all over, not just my hands."

"Yes, you can." Lily spotted Mack and Braden waiting behind an older couple who were having trouble deciding what they wanted to order.

When it was their turn, Braden ordered the double-meat bacon-cheeseburger meal deal and a chocolate shake. Holly just nodded and said, "The same."

"I'll have a chocolate malt," Mack said, and then nodded toward Lily.

"A vanilla ice cream in a cup, please," she said.

Lily took her credit card from her purse, but Mack had already laid money on the counter. "It's on me tonight," he said.

"Thank you. Seems like I keep telling you that all the time," she told him.

"I like doing things for you and the kids." He grinned. "Let's go find a booth and get these starving kids fed."

The kids rushed ahead to claim the bigger round booth in the corner, but they weren't arguing, which meant they still weren't over the fear.

"Don't let the smile fool you," Mack said out of the corner of his mouth. "I'm trying to keep my cool, but it's not easy."

"I'll be fuming for a week," Lily said. "Should I call him or wait and let him go crazy about where they might have gone?"

"That's your decision. I think the man is already insane for treating those kids like that, but he deserves to know what happened to them. It might wake him up," Mack said.

~

When they got home, Holly went straight to the bathroom even though she was supposed to wait for her brother to have the first turn. Braden wanted to go check on the goats, so Mack got a flashlight and took him to the barn. Lily paced the living room floor—around the sofa several times, to the window looking out over the big front yard, and back to circle the sofa again.

After half an hour, Holly yelled down the stairs. "Mama, will you come up here, please?"

Lily took the steps two at a time and found Holly sitting on the side of her bed. Her white bathrobe was belted tightly around her waist, and a towel turban was wrapped around her head.

"Are you okay?" Lily asked.

"No, I'm not, but I'm not scared anymore," Holly said. "Now I'm pissed—I mean, really angry. How could Daddy do that to us? You moved us here, but you never left us alone in a place like that. And you've never put anyone before us, like he does Victoria." She rolled her blue eyes toward the ceiling. "I wish Mack was my daddy. He came and rescued us and fed us and brought us home. And now he's out there in the goat pens with Braden, making him feel comfortable and not afraid."

"Your father was mad because you kids don't like his wife." Lily sat down on the edge of the bed beside Holly. "I'm sure that he was thinking that he'd go back to the motel by your bedtime"—she checked her watch—"which is in about an hour. He thought you'd be all repentant and ready to do what he wanted you to do tomorrow."

"It don't work that way," Holly said. "When we're scared, we call you and now Mack. Y'all don't throw us in a garbage can like that motel like we're trash. I felt so sorry for Braden. He was really scared."

Lily moved over and put her arm around her daughter. "I'm so sorry that this happened."

Holly snuggled closer to Lily. "Daddy always takes us to a fancy place with no bugs or mice, and he's never driven off and left us all alone like he did tonight. If I have a nightmare, can I come sleep with you?"

"Of course you can." Lily hugged her even tighter. "Right now, I'm going to take a quick bath before Braden gets back from the goat pens. But I'll be right across the hall, and honey, nothing is going to hurt you. He's never taking you anywhere ever again."

Holly tucked her chin against her chest. "Promise, Mama? He's going to be really mad."

"I promise, and he can get glad in the same britches he got mad in." Lily managed a weak laugh.

Lily went to the bathroom, ran another tubful of water, and eased down into it. She knew exactly how her daughter felt. Even though Adam had had a sock on his foot when he ran it up her leg and she'd been wearing skinny jeans, her leg felt violated as much as her hands had before she washed them. She scrubbed herself clean, got out, and put on a clean pair of pajama pants and a T-shirt.

Holly had gotten under the covers, and her eyes were closed. Braden stormed up the stairs, and Holly roused for a second, saw that her mother was standing right there, and went right back to sleep.

"Shhhh." Lily put a finger over her lips. "Your sister is already asleep."

Braden made a production of tiptoeing to his room and crooking his index finger for his mother to come over there. He'd put up his Harry Potter posters since the last time she'd peeked into his room, and now it looked more like his old room in Austin. He patted the bed, and she sat down beside him.

"Holly was real scared, Mama, and I mean *for real* scared," he whispered. "She was afraid that we wouldn't be able to use the hotel phone to call you. It was so old and had a cord like the one in the kitchen. She read all the directions about how to make a call and punched the right button when they asked for permission to charge it to the room. I guess Daddy told those people to let us do that so we could call him." Braden hesitated and went on. "I told her to call Daddy—that I'd go to the stupid old dinner with him and Victoria and to the Alamo. I didn't want to, but I didn't like seeing her that scared. It's all right with me if you give her cell back to her before summer. I don't care if you keep mine, but if we have to go with him again, she needs her phone."

"You won't ever be going with him again." Lily gave him a hug. "Now go take your bath and read for a little while. If your light is still on when I go to bed, I'll turn it out."

"Thanks, Mama," Braden said. "I ain't never been so glad to see anyone as I was you and Mack."

"I've never been so glad to find my two kids safe." Lily kissed him on the forehead and left the room. If there was ever a night when she really needed a shot of whiskey, this was it. She tucked her phone into her pocket and headed toward the kitchen.

Mack was already there with a beer in one hand and a shot glass in the other. His broad shoulders and biceps stretched the fabric of a snowy-white T-shirt. Red-and-black flannel pajama pants hung low on his narrow hips, and he was barefoot. What Holly said about wishing he was her daddy came back to her mind. He'd make a wonderful father because he always put other folks before himself.

"You read my mind," she said as she reached for the glass and Mack poured for her. "This has been a double-shot night."

"Or a triple," Mack suggested. "I got to admit, that terrified the hell out of me. I kept thinking what if someone kidnapped the kids? What if they weren't there when we arrived? Did you call Wyatt?"

Lily threw back the first shot. The heat from it traveled from her throat all the way to her stomach, warming her all the way—maybe not in the same way as much as seeing Mack in that shirt and pants did— but it calmed her frayed nerves. She held out the glass, and he filled it again. Then he took her by the hand and led her to the living room.

Lily sipped on the whiskey that time, enjoying the sweet, smoky flavor. Mack sat down on the sofa, pulled her down beside him, and hugged her to his side. Having him simply hold her meant more to her than words could ever describe.

She'd snuggled up even closer to him when her phone rang. She took it out of her hip pocket, saw that it was from Wyatt, and let it go to voice mail.

"You're not going to give him a piece of your mind?" Mack asked.

"Not until I'm ready," she answered.

The phone rang again, and she ignored it again. Barely a minute passed before it rang a third time. On the fourth ring she picked up.

"Hello, Wyatt." She kept her voice as calm as possible.

"Lily, have the kids called you?" His voice sounded frantic.

"They don't have phones until summer. You'd have to let them use yours to call. So I suppose you're not letting them use yours?" she answered.

He ended the call without another word.

"I see you're going to let him go a little crazy," Mack said.

"Yep, I am," she answered. "And that's the least of what I'd like to do to him after this stunt."

"Mama!" Braden called out from the foyer in a loud whisper. "I'm going to get some milk and a banana."

She moved to the other end of the sofa. "Thanks for letting me know."

He stuck his head in the door and grinned. "I tried to be quiet so I wouldn't wake Holly up. I'm still hungry."

Lily's phone rang again, and she ignored it. Only a minute went by before another call rang. She waited until the fifth ring this time. Let him stew.

"Wyatt, for God's sake, why are you calling me again?" she asked.

"The kids are gone," he said. "Victoria says we need to call the police, but I think they may be trying to get back to you."

"What do you mean? Gone?" Lily asked. "Why would they be gone? Aren't you in the room right next to them? How could they leave without you even knowing it?"

"I'm going to keep Braden company while you take care of this," Mack whispered.

"I'm at the hotel where they were, and they're not here!" Wyatt yelled frantically.

"What do you mean the hotel where *they* were? Didn't you book rooms for them in the same one with you? God Almighty! *What have you done, Wyatt?*" She raised her voice.

"I was teaching them a lesson." His tone turned cold and harsh. "I didn't intend to leave them here all night, just until bedtime to show them how good they have it when they're with me."

"You sorry son of a bitch!" She'd finally had enough. "They were terrified out of their minds! They called me, so Mack and I went and got them. We had to kick the roaches and rats out of the way to get to them, but they're safe now." She stopped for a breath. "And just so you know, we left the cold, burned pizza there for the mice. We got them burgers on the way home."

"Don't you get all self-righteous with me." His voice got louder and louder. "You took them to Comfort when they misbehaved. I wasn't doing anything worse than that."

"I didn't leave them alone in a cheap motel, and I *damn* sure didn't leave them to scrounge money for a nasty pizza, or tell them I wouldn't be back to get them until checkout time the next day!" Her voice sounded like an owl's screech in her own ears. She hoped that it pierced through *his* ears and into his brain like a knife.

"Tell them we'll try again next weekend," he said. "Victoria's business in San Antonio won't be over for two more weeks."

"Over my dead body," Lily said. "When the kids decide they want to see you again, it will be supervised visits right here at our convenience."

"I can take you back to court for visitation or maybe even custody," he threatened.

"Go ahead," she told him. "Both kids are old enough now to tell the judge where they want to live. And we do have pictures of the vermin in the room where you left them. I imagine that you'll be spending your money for nothing."

A long silence on the other end made her hold the phone out. That's when she found out that he'd ended the call, but Lily wasn't finished. She called him right back.

"Hello, Lily," Victoria answered in a cool, calm voice.

"Give the phone to Wyatt," Lily demanded.

"What you did is inexcusable," Victoria said. "But it has shown us that you're a bitch. You should have called us and told us you were taking the children."

"Is that the pot calling the kettle black? Why should I call you? You let him leave them in that dangerous place," Lily said.

"Honey, it was my idea." Victoria chuckled. "Those ungrateful little snots needed a lesson in manners. You damn sure don't teach them much out there in the boonies."

"I'll be calling my lawyer tomorrow to file a motion for supervised visits only," Lily threatened.

"Don't bother," Victoria said. "Save what few pennies you have. If I wanted those kids, I'd have them in less time than it takes me to snap my fingers, but I don't want them and never will. Wyatt knew what he was giving up when he married me, so you won't be hearing from him again."

Another long silence. When Lily looked at her phone, the call had ended, again. Red-hot, searing anger filled her heart and soul. She wished she had Victoria by the throat, squeezing until the woman turned blue. Wyatt should simply be shot for letting her control him. She threw a hand over her eyes, but the throbbing pain in her head wouldn't stop. If she didn't get ahold of herself, she'd stroke right out. Then Wyatt would get immediate custody of her children. She took several deep breaths and let them out slowly until she stopped seeing red spots, and then she shut her eyes and imagined that she was somewhere on top of a mountain. Snow covered the ground, and there was Mack coming toward her.

"You all right?" Mack sat down beside her. "Braden is back in bed, but your face is red as fire."

"Victoria says that Wyatt will never call again. I feel bad for the kids," she whispered.

"It will all work out." Mack laid a hand on her shoulder.

"I hope so," Lily said. "Thank you for everything tonight, Mack."

"Hey, we're a family." He grinned.

"I guess we are." She smiled back at him.

Chapter Seventeen

Lily woke on Saturday morning to find Holly snuggled up to her right side and Braden on her left. What she thought was her alarm clock making the noise on the nightstand turned out to be her phone. She reached over Holly and answered with a sleepy "Hello."

"This is Sally, and I've got this big favor to ask. Can you possibly keep the shop until right after lunch? There's a huge estate sale at the north edge of San Antonio, and I would love to go," she said.

"Of course." Lily yawned. "All right if I open at nine?"

"That's great," Sally answered. "I'll be back as soon as I can, and thanks. You're the best."

"What?" Holly sat up and rubbed her eyes.

"I've got to go to work this morning. Want to go with me?" Lily asked.

"Yes!" Holly bounded out of bed. "I'll get dressed and put on my makeup."

Braden got out of the bed and disappeared out into the hallway. Lily followed him, expecting him to go to the bathroom, but instead he went to his room, got back into bed, and pulled the covers up to his chin. She caught a whiff of bacon and coffee all mixed together as she went downstairs. She found Mack sitting at the table with a mug of coffee and the last few bites of waffles in front of him.

"Good mornin'," he said. "I thought y'all were going to sleep in this morning. Can I make you some waffles?"

"Just coffee." She poured a cup. "Sally needs me at the shop. Holly wants to go with me."

"I'm going to Kerrville this morning to look at a couple of goats," Mack said. "Reckon Braden would want to go? I'm not leaving for a couple of hours."

"I'm sure he would." Lily sipped her coffee. "They were both in bed with me this morning when I woke up. Do you think they'll get over last night's trauma anytime soon?"

"Sure, they will," he said. "They'll be back in their routine on Monday, and pretty soon, it'll just become a good story to tell."

"I hope so." She toyed with her mug. "I can't begin to thank you enough for all you've done for us, Mack."

"Right back atcha." He grinned.

"Do I smell waffles?" Braden rubbed his eyes as he came into the room.

"You sure do," Mack answered. "How many can you eat?"

"A bunch. I'll make them." Braden went to the counter, poured the right amount of batter into the waffle iron, and closed the lid. He nibbled on a piece of bacon while he waited for it to cook. "Holly says she's going with you to work, Mama. I don't have to go, do I?"

"You have a choice," Lily told him. "You can go to the shop, or go with Mack to look at goats to buy."

"Mack!" he said without hesitation. "I just didn't want to be here all by myself. What if Daddy calls or comes? I don't want to see him right now."

"I talked to him and Victoria both last night. You don't have anything to worry about, son. It will be a while before we hear from

214

him. I'd better go get dressed." Lily picked up her mug, refilled it, and carried it with her.

When she got to the top of the stairs, she heard her phone ringing. She couldn't rush with a full cup of coffee in her hands, so she didn't pick it up until the fourth ring. Expecting it to be Sally with instructions about the shop, she didn't even check the caller ID, but answered, "Hello."

"I've called four times in the last twenty minutes," Wyatt growled. "Why didn't you answer your phone?"

"What do you want?" she asked.

"To talk to you about last night," Wyatt said. "Why is it that *you* can discipline the kids, but I can't?"

"When I correct them, my methods are within reason. What you did last night wasn't, and I'm not discussing this with you anymore until you apologize to them for what you did," she told him.

"Are you going to apologize to them for taking them to Comfort?" His tone was iceberg cold.

"This has been an amazing move. They like their school, and they love living here in this wonderful, big roach-free house, so the answer is no. I did what I did out of love. You did what you did out of anger." Little red dots of rage swam in front of Lily's eyes again, so she sat down on the edge of the bed and made herself breathe in and out several times. If Wyatt had been right there in front of her, she would have gladly used the bedside lamp cord to strangle him. How dare he compare her moving to Comfort and getting the kids out of an unhealthy environment to the stunt he'd pulled! "Besides, Victoria called last night to tell me that you won't ever be seeing them again. I guess she's got your balls in a vise, doesn't she?"

"It will be a cold day in hell before I apologize," he said. "And Victoria does not control me."

"I'm not arguing with you anymore. Just remember, when you're old and alone, money makes a really poor companion. Goodbye, Wyatt." She ended the call.

Her hands shook as she got out a fresh pair of jeans and a bright-red sweater. Until yesterday, she had never talked to Wyatt like that, not even when he told her he was leaving her and moving in with another woman. She had always given him his way on everything and never questioned him. Looking back, she could see that Wyatt had been the problem in their marriage from day one, with his control issues. Well, those days were over, and he could just accept it.

That morning, it felt damn good to finally speak her mind, and she wished that she'd stood up for herself sooner.

"I'm ready, Mama," Holly said from the doorway into Lily's bedroom.

"Then go on downstairs and have some waffles before we leave," Lily told her.

"Is there yogurt and strawberries?" she asked.

"There's strawberry yogurt." Lily removed her nightshirt and pulled the sweater down over her head. Wyatt hated for her to wear red. He said that black or dark blue looked classy, but red made her look like a hooker. Come to think of it, how did *he* know about that motel, anyway?

"Good enough," Holly said, and was gone.

Lily had thought her child was strange when she smeared yogurt over her waffles instead of butter and syrup. She figured it was a phase that Holly would outgrow, but she hadn't, and the strange thing was that when Lily tried it, she liked it as well as Holly did.

Her phone rang again, and this time she checked the caller ID. With a long sigh, she answered it. "What do you want now, Wyatt?"

"Victoria and I are on shaky ground," he said. "I love her and want to make this marriage work, so for a little while I won't be calling or asking for the kids."

"Well, honey," she said with a saccharine voice, "you're her fourth husband, and each one has gotten younger. Maybe she's got her eye on someone else already. After all, when she enters a room with a boy toy at her side, it makes her feel the same age. When you reclaim your balls, give the kids a call. I expect they'll be grown by then, so it'll be their decision whether to let you back into their lives. Don't call me again." She ended the call and dropped the phone in her purse.

"And that is what you call real closure," she said out loud as she finished getting dressed for work.

~

Mack woke on Sunday morning to the rattle of pots and pans in the kitchen. The sun had just begun to peek over the horizon, throwing a little light into his bedroom. He laced his hands behind his head and thought about where his life had been, where it was now, and where it was going. He liked the picture that had developed in his head, and sent up a little prayer that the third time was really the charm.

He got out of bed, dressed in his old jeans and a faded shirt, and padded across the foyer and into the kitchen in his bare feet. "Good morning. You look nice."

"Thank you." She smiled shyly.

Damn that Wyatt! The expression on her face said that she sure didn't get any compliments like that very often, and Lily was the kind of woman who deserved them every day—hell, every hour wouldn't be too often.

She poured barbecue sauce over a chicken that she'd cut up and put into a deep cast-iron pan. He opened the oven door for her. "I love barbecued chicken."

She slid the pan in beside a pan of biscuits that were baking. "It makes for a good Sunday dinner. Just be the three of us since Holly is going to Granny Hayes's again."

Mack poured himself a cup of coffee, sat down at the table, and rubbed his eyes. "Guess I'm going to have to wear my glasses for a few days. Damned allergies are already starting, and nothing is pollinating or blooming yet. At least I'm not allergic to goats, so that's a blessing." He wanted to slap himself—he should be complimenting her again, not talking about his stupid allergies.

"I rather like a fellow in glasses who makes waffles on Sunday morning and tells me I'm pretty when I look like hammered owl shit."

He chuckled. "Been years since I heard that old saying, but you are pretty."

"Mornin'," Braden grumbled as he sat down at the table.

Holly slid into a chair beside him. "Can we have sausage gravy and biscuits for breakfast?"

"Already have the biscuits in the oven, and the sausage is browned," Lily replied. "I was just waiting on you two sleepyheads to get down here before I made the gravy."

"I have a request." Mack was more than a little nervous, but he really wanted the kids to know that he was there for them.

"If you're going to ask for scrambled eggs, too, then I'll take some," Braden said.

"No, it's a little more serious than that," Mack told him. "I want you kids always, always to do exactly what you did Friday night when you feel uneasy about anything. Call me or your mother, or both of us, and if you have to use a phone and call collect, do that."

"What's collect?" Braden asked.

"It's when, if you don't have a cell phone, and all you can get to is a landline, that you call the operator by pushing zero and tell her that you want to make a collect call. It means that we'll pay for the call on our end and is easy for you," Mack explained.

"I promise I'll do it," Holly said.

"You don't have to worry about me." Braden got out the milk. "I don't never want to be in a scary place like that again. You can bet I'll call you for sure."

So this is what being a real father would feel like.

Chapter Eighteen

*L*ily could hardly believe that more than a whole week had passed since the incident with Wyatt leaving the kids at the motel. She still got mad when she thought about it, but that morning when they went to Sunday school and church, she tried her best to get rid of all that negativity and enjoy the beautiful sunshine.

As usual, Sally met Lily in the sanctuary. "Does that invitation to eat dinner at your house still stand?"

"Of course," Lily said. "But dinner isn't at the house today. We're going to the pizza place. Want to join us?"

"Sure." Sally nodded.

When Sunday school and church services had ended and the benediction had been given, Holly hurried to the back pew to talk to Granny Hayes. Braden took off toward the center aisle to talk to Isaac, leaving Lily and Mack alone. She was putting the hymnals back in the right spots when she giggled.

"What's so funny?" Mack asked.

"I was just thinking that I'm glad Holly wore pants because she'll be riding double with Granny Hayes," she said.

Mack shook his head. "Nope, she won't. Granny Hayes is one step ahead of you, sweetheart. She brought her wagon to church today. Didn't you notice it parked out at the edge of the lot? She likes to put it there so her mule can eat the grass on the other side of the driveway while he waits on her."

"I was so busy wondering why the kids weren't arguing this morning that I didn't pay a lot of attention." Lily slipped her hand into his. "But riding on a buckboard will be an experience for Holly."

"Yep, it will." Mack gently squeezed her hand.

"Mama! Mama!" Braden and Isaac ran up in front of her. "Can I go home with Isaac? His mama says it's all right with her if you don't care."

"We've got to come back to town at three to visit my grandma in the nursing home, so we can bring him home then," Isaac said.

"Pleeeease." Braden looked up at her with his big brown puppy-dog eyes.

"It's fine with me, but be home on time. You've still got math homework to do," Lily told him.

"And I've got to help with the goats," Braden said. "Thanks, Mama." He and Isaac disappeared into the crowd.

"Looks like it's me and you for Sunday dinner." Mack grinned.

"Sally is joining us. Hope you don't mind," she said.

"Not a bit," Mack replied.

Lily reached out to shake Drew's hand as they passed by him. "Want to join us at the pizza place for dinner?"

"Thanks, but I wouldn't dare. The sweet wife has made my favorite meal, and the boys are all home. Maybe another time," Drew said, and then lowered his voice. "I was sad that Holly hasn't been joining us for youth group."

"She'll be back, I'm sure," Lily told him.

"That's good to hear," Drew said.

"We'll have to make plans for y'all to come to the house some evening for supper," Lily said.

"Love to." Drew dropped her hand and extended it to the man right behind Lily.

They were in the truck and headed to the pizza place when Mack took her hand in his. "Why did you invite Drew to join us for dinner?"

"I want to get to know his wife better, and he's your friend, and it seemed like the thing to do," she answered. "Why are you asking?"

"You're not worried about us being alone?" He countered with another question.

"No, Mack, I am most certainly not." She chuckled. "But remember, Sally is joining us, too. And to be truthful, I'm actually looking forward to a dinner with no bickering kids and some adult conversation that doesn't revolve around who ate more slices of pizza."

He made a right turn into the restaurant's parking lot. He snagged a good parking spot, and Sally pulled in right beside him. "Do you ever wonder if Sally will ever remarry or have children?"

"Whatever brought that question out of the blue skies?" Lily asked.

"I guess I'm wondering about you and Sally both," he answered.

Lily shuddered at the idea of a baby at her age.

"I don't know about Sally, but I really wouldn't want to start over. Do the math—if I had another child now, Holly would be almost thirty when that child was just starting high school. What about you?"

"I wouldn't mind a ready-made family." He shrugged.

"Wouldn't your folks want grandkids of their own?" she asked.

"Dad wouldn't know if they were his biologically or not, and Mama gave up on that idea years ago. Adam can't have children, and I . . ." He hesitated. "You know my story. Until you came along, I didn't trust women anymore."

"You've only been around me and the kids a short while," she said.

"But it's been a good time," he declared.

Sally tapped on the truck window and motioned for her to lower the window. "We better get in there while there's still a table."

Lily nodded in agreement. "You're right. It'll fill up quick now that church is over."

This time Sally beat Mack to the punch when the lady at the counter told them the cost for three of them to eat at the buffet that day. "My treat," she said, "since I elbowed my way in on what could have been y'all's private dinner."

"The more the merrier," Mack said, "but thank you."

"Yes, ma'am," Lily said. "Thank you. Next time maybe I'll even have something cooked at home."

"That's why I'm bein' nice." Sally picked up a bowl and filled it with salad from the buffet.

Once they'd sat down in a booth, Sally said, "Hey, Ruth-Ann came by yesterday, mainly just to snoop like always, but—oh, hey!"—she waved and motioned—"y'all don't mind if Teena joins us, do you?"

"Not a bit," Mack said. "We've got an extra chair."

"Anyway, the newest gossip is that you're pregnant, Lily, and that I'm getting married this summer to a guy I met on the internet," Sally said.

"Well, damn!" Mack grinned from ear to ear. "I guess you'll have to make an honest man of me. When does Ruth-Ann say we're getting married?"

"She's not sure, but she's positive that it could ruin your career as a teacher, Mack, and she just wondered"—Sally put air quotes around that last word—"if you and I might be going to raise our tagalong kids together."

Lily almost choked on a sip of her sweet tea. "Are you kiddin' me?"

"Not one bit," Sally giggled. "But now it's time to 'fess up. How in the hell did you and Mack get a baby started so fast? Me and my imaginary boyfriend, according to Ruth-Ann, have been seeing each other since Thanksgiving, but good Lord, you and Mack have only been living together for weeks."

"I heard that, too." Teena sat down with them. "I'm jealous that y'all get to be pregnant together, and I didn't get invited to join y'all."

Mack chuckled. "Don't you just love small-town gossip?"

"Hey, next week, it will all change," Teena said. "Since we're having dinner together, I'd bet that the newest will be that you're the father of both their babies, and having an affair with me, too."

"I'd better take vitamins to keep up with all that," Mack told them.

Lily felt a slow heat moving from her neck to her face. Sure, they were joking, but after what she and Mack had been discussing in the truck, she couldn't help but wonder what a child of Mack's would look like.

~

Lily had lived in this same house her whole life, but today, the gray stone place looked warmer and more inviting when she walked up on the porch with Mack by her side. A rush of warm air met them when Mack opened the door for her. He helped her with her coat and followed her to the kitchen. He put on a pot of coffee, and she got down a couple of mugs.

Comparing two men was like comparing apples and oranges, or maybe pineapples and pecans, but she couldn't help doing it. Wyatt had never helped her do one thing in the kitchen throughout their marriage. She worked as many hours as he had, but since she had done her job from home, that hadn't mattered to him. He'd always been too busy building his career to have much interaction with the kids even before the divorce.

She wondered what would become of him if Victoria did find a younger man. He'd given up his job at the firm, where he'd worked so hard to climb the corporate ladder, and had gone to work for Victoria a few months after they were married. If he got kicked out of the love nest now, he'd basically have to start all over on the bottom rung. *Good.*

"Penny for your thoughts," Mack said.

"I was just thinking about how nice it is to have help in the kitchen. I appreciate you having the coffee made and sometimes even breakfast when I come downstairs." That was the truth, even if it wasn't the whole truth and nothing but the truth.

"Mama used to tell me that you get to know someone best when you work beside them, and I love any time we can spend together." He took down two plates and got the cutlery from a drawer. "When I first moved in here, it seemed strange to use your mother's dishes and pots and pans, but after I'd settled in, it made me feel like family."

"What did you do with what you had?" she asked.

"I'd been living in a little trailer behind Mama and Daddy's place north of town. It was furnished, and I pretty much used paper plates when I didn't eat with the folks. When they sold the place, the new owners wanted the trailer for a grandfather who was going to live with them. This place was a godsend what with everything already here. I just moved your folks' bedroom stuff up to the spare room and bought myself new furniture," he said.

"Did you unload that old secretary before you moved it?" she asked.

"Nope," he answered. "I collected up four of my FFA boys, and they helped me."

Lily decided right then that she wasn't bringing a single bit of her furniture from Austin. She'd sell it all and put the money in the velvet bag for a vacation next summer. The past was going to be left in the past. Her future was in Comfort in her old two-story stone home, and hopefully Holly's jury would come in with a positive verdict.

～

After dinner she and Mack cuddled together in front of the television to watch episodes of *Justified*. Her head was on his shoulder, and being there with him on a buttery-soft leather sofa that her parents had bought twenty years ago felt right. Having his arm around her as they talked was comfortable and yet exciting at the same time.

Her thoughts wandered back to the journal, to the last entry that Jenny had written, about her father leaving the family for another woman. Someday, like Lily had told him, Wyatt was going to wake up and realize what he had given up for Victoria. Maybe it would take until he never met his grandchildren, but he'd realize it.

She snuggled down closer to Mack and fell asleep with his arm around her.

"Mack! Guess what?" Braden came into the house yelling loud enough to wake the dead over in the next county.

"What?" Lily opened her eyes but didn't move away from Mack.

"We're in here, and what happened? This time he said, 'Mack,' not 'Mama.'" Mack whispered the last part.

Lily glanced over at the grandfather clock just as it chimed three times. Braden rushed into the room. "It's snowing! Look!" He bent forward. "It's still in my hair."

Mack pointed toward the window. "Well, would you look at that? Maybe we'll have enough to make a snowman tomorrow after school."

Braden threw up a hand to high-five with Mack, and then with his mother. "We've never got to build a snowman before. Where's Holly? I got to tell her."

Mack stood up and stretched. "It's time to go get her. Want to go with me?"

"I think I'll stay in where it's warm." Lily got to her feet.

"I'll go with you," Braden said. "Bet I can beat you to the truck."

"You just want to go outside and catch snowflakes on your tongue," Mack chuckled.

"Yep, I do, but you and Mama are old, so y'all can't run as fast as me, and besides, you got to get your coat and boots on." Braden was off like a flash of lightning.

The front door slammed, and then Lily and Mack watched him through the window as he ran around with his head thrown back and his mouth open to catch snowflakes on his tongue.

Mack took a couple of steps to the side. "I'll bring you a pretty snowflake when we get back."

"It'll melt before you can get here." She sank down on the sofa and wondered what it would be like to spend some time in bed with him.

"Like that's going to happen anytime soon with two kids in the house," she whispered to herself.

They were gone all afternoon, the pesky voice in her head replied.

"Today was too soon, anyway." She popped up off the sofa and went up to her bedroom. She had about half an hour before Mack would be back with the kids, so she got out the journal and reread the first several pages.

She left the book on the bed and went to the window. The skies were completely gray, and the snow was coming down harder than it had been when Braden came into the house. Mack pulled up into his normal parking spot in front of the house, and the kids jumped out. Small blades of grass peeked out from under the smooth white cover, but in only a few minutes, it had been stomped through. Or else Braden and Holly had rolled up snowballs to throw at each other.

She heard the front door hinges squeak as the door opened, so she made her way downstairs. She met Mack taking off his coat in the foyer.

"Did you bring me a snowflake?" she teased.

He held out a perfectly round snowball. "I brought you a million because you deserve more than one."

She took the snowball from him. "It's beautiful. Thank you. I'm going to put it in the freezer and keep it."

"For real?"

"For absolute real," she said. "This could be the most romantic present anyone's ever given me."

"Aww, shucks, ma'am"—Mack pretended to kick at imaginary dirt—"that's just a snowball. I can do better."

"We'll see about that," she told him as she took the snowball to the kitchen, put it in a plastic bag, and stuck it in the freezer. "Roses and candlelight dinners can't compare to a million perfect snowflakes."

He followed her and sat down at the table. "I'm glad that you like it."

"Mama, I'm freezing." Holly rushed into the kitchen. "Will you please, please make us some hot chocolate, and then can we read more in the journal?"

"Sure thing." Lily got out a pan.

"So tell me more about this journal. I know you and Holly have been reading it for a school project?" Mack opened the refrigerator and handed her the milk, then brought out the sugar bin and cocoa from the pantry.

"I'll show it to you while they have their chocolate," Lily said.

She'd just poured up two mugs of hot chocolate when Braden came through the back door. "Now that's good timin'," he said as he removed his coat and hat.

"Y'all help yourselves to more if you want it," Lily said. "I made extra. Mack and I are going upstairs to see the journal."

"What's that?" Braden asked.

"I'll explain to him," Holly offered.

Lily told Mack about it as she climbed the stairs with him right behind her. "I found it in the secretary. It's all handwritten and the first pages are really brittle. It probably belongs in a museum somewhere. At first I couldn't understand why Mama had the thing. I sure didn't recognize the first person who wrote in it—name of Ophelia Smith. She started writing in it during the Civil War." She took it out and laid it on the bed.

"Good grief, Lily!" He stepped back and stared at the leather-bound book. "That thing really should be in a museum."

"Maybe, but Holly should have it next, so it'll kind of be up to her what to do with it when I'm gone." She carefully closed the journal.

"That's really impressive that you've got something like that," Mack said.

"Mama, are you ready to read yet?" Holly yelled from the foyer.

"Yes, I am," Lily hollered, and then looked at Mack. "We're reading an entry at a time for her history paper. Her assignment is to write about someone in her family."

"Well, it's amazing," Mack said. "I should go now and let y'all get on with the lesson. We wouldn't want our daughter to get bad grades on a history assignment."

It wasn't until he'd passed Holly on the stairs that she realized he'd said *our* daughter, not *your* daughter. Somehow, it sounded kind of nice.

Holly brought her notebooks and spread them out on the bed like she always did, and then looked up at her mother. Lily sat down and opened the journal.

"Look, Mama, the new page isn't as yellow as the ones Ophelia wrote on," Holly noticed.

"Darlin' girl, more than half a century has passed since we first started reading," Lily told her.

Just like that, she thought, *in a twinkling of an eye,* or rather in the time in Comfort, history had been changed. Lily's breath caught in her chest when she saw that a new person had started writing.

"Rachel O'Riley Callahan, August 1920," Lily said.

"But I wanted to hear more about Jenny," Holly moaned.

"Evidently, it's been passed down," Lily said, and then went on:

Mama gave me this journal last week. I've chosen to begin writing in it today since women are now allowed to vote in all the states. In Oklahoma we have had that right for almost two years. I was the first one in line to vote when the law was passed here in our state. I'm glad that I helped fight for the right. Hopefully, it will teach my daughter to stand up for herself and be independent. I'm thirty-three years old and have a wonderful, understanding husband, who has never held me back. We've been married thirteen years, and my daughter went with me on the first day I could vote. I hope she remembers that day forever. Mama still lives on the original homestead, two miles down the road from me, and loves her grandchildren. She misses Granny Matilda, but then we all do. We buried her here in Dodsworth, and we visit her grave often. Mama says it makes her feel closer to Granny Matilda. I hate to think of the day that I lose my mother. She's been a rock to me my whole life, and always encouraged me to take up for myself and never let anyone run over me.

Tears rolled down Holly's cheeks. "I didn't want Matilda to die."

Lily wrapped her up in her arms. "Don't think of it like that. Be grateful that you got to read a little bit about her, and maybe learn that you had a strong woman in your past."

"But, Mama, it's like I know these women for real, not just on the page." Holly wiped the tears away with her sweater sleeve.

"And someday you'll add your pages to the journal, and some young lady will get to know you the same way," Lily assured her.

"I hope so," Holly said. "I want to write about my first days here in Comfort, and tell about my goat and my friend Faith and all kinds of things."

Lily nodded in agreement, and wondered what she'd write on her first pages when she picked up the pen.

Chapter Nineteen

ack's little slip about "our daughter" came back to Lily's mind on Monday as she drove to work. She parked her car behind the shop, opened the back door, and turned up the thermometer when she went inside. Turning on lights as she made her way into the front room, she still couldn't stop thinking about what he'd said. She had seldom even said "our children" when she was talking to Wyatt about Holly and Braden.

She unlocked the front door and flipped the sign over to show that they were open for business. Then she opened the small safe, put enough money in the cash register to start the day, and closed the drawer. The minute she'd stashed her purse and coat, the bell above the door jingled, and Polly came in wearing a big smile and carrying a box from the pastry shop down the street.

"I brought fried pies today to celebrate," Polly said.

"Celebrate what?" Sally came in through the back door and tossed her coat and purse on a chair.

Polly opened the box and took out a half-moon-shaped fried pie. "That Lily and Mack are dating. I *guess* that's what you kids still call it. I've got apricot and cherry. Help yourselves. And"—she pulled a half gallon of milk from her purse—"I brought this to go with the pies. Now tell me all about it."

"Why didn't you call me?" Sally asked Lily. "I'm your best friend. I should have known about this before the whole town did."

"Because it's a rumor." Lily got three disposable cups from under the counter and poured milk for all of them. "But whoever started it has my thanks. I love fried pies. Mama used to make apricot fried pies for us in the summer when she didn't want to heat up the house with an oven."

"Well, crap!" Sally sighed. "You haven't dated since your divorce. I wanted it to be real, and besides, it's Valentine's Day, so we need something romantic to talk about."

"Well, it damn sure ain't goin' to ever happen with two kids underfoot all the time," Polly laughed. "Want me to babysit Holly and Braden some evening? I'd be glad to take them for hot dogs and to a movie so y'all can have some free time to check out that bedroom stuff, and maybe even start dating."

"Polly!" Lily exclaimed.

"Just makin' an offer," Polly giggled.

"If I get a boyfriend who has two kids, do I get the same offer?" Sally asked.

"Honey, if you find a man, I'll take the kids for the whole weekend," Polly answered. "You need to get over that sumbitch you married and move on."

"I'm givin' it my best shot." Sally picked up one of the pies and bit the end off. "I have to find someone who doesn't mind a woman who isn't a skinny trophy girl."

"He's out there," Polly said. "Guess you just got to be patient."

"Hey," Teena called out from the back room, "what's going on in here?"

"We're having a party," Polly yelled. "Fried pies and milk. We'll have cake and champagne at the wedding."

"What wedding?" Teena raised her dark eyebrows. "And who's getting married?"

"Nobody," Lily said quickly. "At least not for a long time, if even then. Lord, we aren't even dating. It's just a bunch of gossip. Don't scare him off by mentioning wedding cake."

"Our daughter" popped back into her mind. "Teena, what's going on in your world?" Lily asked. "We haven't talked in a few days."

"Ryder went back to the university, but he's moving in with Macy this summer. He hates school and really does want to go into the business with me, so I'm going to let him have a chance at it. Macy is going to finish up the first stage of her nursing school, get a job as an LPN and study at night for her RN degree, and they'll be living in her little apartment," Teena said. "Life goes on, and we move on, even after heartbreaks. We've all proven that more than once. I'm just so grateful that y'all have been here with me throughout this whole thing. Support means so much. Sometimes I feel like we're sisters and not just friends."

"Honey, y'all three are sisters of the heart," Polly said, "like me and Vera used to be. I'm like your meddling old aunt—glad for every minute I get to spend with you kids." She sighed. "I also heard that there was some kind of fiasco a while back with Holly and Braden. I've heard all the rumors, but I'm behind on the real stuff since I ain't been to see y'all in a few weeks."

"Well, I heard that Mack took you to meet his parents," Teena said. "Sounds pretty serious to me."

Sally held up her hand. "You better let me tell the story about the kids. Lily's blood pressure still goes out the roof when she talks about it."

"I'll tell it." Lily told Teena and Polly that she was still mad as hell about the horrible hotel incident with the kids as she finished off her pie and wiped her fingers on one of the napkins supplied by the pastry shop. "I need to get over it, but I get angry every time I think about it."

"You've got every right to be upset for as long as you want." Teena nodded. "I vote the four of us take care of Wyatt." She started humming the old Dixie Chicks song "Goodbye Earl."

Polly giggled. "I've got some wooded area back behind my house. We can put the body there. And I also know where there's a real deep well that no one uses anymore." She winked. "Anyone that would treat their own kids like that should be shot for sure."

Just as Lily opened her mouth to say something, her phone rang.

She managed to fish it out of her purse and answer it before it went to voice mail and was surprised to hear a strange guy's voice. "Mrs. Anderson, this is Daniel Wallace, the principal at the Comfort Middle School. We have a problem, and it would be best if you could be here in person."

It took a minute to register the name with the face of the man who'd been in a hurry at the school on the day she enrolled Braden. "Is my son hurt or in trouble?" she asked.

"Both, but there are no broken bones," Mr. Wallace told her.

"I'll be there in five minutes," Lily said, and ended the call. When she turned around, all three women had stunned expressions. "You heard?"

"Daniel's a loud talker," Polly said.

"Go!" Sally said. "We'll all be right here when you get back, and if you need support, just call us, and we'll come running."

Lily's blood pressure must've shot up because she could hear her heartbeat thumping in her ears as she drove toward the school way too fast. Braden had never been in trouble at school. Sure, he might have engaged in quite a bit of mischief outside of it, but Lily had never been called to come take care of a problem. Not once in all of his school days. She burned a few miles off her tires when she braked hard and slid into the parking lot, then again when she whipped into a spot. When she reached the principal's office and saw Braden sitting in a chair in front of his desk, she felt all the blood drain from her face. He had a black eye and a blood smear across his nose. He was holding a bloody tissue, and his lip was cut.

"What in the hell happened to my child?" she demanded as she clamped a hand on Braden's shoulder. "Are you all right, son? Who did this to you?" Then she whipped her head back around to glare at the principal. "What are you doing to the kid who hit my son?"

Braden patted Lily on the arm and said, "I kinda got into a fight, and the other two look worse than I do, Mama. They're over there in another room. Isaac done told his story, and he's gone back to class."

"You were fighting with Isaac?" Lily's eyebrows shot up. "He's your best friend."

"No, it was kind of *because* of Isaac," Braden started to explain.

Mack pushed through the door before he could say anything else. His expression reminded Lily of a violent Texas tornado tearing up everything in its path. If he was that angry at Braden without even letting him explain, then he could damn well pack up his goats and get off her property.

Mack dropped down on one knee in front of Braden and gently touched his eye. "Who did this to you, son?"

"We had a dustup out front just before school," the principal answered for Braden. "He wouldn't say a word to defend himself until both of you got here. We've been waiting."

Both? Why would her son want both of them there? She was the parent, and only parents got called to solve problems. Mack was only her roommate. No, that wasn't right—he was more than that even if she couldn't put a name to what they were. Even so, he wasn't Braden's father.

"Braden?" Lily said.

"Other than your eye, are you all right?" Mack's face relaxed a little as he got to his feet.

"It's kind of like this"—Braden inhaled and let it out slowly—"Lester and Martin are in the eighth grade, and they've been pickin' on us. They mostly just called us names and said that we—" He blushed and shrugged. "I can't say the rest of what they said. It's too nasty to say out loud."

"Isaac wrote it down," the principal said.

Braden took a deep breath and went on. "Yesterday they made us give them our lunch money, and today they were going to do it again. I wasn't going to do it, but they said if we didn't, they were going to"—he swallowed several times—"they said they were going to hurt our sisters. I told them that my sister could whip them both with one hand tied behind her back, but they just laughed at me and said they had high school buddies that would hold her down for them. And they told us just how they were going to do it, so we didn't fight them. This mornin' when I got off the bus, they had Isaac on the ground. They were goin' through his pockets, and when I yelled at them to stop, they threw me in the dirt and tried to pull my jeans off. Lester's elbow hit me in the eye when I was tryin' to get free."

"What did you do?" Mack asked.

"I got up and kinda whupped them both," Braden said.

"You did what?" Mack gasped.

Braden went on. "I told them I knew martial arts. Before we came here, I kinda watched videos on it and practiced. Me and Holly both did in case we got into trouble with a gang or something, but they just laughed at me. Lester had me pinned down, and Martin was undoing my belt. I showed them some tae kwon do and some jujitsu. I kicked one of them in the nose, hopped up, and did a spin and put a heel in the other one where it hurts real bad."

"We have a no-bullying policy here," Mr. Wallace said. "Why didn't you come tell me that these two boys were being mean to you and Isaac?"

"I didn't want them to hurt Holly and Faith, and what they said they were going to do to them made me want to throw up," Braden said. "Did I do wrong when I fought them off me and Isaac?"

"Absolutely not!" Lily shot a look toward the principal. "If anyone tries to take your pants off, you do exactly the same thing next time."

"I wholeheartedly agree with your mother." Mack laid a hand on Braden's other shoulder.

Mr. Wallace hit a button on his desk and said, "Would you please bring in Lester and Martin?"

The two boys were ushered in by a short guy wearing glasses. One of the boys had bloody smears all over his shirt. The other one was still a little pale and walking like a ruptured duck. Lily didn't care if they had to crawl into the office right then. She had no time for bullies.

Both sets of their parents crowded into the room, all four of them demanding answers.

The principal held up a hand. "I've gotten Isaac and Braden's statements. Now, do you two want to tell us what happened out there this morning?"

Martin gave Braden a go-to-hell look. "He bloodied my nose for nothing, and he kicked Lester so hard that he's still walkin' funny."

"What did the two of you do that caused him to do something like that?" the principal asked.

"We was just jokin' and playin' around with him and Isaac." Lester's voice really did sound a little high for a big boy his size.

"Stealing lunch money is playing around? Threatening to hurt girls is just joking?" The principal stood up. "You two boys have in-school suspension for the rest of the year. I would suggest that you keep your distance from Braden."

"You picked on two little kids half your size?" Martin's daddy asked. "Well, son, you just got your phone and television privileges taken away for the rest of the school year."

"And you"—Lester's father pointed at him—"will be doing double chores for the next month. I'm ashamed of you for picking on a kid half your size."

"What's he gonna hafta do?" Lester glared at Braden. "He hit us, too."

"Probably get a medal," Mr. Wallace said.

"What about school activities like the junior livestock show and the rest of the basketball season?" Mack folded his arms over his chest.

"The policy book says that while a student is in ISS, they cannot participate in any extracurricular activities. So no basketball, baseball, or anything else for these two boys the remainder of this year," the principal said, and hit the desk with the policy manual so hard that the noise made both boys jump. "Next, you two will clean out your lockers and report to ISS. Mr. James runs a tight ship over in his building, so you should know that if you get in trouble there, you will be expelled."

"This ain't fair," Lester said. "I'm the star of the junior high basketball team."

"And I got show goats ready for the livestock show," Martin said.

"Too bad," his father said. "I paid a lot of money for those goats. You can work it off on Saturday and Sunday afternoons after your regular chores are done."

"Can't we do something else? Pick up trash or do Saturday school?"

"No, son, you can't." The principal shook his head. "You were here the first day of school when I told the whole student body what would happen if there was any bullying. All y'all signed the contract. Now you can suffer the consequences. I've taken a picture of Braden's black eye and have his height and weight on file. He and Isaac gave me permission to record their statements. Isaac went into full detail about what you threatened to do to their sisters and the language you used. Should I play that for your parents?"

"I don't even want to hear it," Lester's mother said. "I'm very sorry my son has behaved like this, and he will take his punishment like a man. If there's any more bullying, call us, please."

The four parents filed out of the room without a backward glance at their kids.

"Now you can go to the bathroom and clean the blood off your face," the principal told Braden, "and if your folks don't have any more questions, we'll all go about our business now."

"Yes, sir." Braden stood up and extended a hand to the principal. "Thank you, sir."

Mr. Wallace shook with him and said, "From now on, son, bring problems like this to me first."

"Yes, sir, I will," Braden said. "Mama, I'll see you and Mack at home."

The principal pointed toward the other two boys. "You two can sit on those chairs. Our ISS director, Mr. James, will be here in a few minutes to take you to his room."

Lester and Martin slumped down into the chairs, folded their arms over their chests, and scowled at the principal. Mr. Wallace followed Mack and Lily out of the room and closed the door behind them.

"You've got a good kid there," he said. "I just wish he would have come to me before things escalated to this point."

"I'll remind him again about that this evening." Lily could almost breathe again. Her chest didn't ache as bad, and the thumping noise in her ears was slowing down. A tiny bit of guilt over the fact that she didn't even know that Holly and Braden were practicing martial arts still plagued her, but she was sure glad they had.

"Thanks for not putting him in ISS with them," Mack said.

Mr. Wallace chuckled. "When everyone in school hears that they got their plow cleaned by someone Braden's size, I imagine they'll be glad to hide in ISS to avoid the shame."

"Should I warn the high school principal that my daughter, Holly, has taught herself some martial arts, too?" Lily asked.

"Might be a good idea," Mr. Wallace said.

Mack put his arm around Lily's shoulders, and they left the building together. When they were outside, he chuckled and then laughed out loud. "Why didn't you tell me we had a couple of lethal weapons living in the house?"

"I didn't even know. Just goes to show that I needed to get out of Austin and get more involved with the kids," she answered. "Why is that funny?"

"You'd have to be a boy to understand." Mack walked her to her car. "I'm just glad he took up for himself, and even more glad that he wanted me to be there."

Our daughter—should I have taken his earlier comment as a premonition about them both? She got in her car and drove back to work. After she'd figured out that Mack was there for support and not to fuss at Braden for breaking the rules, his presence had been a big comfort.

Chapter Twenty

*H*olly and Braden could argue until the sun came up in the west and the moon fell from the sky, but the look Holly got on her face when she saw her brother's black eye proved that no one else had better get between them. Lily was sure glad that the school bus stopped at the junior high school before it picked up the high school kids. Holly had threatened to burst into the ISS room, take hold of those two bullies, and finish what Braden had started. If they thought for one minute that they could threaten her and Faith, she'd be glad to treat them to what a girl could do to them.

"And on Valentine's Day at that," she fussed. "Me and Braden were going to take selfies of us together this evening and print them for your present, Mama. We rescued a frame from the trash when we first moved in to put it in and everything."

"I'll take it, anyway." Braden grinned and then winced. "It'll be proof that I got in a fight and won."

Mack arrived before Holly could say anything. He held three pretty boxes of chocolates, handed one to each of them, saving the biggest one for Lily. "Happy Valentine's Day to all y'all."

"For me?" Holly held the heart-shaped box to her chest. "That's so sweet, Mack. Thank you."

"I'm opening mine right now," Braden said as he took off for the kitchen.

"Thank you. We didn't get you anything at all," Lily said.

"Yes, we did." Holly brought a picture from her backpack. "We kinda rescued this frame, too, and we made a collage. Happy Valentine's Day, Mack."

Lily noticed that Mack had to swallow a couple of times as he looked at the pictures. "How'd you do this without a phone?"

"I've got a camera. It's kind of old, but it'll still take pictures, and then the librarian let me print them at school. Do you like it? There's at least one of all of us in the frame, and one of War Lord and one of Star, and that right there is the mama cat and her kittens at Granny Hayes's place." Holly pointed at them as she talked. "That one is of you and Mama in the kitchen. I had to sneak around and take most of them so it would be a surprise. We wanted to take the one for Mama on this very day, but now Braden looks like he went up against a grizzly bear."

"I'll love it, anyway," Lily declared.

"Holly, I'll trade you my orange chocolate candy for a caramel," Braden yelled from the kitchen.

"You got a deal." She headed that way. "But first we got to do our selfie for Mama and then beg her to let us print it out on her printer."

"Of course I'll let you," Lily said. "After all, it's Valentine's Day, and what I got for each of you is on your beds."

They both stormed up the steps and squealed when they found their tablets lying on their beds.

"What's that all about?" Mack asked.

"They get their tablets back," she said.

"But not their phones?"

"They still have a ways to go before they earn those." She set her candy on the foyer table and hugged him. "Thank you for remembering us."

He tipped her chin up with his knuckles and kissed her. She tiptoed and wrapped her arms around his neck. When it ended, he took a step back. "Best Valentine's Day ever."

"Absolutely, the very best ever," she agreed.

~

Holly was still fuming at the breakfast table on Saturday morning. "I still think I should get at least five minutes with those punks," she said as she slathered butter on a biscuit.

Lily was reminded of what she'd read in the journal about Rachel's temper and determination. If Holly had lived in those days, the law to let women vote might have been passed a lot sooner than it had.

"You don't need to take up for me," Braden said. "I can take care of myself."

"I'm not taking up for you, raccoon boy," she smarted off. "I need to teach those sorry punks not to threaten me and Faith. If a girl whips their butts, they'll sure know to leave everyone alone."

She fussed about it all weekend, but by Monday afternoon she had settled down a little bit. When she got off the bus, she and Braden dropped their school things in their usual places and rushed into the kitchen, both of them talking at once.

Lily held up a hand. "One at a time, please."

"Isaac and Faith want us to come to their house Saturday night for snacks and a movie," Braden blurted out.

"Their parents said it would be okay, and we really want to go," Holly said.

"And we won't go to their house until after supper, like around six," Braden butted in.

"We'll be home by ten," Holly said.

"That's fine with me, but we'll have to plan a night for them to come here real soon," Lily answered.

"Are you going to marry Mack?" Holly asked out of the clear blue sky.

Lily's mouth went dry, and her hands got clammy. "Why would you ask that?"

"You went to meet his parents, and they're coming here to meet us," Braden chimed in. "Me and Holly talked about it, and we really like Mack, but what if his mama and daddy don't like us? I mean, they canceled the last time when they were supposed to come, and now they're really coming, and . . ." His voice trailed off.

"Why wouldn't they like you?" Lily set a bowl of fresh fruit on the table and poured two glasses of milk.

"I smoked pot. Braden's still sporting an eye that says he got in trouble at school." Holly sighed as she took a banana from the bowl. "What if they don't like us, and Mack moves out?"

"I'm sure that isn't going to happen," Lily reassured them. "But we do need to talk about something here. Mack's dad is Orville, and he has Alzheimer's. Do either of you know what that is?"

"Nope," Braden said.

"Is that when a person gets old and their hands start to shake?" Holly asked.

"No, that's Parkinson's. What I'm talking about is when people begin to get something known as dementia, and they don't remember things very well. Sometimes they get mad because they can't remember, or they think you're someone else. Other times they're better at remembering, so y'all need to keep that in mind." Lily tried to explain.

"Is Mack going to get like that someday?" Holly's eyes were wide. "We've been studying a little about genetics in science class. We kind of learned why some of us are short and some are tall, and some have blue eyes and others have brown ones. Is this something Mack might get? I don't want him to not know me."

"I don't think so," Lily answered.

"Good," Holly said. "I'll have to do some research on it when I get back to the library."

"Does his mama have it, too?" Braden asked.

"No, she doesn't. Her name is Nora, and she reminds me a lot of your Granny Vera. I would appreciate it very much if you spent some time with them."

"All right." Holly nodded. "But you didn't answer our question. Are you going to marry Mack?"

Lily said honestly, "I can't answer your question very well. We haven't even been on a real date, and—"

"For God's sake, Mama." Holly butted in before Lily could finish. "We aren't living in caveman days." Holly's tone was full of dramatic exasperation. "You *can* ask him out if he don't ask you."

"We've only been here a short while," Lily countered.

"But we've lived together in one house for like what? Six weeks now?" Braden rolled his big brown eyes toward the ceiling. "So if you were dating him, it would be like a gazillion dates."

"The only answer I can give you right now is that we'll have to wait and see what the future holds. We can't rush time," Lily told them.

"Well, I'd be all right with it." Holly finished her banana and milk.

"So you're ready to stay in Comfort and not move back to Austin?" Lily asked.

"Duh!" Holly rolled her eyes. "Of course I want to stay here. This is way better than Austin, and besides, Sally said I can work in her store when I get sixteen, and who'd have Sunday dinner with Granny Hayes if I wasn't here?" She did a head bob and then changed the subject. "Hey, when I get my homework done, would you and Mack play a game of Scrabble with us after supper?"

"Where'd you get a Scrabble game?" Lily asked.

"She was snooping in the old buffet in the dining room and found a whole bunch of board games," Braden tattled. "I told her I could beat her because I used to play online on my tablet, back when we had Wi-Fi. Are we ever going to get it here?"

"I wasn't snooping," Holly argued. "I was just looking for something."

"What?" Braden grinned. "A joint?"

Holly shoved a finger so close to his now multicolored eye that he jumped and almost fell out of his chair. "I was not, and I haven't drank or smoked since we left Austin."

"What's going to happen when you get your phone back?" Braden argued. "All your pot-smoking, partying Austin friends are going to be texting and calling."

Holly did one of her famous head wiggles. "I'll take care of it. Are you going to run away and go back to your little hoodlum friends?"

"Nope," he responded with a perfect imitation of her head roll. "I'm going to join 4-H and then FFA."

Holly sighed loudly. "He's horrible, Mama. Why didn't you give him away at birth?"

"Because you needed me to take care of you," Braden laughed.

At his last word, she stormed out of the room.

Someday they were going to stop their incessant arguing and be friends. At least Lily hoped so. Supper was in the oven—dessert in the refrigerator. She had a few minutes, so she wandered upstairs to see what, if any, other entries Rachel might have written in the journal.

"You got time to read another passage in the journal?" She rapped on Holly's open door.

"Yes, ma'am." Holly beat her mother to Lily's bed.

Lily opened the flap of the old oak secretary, took the journal out, and opened it to the page where she'd left her bookmark. She was glad to see Rachel's name on the next page, but sad that again so much time had passed between the new date and the previous one.

She read, "Rachel O'Riley Callahan, June 1926."

"Yay!" Holly squealed. "We still got Rachel."

Lily went on with a smile on her face:

"My sweet daughter Sophia has married and left Oklahoma. She fell in love with a man named Fred, who came to our parts a few months ago to buy cattle for his place in Texas. They corresponded when he went back to his home, and he asked her to marry him. I can't say I'm happy about it. He still lives with his German parents, who I understand are very set in their ways. But she is eighteen and her mind was made up. It was either let her marry him or else she would have run away and done it anyway. She writes me a letter once a week. I learned that she hasn't settled into the town or the place so well. I didn't realize what a good friend she was to me until she wasn't here anymore. To say that I miss her would be an understatement. I read her letters over and over and wish she would have listened to me. I could see that Fred was a controlling man, probably much like his own father. She wasn't raised to bow down and kiss a man's feet. I swear that I will be a nosy mother and give my boys a talking-to if they ever treat a woman like they own her. I just wish I could do that for Sophia. She sounds so homesick and miserable in her letters. I've told her that she can come back home, but she said that she made her bed and she will lay in it."

"I don't like that name—Fred," Holly declared. "I'll never marry a man with that name."

"It's not the name," Lily told her. "He could be named Dixon or even Benjamin and still be a controlling fellow."

Lily could hardly believe that a daughter of Rachel's would take that kind of treatment. To think of a man controlling a woman like that fired up a mad spell in her. She closed the journal, wishing that she hadn't even read that page. Then she realized that her anger was directed not just at Fred but at herself, too. She'd let Wyatt control her. He'd wanted a son to carry on the Anderson name since *he* was an only child and his father had been one, too. To him, having a son had been very important, and he wanted one *immediately*. Even though Lily had wanted to wait a couple of years, she'd thrown away her birth control pills on their wedding day. A year later, she'd given birth to Holly. Wyatt had been very disappointed, and childcare had been expensive, so he'd talked her into giving up her job and working from home. He'd been so good at manipulating her that she had actually thought for years that the idea had been hers. Then Braden was born, and she thought Wyatt would be happy. He was for a little while, but then he began to work more and more, spend less and less time with her and the kids, and their marriage had simply died in its sleep.

"Mama, what are you reading?" Braden asked from the doorway.

"An old journal I found in your grandmother's secretary," Lily answered.

He came on into the room and touched the book's leather binding. "It looks really old. What's in it?"

Holly air slapped him on the arm. "I told you about the journal days ago."

"It's a family journal," Lily said. "The first entry was made in 1862 during the Civil War, and it seems to have been passed down from mother to daughter. So far what I've read has been about the lives of our ancestors. Holly and I have been reading it for her history project."

"Hey, Mama." Holly joined her brother right outside her mother's door. "I'm going out to the goat pens with Braden and Mack to check on the goats. Can I please have a pair of rubber boots?" she asked. "I've been wearing the ones that belonged to Granny Vera, but they're getting cracks in the soles."

"I imagine we can get you a pair tomorrow," Lily said. "Maybe I'll go with y'all out to the barn and pens."

"That'd be great." Holly's eyes lit up. "You haven't seen Star in a couple of days, and she's growing more and more all the time."

Lily said a silent prayer as she followed her daughter downstairs. *Please, God, don't ever let her walk in Sophia's shoes. Give her the courage to stand up for her rights, and don't let what she thinks is love shade her judgment.*

~

Lily was glad to see sunshine on Saturday morning. The week had gone by fast, like most of the time had since they'd been in Comfort. She put a pot roast in the slow cooker before she even made breakfast, and then she stirred up a rising of hot yeast rolls. By getting things organized and ready before time, she and the Coopers could spend more time visiting and less time in the kitchen. She remembered that Nora was friends with Polly as well as her mother, so she invited them over for midafternoon snacks. She'd just made a run up to her bedroom to freshen up a little when someone rapped on the front door. She finished brushing out her dark hair, checked her makeup one more time, and was hurrying downstairs when she heard Holly talking.

"Come in," Holly said. "You must be Mrs. Cooper. I'm Holly. Where's Mr. Cooper?"

"I left him at the barn with Mack and your brother," Nora answered.

"Hello," Lily said when she made it to the foyer. "Just hang your coat there on the hall tree and come on into the kitchen. I'm going to take out the dinner rolls so they can rise. Can I get you a glass of sweet tea?"

"That would be wonderful." Nora removed her long coat to reveal jeans and a sweatshirt. "I didn't get dressed up. Sometimes Orville insists that I stay out at the goat pens with him, but he's having a pretty good day today."

"No need to dress up to come visit here." Lily looked down at her own jeans and T-shirt. "You're family."

"Thank you for that." Nora followed them into the kitchen.

"I'll get us all a glass of tea." Holly made her way around them.

"Except for that blonde hair, she sure reminds me of Vera. Your grandmother, Vera's mama, was a blonde. Maybe that's where Holly got that pretty hair." Nora followed Lily into the kitchen and sat down at the table.

"We never knew Mama's granny. Did you?" Holly asked as she poured tea into glasses and set one in front of Nora.

"She died before I was born, but Mama had a picture of her," Lily interjected. "It's probably in one of the albums stored up in the attic."

"Can we go up there and bring them down?" Holly asked.

"Sure, but not today. We'll probably have to fight the dust bunnies to even find the albums." Lily punched down the bread and pinched off pieces for rolls. "Mama talked about her a lot. What do you remember about her, Nora?"

"Well, she lived here with your folks when your mama and I were little girls. She was the sweetest lady I ever met, and she loved to cook. This was one of the bigger houses in Comfort at that time, so she'd let Vera invite me and Polly over here to spend the weekend whenever we wanted. She had this big garden out back. Your grandpa had cattle, but no goats. I remember that he worked right here on the ranch—" Nora stopped and took a long drink of her tea. "Seems like I heard he'd been a foreman here for years."

"And she had blonde hair?" Holly pressed her for more.

"Oh, yes." Nora nodded seriously. "A great long mane of beautiful hair. She braided it and wrapped it around her head like a crown. One night when we were all here, she took it down and we brushed it out for her. She sat in a kitchen chair, and her hair almost went to the floor."

"And my grandfather?" Lily asked. "Mama never talked a lot about him except to say that he was a good father."

"Albert walked with a limp. He'd had an accident when he was young that left him with one leg shorter than the other," Nora said. "He had red hair and a million freckles and the clearest blue eyes you've ever seen. He was a man of few words, but he adored Annie."

Lily thought of poor Sophia, who had married a man who apparently didn't love her like that, and wondered what had become of that woman.

"Now let's talk about you, young lady." Nora focused on Holly. "What do you want to be when you grow up?"

"I want to be a teacher. Not for big kids, though. I want to go into early-childhood development and teach the little kids," Holly answered. "Braden, my brother, wants to be a vo-ag teacher just like Mack. But I really haven't made up my mind for sure. Sometimes I think about going to the air force like Faith Torres. It would be great to be a pilot."

"Those are good and noble ambitions," Nora said. "I always thought I'd like to teach little kids, but I got married and had twins. Orville was a bank president here in Comfort, but he had the goat farm on the side, and I took care of it a lot of the time."

"I'm not getting married until I'm thirty," Holly declared.

"That's smart," Nora agreed.

Lily remembered when Holly wanted to be a rock singer, and Braden declared he was going to be a fireman. They would probably change their minds a hundred times before they graduated high school, but it was good to hear that their goals were a little more grounded and realistic.

~

Mack had set three chairs up on the south side of the barn so his father would be sitting in the warm sunshine that morning. Orville was wearing his rubber boots and his old work coat, and he was having a good day. Could it be, Mack wondered, because he felt at home in the presence of goats and was dressed in old familiar clothes?

"What makes you like goats?" Orville had asked Braden first thing when he'd sat down.

"They're cute and they're little," Braden answered honestly. "Cows and horses kind of scare me. My mama is short and so is my dad, so I'm probably not ever going to grow up to be tall like Mack. I can hold my own with a goat. I might not ever be able to do that with a big animal."

"Where'd you get that black eye?" Orville asked.

"Well, sir, it was like this . . ." Braden started telling the story of the day before the fight when the two bullies had taken his lunch money, and ended with, "I guess I had just had enough of them."

Orville chuckled. "Boy, I don't reckon you'd have a bit of trouble with a big animal."

"Thank you. Why'd you raise goats?" Braden asked.

"I raised premium goats, and I sold them to kids from all over Oklahoma and Texas for their livestock shows. What I didn't sell went to the market once a year and paid for two boys' college educations. See that one out there with the star on her face? She'll be a prime show goat next spring. And that young ram over there that you call War Lord could take the prize home when you show him. My son . . ." It was evident he was trying hard to remember a name. "My son Adam—no, that's not right. Aaron is the one that likes to go with me to take care of the goats."

Mack nodded in agreement. "That's right, Dad. Now tell me about the rest of my new herd. Which ones should I sell as premium stock, and which ones will bring less money?"

"Aaron?" Braden asked.

"Aaron Matthew Cooper is my birth name," Mack explained. "They started out calling me Matt, but my brother could only say Mack, and that's what I've answered to ever since."

"Adam is at college. He's coming home this weekend," Orville said. "But he doesn't like to do anything that gets his hands dirty. See that black-and-white one over there, Mack? The one that looks like a Holstein cow—that's your best one of the lot. I hear you're steppin' out with that Miller girl. She comes from good people. You should marry her."

Mack felt the heat rising from his neck to his cheeks. Of all the things for his father to say in front of Braden, that dang sure wasn't what he wanted Orville to get started about. "Yes, she does, and she's a good woman. Now how about that brown goat out there? The one jumping up on the hay bale—you think she's top-notch?"

"She's a grade below the black-and-white one but still ain't too bad. Have you moved in with the Miller girl? You moved in with Brenda, and Adam married her. Maybe you better not live with Vera's daughter."

"Maybe not," Mack agreed.

"But he already lives with my mama, only he lives downstairs and we all live upstairs," Braden told him.

Orville acted like he hadn't heard. "I'm getting hungry. You reckon your mama has dinner ready yet?"

"Maybe," Mack answered, glad that his dad was getting away from the subject of Lily and marriage. "Why don't we go see, and if she doesn't, I know that she keeps the cookie jar filled."

Orville stood up and started walking straight out from the barn. Mack stood up and hurried to catch up with him. "We'd better go this way, or we'll have to climb a fence."

Orville chuckled. "I got turned around a little."

~

Lily leaned her head back on the sofa that evening and let out a long whoosh of air—something way beyond a sigh. Mack had taken Holly and Braden over to the Torres place, and now he was out doing the evening chores. Thank God she had thought to invite Polly over for the afternoon. Orville had gone to Mack's room for a nap, and Polly had caught Nora up on all the town gossip.

It had been years since she'd had an all-day event with anyone, including her two best friends, Sally and Teena, or even Mack. On Saturdays, he was usually in and out of the house, doing one thing or another out around the place. Lily closed her eyes and had started to doze off when her phone rang. She fumbled across the end table for it, barely opened one eye a slit to find the right icon to answer it, and said, "Hello." She halfway expected it to be one of the kids wanting to know if she'd bring them the Harry Potter collection of movies.

"Is that you, Lily?" Wyatt asked. "Your voice is even huskier than usual."

Her eyes popped wide open. "What? It's me. Why are you calling?"

"Victoria kicked me out and moved a younger man into her house and into her life," he said flatly. "I'm in a hotel in San Antonio with no job and no place to live. I lived on room service and paced the floor for two days before I decided to go to a therapist. After two sessions, I figure I owe you an apology."

"Accepted," she said. "Goodbye."

"Wait a minute!" he almost shouted. "Give me a little time here. I want to come clean. Victoria wasn't my first affair. I started cheating on you right after Holly was born. I tried to straighten up after Braden came, but"—he hesitated—"I couldn't do it. I liked the thrill."

Lily closed her eyes and counted to ten. "Are you trying to torture me by telling me this crap?"

"No, I just want you to know so you can move on with your life, too. I was smart enough to save my paychecks for the last year, so I can survive and won't be begging off you. Evidently, I got my comeuppance with Victoria. I've been faithful to her, but she prefers younger men. I'm sorry for the things I did, and you deserved better than you got from me, and I hope you find it. I'm interviewing Monday for a job, and when I get my life in order, I want to be a better father and have a better relationship with the kids."

"Well, I guess you'd better get started because that's going to take a while after that motel stunt," Lily said.

"Probably so," he relented. "Now, a question, and you don't have to give me an answer right now. You can think about it. If you aren't coming back to Austin, will you sublet your apartment to me? The kids told me that their furniture is"—another long pause—"still there, and when I do get things right in my life, maybe they'd feel more comfortable coming to visit me there than in hotels. I'll understand if you say no, but would you think about it?"

"I will," she agreed. "Anything else?"

"You have my number. When you make a decision about the apartment, give me a call. Good night, Lily."

The line went dead, and she sat there in stunned silence until Mack joined her. Smelling like soap and shaving lotion and wearing pajama bottoms and a snug-fitting tank top, he eased down on the sofa beside her. "It's been a day. Dad was having a fairly decent day, and I loved having him and my mother here." He slipped an arm around her shoulders. "But now I'm glad to have some time alone with you to unwind."

"Wyatt called," she said, and then she told him what the man had said.

"It's your decision about the apartment," he said. "I hope he *will* straighten up. He's got two beautiful kids, and he's sure missing out on a lot of their lives. They'll be grown in a few years, and they won't even know him. Dad asked me today why I didn't marry you."

Lily appreciated that Mack had said whether or not to sublet her apartment was her choice. Wyatt would have made the decision for her, much like she figured Fred had made all the decisions for Sophia. "Braden asked me if I was going to marry you."

"Would you ever want to marry again?" Mack asked.

"Maybe." Lily laid her head on his shoulder. "Mama would tell me not to judge the whole barrel of apples by one bad one."

"That's good advice," Mack said. "You've got to have trust issues after the way Wyatt treated you, and you've been on your own for a long time. And you can see what I've got in my gene pool—the possibility of Alzheimer's like my dad and a stupid ass for a brother."

"I'd trust you with my life and with my kids as well, Mack. Besides, my mother died at seventy, my dad at the same age a year before her. Mama said that my Granny Annie only lived to be seventy, so . . ." She trailed off.

"I've learned to never look that far ahead." He tipped up her chin with his forefinger.

She barely had time to moisten her lips before his mouth covered hers in a kiss that held so much promise that it made her forget everything and everyone. Like two love-starved teenagers, they made out on the sofa for a while, their hands moving over each other's bodies. Finally, she pulled away and locked gazes with him.

"We're headed to a place in this relationship that will be far more comfortable in the bedroom," she whispered.

"Your place or mine?" He stood up, scooped her into his arms, and left the living room.

"Do your springs squeak?" she asked.

"No, ma'am," he answered.

"Then your place. It's closer," she said between short breaths.

Kissing her again and again, he carried her into his bedroom and kicked the door shut.

Chapter Twenty-One

S ally slipped into church just as the congregation was finishing the first hymn that Sunday morning. She tapped Lily on the shoulder and then sat down beside her when Lily scooted over closer to Mack.

Sally cupped her hand over Lily's ear and whispered, "I overslept and missed Sunday school. Where's Granny Hayes? Dusty, her old mule, isn't tied up to the post outside."

"I have no idea, but Holly will be heartbroken if she can't go home with her," Lily said.

"If she don't show up, we're going out there to check on her. I've never known her to miss church," Sally said.

"Not even when she's sick?"

"Not even when it snows or rains—she don't get sick," Sally said.

They finished the last chorus, and Drew took the podium. "Are y'all about tired of winter? I'm ready for spring and new growth on the trees and evidence that rebirth is all around us. That's what I'm going to talk about this morning—rebirth in our spiritual lives. Sometimes we get so tied up in our physical life, our work and families and kids, that we forget about our spirit, and it gets as dead as those trees out there right now."

Rebirth—that's exactly what Lily had gotten when she came home to Comfort. Now she had a better relationship with her kids than she'd ever had before. She was flat-out in love with Mack Cooper. She'd loved Wyatt, but there was a difference in loving someone and being in love. The latter went so much deeper than just love. Plus, she had renewed her friendship with Sally and Teena into more than just once-a-month catching-up sessions.

Drew ended the service by asking Mack to deliver the benediction. Mack stood to his feet, bowed his head, and said, "Dear Lord, thank you for this service that reminds us that there is life after this one. Be with each member of this congregation as they go through the week, and forgive us for our sins. Amen."

Everyone began to stand and head toward the door. Mack held out a hand to Lily. "Ready to go home?"

"Yes, I am," she said, and *home* was not Austin.

"But first, we're going to drive out to Granny Hayes's place," Sally told him. "It's not like her to miss church."

"Can I stay with her, Mama? She invited me to come again when Mack picked me up last week. Please, please, please!" Holly begged. "She taught me how to do a crocheted chain, and this week, she's going to show me how to connect it to make a scarf."

"Of course you can stay with her if she invited you," Lily answered.

"Can I see the kittens?" Braden asked.

"Probably not," Sally answered. "She barely lets me come inside the cabin. But I understand she did say that you could have one, and that Holly could have the pick of the litter. That's a big thing for her, giving you one of her kittens. She's pretty selfish with them."

Braden frowned and sighed. "Can we go to Dairy Queen after we drop Holly off out there?"

"Yes, we can," Mack told Braden. "Your mother deserves a day out of the kitchen, so we'll have burgers and malts."

"Or tacos?" Sally suggested. "I love their tacos, so I'm inviting myself to join y'all."

Drew shook hands with each of them as they filed out the door, then asked Sally, "Have you heard from Granny Hayes? It's not like her to miss the services, and today is such a lovely day. A little chilly, but sunshiny and no wind or rain."

"I had the same thought. We're going to check on her," Sally said. "I keep trying to convince her to let me come get her and take her home so she won't be out in the weather. She tells me that Dusty needs the exercise."

"Let me know if there's anything I can do," Drew said.

"Sure will," Sally told him. "Now, who's riding with me?"

"I'm going with Mack," Braden said.

"So am I." Holly had run on ahead and was already getting into the back seat.

"I'll ride out there with you." Lily got into the passenger seat of Sally's business van. "Why'd you drive this today?"

"My car is in the shop getting new tires and a tune-up." Sally got in and turned the key to start the engine. "I get it back tomorrow. So we've got about five or ten minutes at the most. Tell me how the day went yesterday with Nora and Orville."

"It went fine. Nora was so happy to meet Holly and Braden. Orville and Braden really struck up a friendship, and Holly visited with Nora until it was time for her to go to Faith's house that evening. I was so damned—oops, forgive me, Lord, for cussin' right after church—proud of her that I could have shouted."

"That's great," Sally said. "Things are working out just like they should. How're things between you and Mack?"

"I keep waiting for the other shoe to drop. I know something will go wrong because nothing can be so right," Lily said. "The kids like him. His dad asked him if he was going to marry me. Oh, and Wyatt called last night."

"What did that bastard want?" Sally asked.

"Victoria kicked him out for a younger man, and he wants to sublet my apartment. Allegedly, when he gets his life straightened out, he wants another chance at being a father," Lily told her. "We'll see."

Sally drove up to Granny Hayes's yard. Chickens squawked and ran around the house. The ducks on the porch eyed the two vehicles cautiously. "He doesn't deserve it, but you're going to say, 'for the kids' sake,' aren't you?"

"What is that?" Lily pointed to a huge pile of dirt with rocks laid all around it.

"Sweet Jesus!" Sally groaned. "Dusty must've died, and she's buried that big old mule. That's why she wasn't in church this morning. He died, and that's his grave. See that little cross propped up with rocks? It's got his name on it." Sally was out of her van and running toward the cabin before Lily even got her seat belt undone.

"Keep everyone outside until—" she yelled as she cleared the porch and knocked on the door several times. When there was no answer, she tried the knob, and the door swung open.

Holly slid out of the front seat of Mack's truck and was on the porch when Sally came out and closed the door behind her. Lily stopped in her tracks and knew what had happened before Sally said a word. Granny Hayes was dead, and Holly was going to be devastated.

"We can't go in there, not until the doctor comes." Sally's voice cracked, and tears dripped onto the collar of her coat.

"Is Granny Hayes sick? Is she going to be all right?" Holly asked.

Mack pulled a clean white handkerchief from his pocket and handed it to Sally. "I'll call Doc Greene. He usually goes to the Comfort Café for lunch on Sunday, so maybe I'll catch him there."

"She's gone, and probably has been for days, maybe since the night after she got old Dusty buried." Sally dabbed at her eyes.

"No, Mama! She can't be dead. She's my friend, and she can't . . ." Holly threw herself into Lily's arms and wet the front of her mother's sweater with tears.

Sally passed the hankie over to Lily, and she wiped Holly's cheeks with it as she held her and let her cry as long as she wanted. Braden got out of the truck and walked out to the mound of dirt, with Mack right behind him. Lily watched from the corner of her eye as Mack made the phone call and then draped his arm around Braden's shaking shoulders.

"She left a sealed letter with me last month, and then in church last week she handed me another one," Sally said between sobs. "I wasn't to open them until she was gone. She said they had all her wishes in them. I laughed after she'd walked away because I thought she'd live to be a hundred for sure. She was always secretive about everything, but the one thing she told me was that we weren't to take her off her property. No embalming and no big funeral at the church. The rest I'll have to read when I get back to the shop. The letters are in the safe."

Holly plopped down on the top porch step. "We would have helped her bury that old mule. All she had to do was call us."

"Honey, she didn't have a telephone." Sally sat down beside her. "I tried to buy her a simple one, but she wouldn't have it."

"She lived the way she wanted." Lily took a place on the other side of her daughter. "It was her time to go, and now she's with her brothers and her parents."

"She didn't like any of them, except her mother." Holly took the handkerchief from her mother and wiped her face with it. "Granny Hayes said her mother was an angel for putting up with her daddy. She said he was a hard man that demanded a lot from his wife and daughter."

They were still sitting there fifteen minutes later when Dr. Greene pulled in beside Sally's van. He nodded at them, went inside, and came back out in just a few seconds. "She probably went in her sleep last night. Rigor has come and gone. Should I call the undertaker?"

Sally told him what Granny Hayes had set out.

"Well, then, you should abide by her wishes. Let me know if you need me for anything else. I'll get a death certificate ready and file it since she didn't want to go to the funeral home."

"I can't leave her," Holly said. "She was my friend."

"Is it all right if we go inside now?" Sally asked Dr. Greene.

"Don't see why not. She was a strange little bird. I only saw her once about a month ago. She'd never been to a doctor in her life," he said, "but she marched into my office without an appointment. She wouldn't go for tests, but I was pretty sure from her coloring and what she told me about her symptoms that she had pancreatic cancer. I told her if she didn't get treatment, she probably wouldn't make it six weeks. She told me she'd lived a long life and lived it the way she wanted, and she wasn't doing anything but getting her affairs in order. She put you"—he nodded toward Sally—"down as her emergency contact person and gave us permission to tell you anything about her condition if you asked."

"I'll go right now and get that letter. Then I'll tell the cemetery folks what we need to do," Sally said. "I've never been in charge of anything like this, so I'm flying blind."

Dr. Greene patted her on the shoulder as he started down the stairs. "I'm sure Granny Hayes has it all lined up from A to Z. She might have been an odd duck, but she took care of her own business."

Sally got to her feet. "Y'all can go inside where it's warmer."

Holly didn't waste a second. She jumped to her feet, crossed the porch, and opened the door. Lily didn't know how her daughter would react to seeing a dead person or what condition Granny Hayes might be in, so she rushed inside right behind Holly. To Lily's surprise, Holly pulled a rocking chair up to the bed and sat down.

Granny Hayes looked smaller than usual in her flannel nightgown buttoned up to her wrinkled and thin neck. She was lying on her back with the covers pulled up to her chest. Her arms were stretched out beside her body on top of the piecework quilt, and her braids lay down across her breasts and to her waist.

"Are you sure she's not just asleep?" Holly whispered.

"Positive. The doctor has pronounced her dead." Lily brought a ladder-back chair across the floor and sat down beside Holly.

Mack and Braden came into the one-room cabin. Mack crossed the room and stood behind Holly and Lily. Braden sat down on the floor and gathered the mama cat and all three kittens into his lap. "I ain't never seen a dead person except Granny Vera, and she was in a casket. Granny Hayes don't look dead. She looks like she's asleep."

"Are you ladies all right? Can I get you anything?"

Lily reached over her shoulder for his hand, and he laced his fingers in hers. "Not a thing. We'll just sit here with her until Sally gets back and tells us what to do." The touch of his hand brought comfort to the strange but peaceful turn of events that morning. It seemed like time stood still until Sally came through the door with two envelopes in her hand. She dragged a second chair over to the other side of the bed and opened the first one, scanned through it, broke the wax seal on the second one, and read out loud.

My Dear Sally,

If you are reading this, I'm gone on to whatever eternity God has planned for me. Don't weep for me, but be happy that I've had a long life and a happy one for the past near forty years. I've lived exactly the way I wanted, and God blessed me with a dear friend like you, and now a little friend in Holly Anderson. I've gone back into all the births and deaths recorded in my grandmother Mayer's Bible and found that she and I are very distant cousins. That's the only thing that I like about having Mayer blood in me.

This cabin and everything in it are yours. Do with it what you will. Give it to the historical museum if you want. The money in the coffee cans lined up on the mantel is to be given to Lily to use for Holly's education. I always wanted to go to school and maybe even on to college to study, but my father wouldn't allow it. In his eyes, a girl was to be a wife and a mother. If I couldn't do what I wanted, then I refused to be what he wanted me to be.

The rest of the things I want done are in the first letter that I gave to you. Please tell Holly that the days I spent with her were special to me, too. My mama cat and kittens belong to her, and if Mack will let Dusty live out the rest of his life out there with the goats, I'm sure the old boy would like that. Also, the two steers I'm raising for next winter's beef can go with Mack. Anyone who can catch the chickens and ducks can have them.

Live your lives to the fullest, and the way you want.

Sincerely,

Johanna Hayes Mayer

Sally laid that single sheet of paper to the side and picked up the first one. "She says in this one that when she dies, I am to call the funeral home. She's already picked out her casket, which is a plain wooden box like her mother was buried in, and that they have their orders already. She is to be taken to the cemetery from here in her old wagon, and if Dusty is still alive, he is to pull the wagon. If not, then I'm to make arrangements for another mule, but not a horse, to do the job. She does not want to be embalmed, and she'd like to be buried beside her mother at sunset on the day after her death if the ground isn't too hard or wet for the gravediggers to get her space ready. She only wants one song sung, and that's to be 'I'll Fly Away.' The headstone is already in place at the Comfort cemetery right beside her mama, but I'm to let the people know that it's time to put her death date on it." She pulled her phone from her pocket. "I'll call the funeral home right now."

"Do you think they can get things arranged by tomorrow evening?" Mack asked.

"I sure hope so," Sally said, and then talked to the funeral-home director. "He says they will be out here in fifteen minutes and that we probably should leave while they take care of things."

"Can we just stay until they get here?" Holly asked. "I don't want her to be lonely."

"Of course we can," Mack answered. "Maybe we could use that box over there in the corner to put the cat and kittens in while we're waiting."

"And gather up those coffee cans and put them in another box," Sally said. "You might as well take them on home with you, too, since that's what she wanted."

"I'll hitch up the trailer and come get those two calves out there in the corral this afternoon," Mack said.

"It's sad," Holly sniffled. "Everything that she loved, her whole life and everything she loved, is all over and gone in just a day or two."

Mack laid his spare hand on Holly's shoulder and gave it a gentle squeeze. "It's a lesson to us to live every day like it was our last."

Holly patted his hand and then stood up. "I can't believe she was our cousin, or that she's giving her cats to us. That's so sweet. I didn't know her long, but I'm going to miss her so much."

Mack let go of Lily's hand and helped the kids get the mama cat and her three babies into the cardboard box. As he and Braden took the box outside, the undertaker came into the house. He'd taken care of both Lily's parents, and he nodded solemnly at her.

"This will be an unusual one, but we'll do our best to abide by her wishes. Her wooden casket is out there in the hearse, and we'll get her into it. She told me that Sally and your family are the only ones to be at the private burial service, and that once she is in the casket, we are to shut it and not open it again," he said. "Do you want to change any of that?"

Sally and Lily both shook their heads. "Do whatever she wanted."

"I called Mr. Stewart on the way over here. He'll be here tomorrow afternoon with his old mule to pull the wagon to the cemetery. The service will be at six thirty. I think that's about sunset at this time of year. Do you want to tell her goodbye one more time before we get started?" he asked.

Mack came back and picked up the box that had about a dozen old metal coffee cans packed inside it. "Are we about ready to go?"

Holly went to the bed, leaned down, and kissed Granny Hayes on the forehead. "Goodbye, Granny. I loved you, and I should have told you so," she said, and then turned around and, with a fresh batch of tears running down her cheeks, left the cabin.

Sally, Lily, and Mack fell in behind her, and the solemn little parade crossed the porch. "Shall we stop by the—" Mack started and then shook his head. "We have the cats. We'll have to go home and come back."

"I'll call in a couple of pizzas, some pasta, and breadsticks on the way, pick it up, and bring it all to the house," Lily said. "Holly and Braden aren't going to want to leave those cats alone today."

"While they're getting the pizza ready, I'll dash into the Dollar Store and get litter, a pan to put it in, and a small bag of food," Sally said.

Thank God for cats, Lily thought several times that afternoon. Holly informed them that Mama Cat really was the mother cat's name, and then she and Braden discussed what they'd name the other three all afternoon. Every so often Holly would sigh and dab her eyes, but for the most part, she took Granny Hayes's death better than Lily had thought she would. Neither of the kids asked about the coffee cans, which seemed strange to Lily, but then what was money when they had three frisky kittens in the house?

Sally left in the middle of the afternoon to make some phone calls about the chickens and ducks, and Mack hitched up the trailer to go get the Angus steers. By evening they were in their new home in the pasture on the north side of the lane, and the goats were all in the one on the south side.

The whole day seemed surreal that evening, but it got even stranger when Lily and Mack opened the box with the coffee cans. She figured they'd be full of change—dimes, nickels, and maybe some quarters—but each can was filled with neatly rolled hundred-dollar bills. Twenty bills to each roll. Ten rolls to each can.

Lily tried to do the math in her head. Seven times $20,000 was mind-boggling. The total was well over $100,000, and Granny Hayes had kept it in her cabin. Right there on the shelf, where anyone could have broken in and stolen it. Where had she gotten that kind of money, anyway? She certainly didn't make that much selling earrings, scarves, and shawls.

"I'd say that Holly's college fund just took one giant step forward," Mack said.

"Where did she get that kind of money?" Lily finally asked. "Was she growing pot out there on her land?"

"I would imagine that her father had no time for banks, and her mother never used them, either," Mack said. "This is probably her inheritance from them. She probably added to it every year when she sold a steer or two that she didn't need for meat. Did you see that rifle hanging above her fireplace? I wouldn't be surprised if she had done some hunting—maybe deer, quail, rabbits. She would raise the steers, but then when she didn't need them, she'd sell them and put the money in the coffee cans."

"Should we really keep all this money?" Lily asked.

"It's what she wanted, but I would suggest that you take it to the bank in the next few days and get it put away somewhere safer than in those coffee cans. Maybe one of those 529 funds," he suggested. "It's late, darlin'. Kids are sleeping, and I'm yawning. Let's think about this tomorrow after the graveside services." He walked her to the bottom of the staircase and kissed her good night.

"I'd like to spend the night in your bedroom and wake up cuddled up next to you," she whispered. "But I don't think that would be a good example for Holly and Braden."

"No, it wouldn't." Mack drew her close to his chest and raised her chin with his knuckles. His dark lashes rested on his high cheekbones, and he found her lips with his eyes closed.

When the kiss ended, she turned and went right up to her bedroom, but she was too wound up after the whole day's events to ever go to sleep, so she got out the journal and opened it to the next entry.

Holly eased into her room and said, "Mama, I'm still awake. Can we please read some more in the journal?"

"I've already got it out, and it looks like Sophia has gotten married again. This will be my grandmother that's writing now, and your great-grandmother," Lily said, and began to read:

Sophia Ann Callahan Mayer Johnston, July 1946: Mama gave me this journal to add my story to hers and my grandmother's when Fred died and I went home for the first time since I left Oklahoma and moved to Texas. It didn't take me long to figure out that he wasn't the same man I dated once we were married. He was as controlling and mean to me as his father, Hermann, was to Fred's mother. I hated living in this house with him and them, and the only bright spot in my life was my mother's letters and getting to visit with Albert, the foreman, on my daily walk around the place. If Albert hadn't been there to talk to me for all those years, I might have taken a whole bottle of my mother-in-law's sleeping pills and simply gone to sleep forever. I thought things might change when his parents passed, but they only got worse. I wasn't allowed to go anywhere without him, not even to church. He blamed me for us not having children, and then when I did get pregnant after years and years of marriage and was almost past childbearing age, he said the baby didn't belong to him. Fred drank too much one evening and fell down the stairs. He died when I was three months pregnant. Albert declared his love for me, and we were married when my daughter was two years old, and he adopted Vera. He'd always called me Annie, not Sophia, and I liked that, so when Fred was gone, that was the name I adopted. I think it was more of an effort to draw the line between the horrible life I had with Fred and the wonderful life Albert and I started, rather than an effort on my part to be someone else. Someday I'll pass this journal on down to Vera Ann, and she'll understand why she lives in this house and why I didn't want her to be a Mayer.

"I'm confused, Mama," Holly said. "So Grandma Vera was really a Mayer, and that made her kind of kin to Granny Hayes?"

"Yes, it did," Lily answered. "Shall we go on?"

Holly nodded. "I like that I'm kinda kin to Granny Hayes."

"Me, too," Lily agreed. "She was a wonderful woman."

Lily flipped to the next page to read:

Annie Callahan Johnston, August 1950: Vera is now five years old and will go to school next year. She reminds me of my mother, Rachel, who passed away last summer, but she has Albert's kind and sweet heart. Life goes on here on the place, and as the saying goes, the seasons come and the seasons go, but I'm happy in my lot. I have Vera and Albert. We were both forty-two this year on our birthdays, which are only three weeks apart. We are at war again, this time with Korea. The newspapers call our involvement a police action, not a war. I'm glad that Vera was a girl and not a boy who could be drafted. That's selfish, I know, but the thought of sending my child to war terrifies me.

"One more, please, Mama? We're to the part now when Granny Vera will start writing in the journal, right?" Holly begged.

"I think there is only one more, so we'll read it and then you've got to get to bed," Lily told her.

"I promise I will," Holly said.

Vera Johnston Miller, December 1990: I found this in an old trunk in the attic when I was cleaning it out last week. I don't know why Mama never mentioned having it. I would have loved to have read all this before now. It's strange to think that I am biologically related to the people on the historical plaque out in front of this house, even stranger to think of all the women in the family who have written in this journal for more than a hundred years already. I feel an obligation to write my story in this book, but I'm not sure where I should begin. Mother and Daddy are both gone now. They passed away within six months of each other. Like my mother, I was married several years before I had a child. Then I had two beautiful daughters within two years—Rosemary Ann was born first and then Lily Joann. We lost Rosemary before her eighth birthday to a rare form of cancer, but Lily is now nine years old. I held my breath until she passed her eighth birthday, always fearing that I might lose her, too. Mother passed away when Rosemary was only a few months old, but she told me often that she had finally gotten her official badge of honor and was really a grandmother, so her life was complete.

Lily couldn't put the journal down, though it was getting late. She turned the page and continued to read:

Vera Johnston Miller, June 20, 2004: Today is Lily's wedding day. I worry about her so much. She has finished college and has a good job, but Wyatt Anderson, her fiancé, is controlling like Mama's first husband, Fred. He's not as blatant about it as I imagine Fred was, but the wedding is basically what he wanted, not the small, intimate event that Lily had in mind. She assures me that she loves him, and I only hope that he will change. He's a very handsome and charismatic young man, but he has a wandering eye when it comes to pretty women. I hate to think of him breaking her heart. It's time for me to set the veil on her head so the photographer can take a picture. With motherhood comes worry and fears—that's just life and it can't be changed. My mama, Annie, always said, "Once a mother, always a mother, no matter the age or the era." Truer words have never been spoken.

"So Granny Vera didn't like Daddy so much," Holly said. "Well, I don't like him so much right now, either, Mama."

"Give it time. He could change." Lily hugged her daughter. "Now off to bed with you."

"I don't want the journal to end. I like reading it and talking about it with you," Holly whined.

"Well, someday you can have it and read what I write in it," Lily promised.

"Will you write about me?" Holly's grin was downright impish.

"Most likely. Good night," Lily said.

Holly hugged her tightly. "Night, Mama."

When Holly was gone, Lily tucked the journal into the secretary. "Why didn't you write more, Mama? I want to know more. What about those years after I left home and you passed away?"

It's your life and your journal now, the voice in her head said bluntly.

Chapter Twenty-Two

The sun was still a full orange ball on the horizon that evening when five people gathered round the wooden casket. Holly hadn't even put on makeup, because she said she'd just cry it all off. She stood between her mother and Sally, with Mack and Braden on the other end of the small crowd.

Sally nodded at the funeral director, and he pushed a button on a CD player. Alan Jackson's voice singing "I'll Fly Away" floated out across the rolling hills as the sun dipped behind the bare mesquite trees. Mack handed clean white hankies to each of the three women when the song started. When it finished, Sally took a step forward, opened a well-worn old black Bible, and read, "To everything there is a season, and a time to every purpose under heaven. A time to be born and a time to die." She closed the Bible and handed it to Holly. "She would want you to have this since so many of your ancestors' births and deaths are recorded in this book. Granny Hayes wanted to be buried as the sun was going down. It seems appropriate, but I like to think of her in a place now where there is no night or day, no age or youth, and time doesn't matter anymore. That's all I have to say, but I thought we needed a little more than a song."

"Amen," Lily said.

Holly laid a yellow daisy on the casket. "You weren't a rose, Granny Hayes. You were a wild daisy, doing what you wanted. I really loved you."

That reminded Lily of a Dolly Parton song, "Wildflowers." She pulled it up on her phone and turned the volume up as high as it would go. The lyrics said that wildflowers didn't care where they grew, and that she'd grown up in a different garden than other folks. There wasn't a dry eye among the bunch of them when the song ended.

The sunset was beautiful with the bright array of oranges, yellows, pinks, and purples that evening. Lily was sure that God had planned it special for Granny Hayes, just as surely as she'd felt that He had answered her prayers that morning when the sun came out bright and warm. It just wouldn't have been right or fair for that particular Monday to have gray skies and rain.

Holly was sobbing and wiping her eyes with the hankie Mack had given her when the song ended. "Mama, that song was perfect for Granny Hayes. Thank you for playing it for us." She wrapped her arms around Lily.

"I should go visit Mama and Daddy's graves." Lily motioned toward her right. "They're over there and . . ."

"I'll take the kids to Dairy Queen. We'll meet you there," Sally whispered.

"Thank you." Lily gave her a quick hug. "I don't think Holly can take much more today, but I haven't been . . ."

"I understand." Sally shushed her with a wave of her hand. "Go on. We'll get a table and be waiting for you."

Mack took her hand in his, and together, they walked across the brittle grass. Several of the graves still had poinsettias from Christmas on them, but the first thing she noticed when she got to her folks' grave was a lovely arrangement of yellow tulips in the vase at the end of their tombstone.

"I should have been here to take care of this, rather than leaving it in Sally's hands," she said.

"There is a time for all seasons," he quoted Scripture. "A time to break down and a time to build up. You've had your time to break down, and now it's your time to build up. Don't punish yourself for what you didn't do. Just put all that behind you and move forward."

"I love you, Mack Cooper," she said.

"And I love you, Lily." He drew her closer to his side. "Times like this, when we send a person on to their eternity, or when I see my father slipping away a little at a time, those things remind me that we should say what's in our hearts more often."

She'd thought that her heart would flutter if and when Mack ever said those words to her, but instead of a rush of excitement, there was simply peace and happiness. What they'd had in the bedroom had so much heat that she'd been surprised that it didn't fog the windows. She had no doubts there would be plenty of love in their lives.

"You are so right," Lily said as she let go of another bit of her past. What Wyatt had done or hadn't done was on him. She had a bright future ahead of her—hopefully sharing every minute of it with Mack and her children.

Something that her mother had asked her just before she walked down the aisle to be married to Wyatt came back to mind.

"Do you like Wyatt?" Vera had asked.

"Mother, I love him," Lily had told her mother.

"I didn't ask if you loved him or even if you were in love with him. I asked if you like him. There's a difference between love and being in love, and also in liking a person. Love is akin to lust, and lasts a few minutes a day. *In love* is deeper than that. But, honey, you better like him first and foremost, because that goes beyond all the rest. It's what's left when you're old and lust isn't there anymore for health reasons. It's the glue that holds a marriage together," Vera told her.

Lily didn't remember how she'd answered her mother that day, but looking back, she didn't think she'd ever liked Wyatt, with his ego and his manipulation. She'd loved him, but she had doubts that she was ever in love with him. She was in love with Mack, and even better, she really, really liked him.

"I'd ask you to move in with me"—he chuckled—"but you kind of already have, and besides, it wouldn't be a good example for the children for us to sleep together with them in the house. So what are we going to do about us?"

"I guess we'll take one day at a time and do the best we can with whatever life throws at us. I'm glad you're here with me to help me with whatever that might be," she answered.

"I want so much more than just friendship or even this relationship we're in right now," he said.

"So do I," she admitted.

A soft southern breeze blew her blonde hair across her face. Mack reached over and tucked it back behind her ear and then kissed her on the cheek. "I'll leave the timing to you, but I do want you to know that I'm ready when you are."

"Mack, are you proposing to me?"

"Not in a cemetery." He shook his head. "Although I like to think that maybe your mother wouldn't mind, since she's right here with us. I'd rather my proposal be a little more romantic, though. Maybe this is just a commitment toward that end, if you'd be willing for that much."

"I'm willing." She laid a hand on her parents' tombstone. Her mother's name was on one side, her father's on the other. Their marriage date was engraved below a set of entwined wedding bands. There it was right there—dates of birth, dates of their deaths, and the most important thing to Lily that day, a symbol of their commitment to each other. That's what she wanted when she was finished with this life and Holly took over the family journal. She had been born. She had died.

But the most important thing in her life, other than her children, would be when she became Mrs. Mack Cooper.

"Ready?" Mack asked.

"I am," she said as she tucked her hand into his. "I'm ready for more than just today, Mack. I'm going to let Wyatt have that apartment, but I'm going to add the furniture into the rent, heavily. I'm happy here working at the shop with Sally and living at the house with you. Life is"—she paused and cupped his face in her hand—"I'm not sure the right word is *peaceful* when we have two kids that bicker about everything, and after that scorching-hot time in your bedroom, but that's what comes to mind. The other thing is happiness. I didn't realize how much I missed that in my life until I found it again."

"Me, too, on all of what you just said," Mack told her.

"But before we take another step, I want you to think long and hard about something, and that's children. We're not too old to have a child between us, but do we want to do that? We need to give it a lot of thought and maybe even pray about it," she said.

"Honey, we have two beautiful children. I'd just as soon not plan any more, but if an accident should happen, we won't be upset. We'll just figure . . ." He hesitated. "We didn't use protection the other night."

"I'm on the pill, not so much for protection, but for irregularity at my age," she said. "Don't worry. Everything is fine."

He led her back toward his truck about the time the gravediggers lowered Granny Hayes's casket into the ground. Lily stopped and watched them, then walked over to the grave, picked up a handful of dirt, and sprinkled it on the wooden box. "Thank you for what you meant to us, Granny. Rest in peace."

"She would have liked that," Mack said.

"I feel like my eyes have been opened after I'd been in a deep sleep since I came home to Comfort," she said as she brushed her hands together to remove the last of the dirt. "First finding the journal with all my ancestors in it, and then reuniting with my friends and realizing how much they mean to me, and then there's you."

"I came in last?" he teased.

"No, I just saved the best for last," she told him.

He opened the truck door for her, put his big hands around her waist, picked her up, and set her in the passenger seat. "I'll take being last all the time if that's the case."

"Let's go home," she said, and she meant it as *home*—permanently.

Chapter Twenty-Three

Thirteen months later

Lily took a dozen pictures of Holly that beautiful April evening before her daughter left her bedroom. With her long blonde hair all swept up in curls and wearing a lovely light-blue prom dress, she looked even more like Vera's wedding picture than ever before. Preacher Drew's son, Clay, waited for her in the living room. Looking all grown up in his black tuxedo with a blue vest that matched Holly's dress perfectly, he was right at home in the old stone house. But then, he should have been—he'd been dating Holly for the past year and spent lots of time there.

"Oh. My. Goodness!" Clay stood up and his eyes widened. "You are so beautiful, Holly. I'm going to have the prettiest date at the prom."

She smiled, a little shyly for Holly Anderson, but then Clay brought out the best in her. "Thank you. I'm going with the most handsome boy in the whole school."

"If y'all are through kissin' up to each other, let Mama take some pictures of you putting that corsage on her wrist so me and Isaac can get back to watchin' our movie." Braden's voice had gone through the cracking changes. Now his drawl was even deeper than Mack's and sounded like it came from a much bigger man.

"Little brothers are such a nuisance," Holly fussed. "I'm never having sons. I'm only having daughters."

Lily snapped several more pictures and then a final one of their backs as they were walking off the porch. Mack draped an arm around her shoulders.

"Time kind of gets away from us, don't it? Before you know it, we'll be watching her leave with some guy. Only she'll be wearing a white dress and veil," he said.

Lily shoved her phone into her hip pocket and turned around to face Mack. She put her arms around his neck and tiptoed to kiss him. When the kiss ended, she leaned her cheek against his broad chest. "I don't want to think about that day, but I do hope that she finds a man who treats her as good as Clay does, and as good as you treat me."

"We make a pretty good couple, don't we? So have we got everything in order for our belated honeymoon at the end of next month?"

"All we've got to do is pack our bags and drive to the airport. From there it's all planned out for us. The kids are excited to go on a ten-day Alaskan cruise," she answered.

"I'm looking forward to it, too," he said. "Ten days to celebrate our marriage."

"That happened a year ago." She tiptoed and kissed him on the cheek. "And we've celebrated it every day since."

"But not on a big ship. Maybe we should do this every year," he suggested. "But right now I'd better go take care of the evening chores."

"I'll have supper on the table when you get back," she told him.

He left by the back door, and she sat down on the bottom step. It had been a good year, but somehow she'd never gotten around to writing anything in the journal. She had meant to—she really had. The time just never seemed quite right.

"No time like the present," she said as she stood and went up to her old bedroom, which was now her office. She opened the oak secretary, pulled down the flap, and took out the journal. She thumbed through the pages, scanning more than a hundred years of handwriting from her ancestors. Happy times. Sad times. Deaths. Births. Life in general. It was all there to show her that her life was what she made it and that her choices would have consequences. When she reached the first clean page, she reached for an ink pen and began to write:

Lily Miller Anderson Cooper, April 2020: I've never been happier than I am right now. My life is not perfect by any means, but then, no one ever promised it would be. I just watched my daughter, Holly, leave for her very first prom with Clay. He's the preacher's son and is a young man that I both admire and appreciate for his convictions and values. Six years ago Holly's father walked out on us— Holly, her younger brother, Braden, and me—and for five of those years I was little more than a zombie. Then one day circumstances made me sit up and take notice. I realized that my kids were completely out of control, and it would take drastic measures to put them back on the right track. I took them out of the environment they were in and brought them to Comfort, Texas—back to my roots and the house I'd been raised in. It was during those first days that I found this journal, and it has helped me so much to understand that life is what we make it. The kids' father, Wyatt Anderson, is struggling to find his way. They see him about every three months for a weekend, and I have hopes that someday they'll have a decent relationship. That's up to him and them, and I try to stay out of it. I remarried after I came home. Mack Cooper and I said our vows last summer. He's a good man, a good husband, and a wonderful role model for the children. We have an amazing life here on our little goat farm. Holly knows about this journal, and she knows that someday she'll have the same responsibility that I have.

Lily laid the pen down and fiddled with her wide gold wedding band. It still seemed surreal that she and Mack were married. She picked up the pen again and began to write for the second time.

Mama died at the age of seventy, just like her mother. She's been gone six years now, but if I open the bottom drawer of her old dresser and get a whiff of her rose-scented sachet, it seems like she's still here. Braden asked me once if the place was haunted, and I told him no, but I wouldn't mind if it was. I think Mama would be happy that Mack and I are married. She never really trusted Wyatt, and with good reason, but she was wise enough to let me make my own decisions, even if they weren't good ones. I pray that I can let Holly make her own path and support her like Mama did me.

Lily reread what she'd written. It wasn't good prose and didn't say as much as some of the previous women had written about, but it was from the heart. She put the journal back into the secretary and was on the way downstairs when she heard Sally yell from the front door.

"Hey, where are you?" Her voice floated up the stairs. "I brought a cheesecake for dessert with hopes that you'd invite me to supper. You said when you left work you were frying chicken tonight."

"I'm on my way down," Lily called out.

Friends and family, and a man who loved her just the way she was. Life didn't get a bit better than that!

Dear Readers

As a teenager I had a little pink diary that locked. I had the only key and was glad that I could keep all my private and most personal writings locked away from prying eyes—such as those of my younger brother and sister, and even more so from my mother. In all the moves I've made since those years, the diary has long since been lost. The writings were those of a dramatic young girl, I'm sure, but I've often wondered what it would be like to read them again. Or better yet, to read something that my great-grandmother or my mother might have written.

With that in mind, the idea for *The Family Journal* came to me a few years ago. Lily Anderson appeared in my virtual world with a story to tell me that went along with the inspiration. She was still in pain from a messy divorce after five years and needed a change in her life. She and her young daughter bonded over an old family journal she found in her mother's antique secretary. Having these characters in my head for all the weeks I worked on this book was truly an experience, and like so many of my other books, it became a book of my heart.

As always, it takes a village to produce a book, and I have folks to thank who abide in that village with me. My agent, Erin Niumata, and my agency, Folio Management, are amazing, and I can't thank them enough for continuing to be there for me. My editors, Anh Schluep and

Krista Stroever—y'all are simply the best, and I love working with you both. All the folks on my Montlake team who proofread, copyedit, and design my awesome covers—and do a fabulous job of promotion—I bow to all your expertise. My husband, Mr. B, who is my biggest supporter, who doesn't mind having takeout so I can finish one more chapter—I love you, and here's to another fifty-three years together.

And to my readers! Y'all are the icing on the cupcake. You are all worth every bit of the work that goes into producing a book. I love your notes, your reviews, and your encouragement.

I'm one blessed author, and I appreciate everyone in my life who helps me be able to say that!

Until next time,
Happy Reading,
Carolyn Brown

About the Author

Photo © 2015 Charles Brown

Carolyn Brown is a RITA finalist and the *New York Times, USA Today, Publishers Weekly,* and *Wall Street Journal* bestselling author of nearly one hundred books. Her genres include contemporary and historical romances, cowboy and country-music romances, and women's fiction. She and her husband live in the small town of Davis, Oklahoma, where everyone knows everyone else, knows what they are doing and when . . . and reads the local newspaper every Wednesday to see who got caught. They have three grown children and enough grandchildren to keep them young. Visit Carolyn at www.carolynbrownbooks.com.